ADVANCE PRAISE FOR NEME*SIS*

"Marshall has written a rare book: a YA novel in which serious themes—divorce, isolation, mental health, bullying, etc.—are considered without admonishing readers or beating them over the head with lessons. Instead, readers progress through sophomore year with Nadine, sharing her daily discouragements and small triumphs. The recurrence of certain problems is only natural; they're part of Nadine's experience, after all. On top of that, Marshall accurately portrays the relative gravity of teenage crushes and friend-group drama—heavy considerations for the high school crowd. A smart choice for teen readers."

- *Kirkus Reviews*

"A well written, engaging YA novel."

- Rhonda Lomazow, advance reader

"This story is very well constructed and the characters are well developed. It sends a strong message about cyber as well as physical bullying. The possible solutions to address these issues are not easy but plausible. It's a credible young adult novel and I would recommend to readers of all ages."

- Brigitte HF, *Mes Livres* book reviews

"This is a fast read that will keep you turning the pages. You will laugh and cry, and cheer the characters on."

- Patricia Statham, advance reader

"A compelling coming-of-age book."

- Rai Bai, advance reader

COPYRIGHT INFORMATION

NemeSIS
Copyright 2017 by Susan Marshall
ISBN: 978-1-988279-21-3 All rights reserved
Cover design and graphic: DigiWriting
Editor: Allister Thompson
Published in Canada by Blue Moon Voices, a division of Blue Moon Publishers, located in Toronto, Canada.

The author greatly appreciates you taking the time to read this work. Please consider leaving a review wherever you bought the book, or telling your friends or blog readers about *NemeSIS*, to help spread the word. Thank you for your support.

This book is a work of fiction. The characters, incidents, and dialogue are drawn from the author's imagination and are not to be construed as real. Any resemblance to actual events or persons, living or dead, is entirely coincidental.

© First Printing April 2017

NEME*SIS*

By Susan Marshall

To Meg,
I hope you enjoy!
Susan Marshall

BlueMoon
PUBLISHERS

For my parents Eleanor and Tony Marshall and my sister Virginia, all avid readers.

CONTENTS

ACKNOWLEDGMENTS

Firstly, I would like to thank my amazing husband Mark, who has always been uber supportive of me, as well as our four wonderful children, Patrick, Daniel, Andrew, and Claire. You are all unique, fun human beings who make our house a lively, chaotic home. Together, we are a tight-knit tribe that I value above everything.

To Blue Moon Publishers, especially Heidi and Talia; you have been fantastic partners — supportive, consultative, smart, and dynamic — every step of the way. I am so thrilled to be part of your family.

Without the insightful critiques, comments, and matchmaking skills of Allister Thompson, *NemeSIS* may never have made it to the finish line. I am forever grateful to you and in awe of your abilities.

I owe a huge debt of gratitude to my sister Corinne Marshall and my dear friend Kathy O'Handley, who are not only excellent listeners and patient readers, but also skilled editors who offered crucial input from the very beginning and, amongst other things, have taught me to write in one continuous tense.

To Carly Wiseman and Christine Castelli who proofed the field hockey sections of the book for authenticity and accuracy, thanks so much for your eagle eyes; I hope I got it right.

For those of you who were subjected to early, rough versions of the book, including Erin, Becca, Hillary, Margot, Harriet, Jen R., Jody, Karen, Dana, Jen Mc., Chris, Marie, Sylvia, and Bev, as well as to Nancy who encouraged me to add "reading" to my writing, I am super grateful to you all.

I would also like to add a special shout-out to a fabulous mentor, hand-holder, fellow coffee enthusiast, and friend, Ali McDonald.

And last but not least, I must extend thanks to Dr. Paul Werstine of King's College, Western University, who taught me many years ago to love the written word largely but to write sparingly.

Susan Marshall

CHAPTER 1

It was lunch hour at Elgin High, and there I was hiding out in the library, again. The whole high school thing just wasn't working for me. While all the other kids were in the cafeteria or at a coffee shop or stuck in detention, I spent every lunch period alone. I pretended to study so I wouldn't have to eat by myself in public. The self-imposed sentence had been going on for over a year. It was the start of grade ten, and basically I was friendless.

Okay, so maybe I did have one friend. His name was Felix, and like me, he was always hanging out in the library. I could see him making his way over to me that day, but I had to quickly shut him down. "Psst, Felix. You have to come back," I whispered. "I haven't eaten yet." Since our friendship was based on food and there wasn't a morsel in sight, the little grey mouse hightailed it away.

And that was a good thing. Moments later, I heard the deep voice of Mr. Khan, which always arrived just before his substantial body. "Miss Nadine, all the studying you do! You must get over one hundred percent in every course."

I felt my face flush. It would at least mean something if all this social isolation translated into perfect grades. But I really didn't accomplish much other than mope. Besides, if I did my homework during the day, what would I do at night? It's not like I had friends to waste time with on Snapchat or Instagram.

"Not quite. I do okay. I guess."

"I am reminded of that saying, 'All work and no play makes Jack dull.' Is that how it goes?" That Mr. Khan. While he didn't get it quite right, he somehow nailed it. *Dull, that was exactly how I felt.* My black shirt and dark jeans completed the mood. In sharp contrast, Mr. Khan was sporting his signature look, a vibrant-coloured polo shirt that flaunted his large belly. Today it was cherry red.

"Yeah, that's pretty much it."

Mr. Khan smiled and then went over to the main library desk. He always made a phone call or two, and soon he was leaning back on his swivel chair and laughing softly into his cell. The timing was perfect; it was getting close to the end of lunch period, and I was pretty hungry.

With Mr. Khan distracted, I opened my backpack and pulled out my food—silence was key here. I leaned in closer to the textbook that I kept propped up on my carrel as I peeled back the tinfoil lid of the yogurt. I coughed to muffle the sound. The goal was to eat as quickly and as quietly as possible so that Mr. Khan didn't catch me in the act of desecrating the school library.

God forbid if jam accidentally got smeared on an encyclopedia. Or imagine the worldwide fallout if a juice box dribbled onto an atlas. I was pretty sure Mr. Khan knew I ate here, but try as he might he still hadn't caught me red-handed, so we kept up this little cat-and-mouse game.

"Nice work on clean-up!" I whispered to Felix, who had returned and was busy nibbling away at bagel crumbs that had fallen onto the beige-carpeted floor. I knew if I stopped eating there, or if I started eating with less spillage, even Felix would abandon me. Our friendship was rock-solid, though, since I had nowhere to go, no one to hang out with, and I wasn't the most careful eater.

Mr. Khan finished the call, so I moved my legs around. That always made the naturally skittish mouse run away. I stashed all the evidence of my furtive lunch in my backpack, coughing again to muffle any sound. All the subterfuge made me feel ridiculous. And really, he had to know I was trying to eat here secretly—that, or I was suffering from tuberculosis.

"Try some play tomorrow, don't be like dull Jack!" Mr. Khan called to me as I headed toward the door, the lunch bell chiming over the speakers.

I knew that he meant well, but seriously, did he think I could just snap my fingers and suddenly get a life?

I choose to humour him. "Maybe, you never know," I replied. But really, who was I kidding? The odds of me getting some "play" were about the same as Felix morphing from a mouse into a man. Zilch. So I knew that I'd be back again. Tomorrow.

*

Around eight o'clock that evening, my stomach was rumbling. I'd had a peanut butter sandwich after school, but that wasn't exactly a complete meal. As I went downstairs to peruse our food selection, a delicious smell wafted out of the kitchen. It was a nice surprise to find my mom already home and a bonus that I wouldn't have to scrounge up the usual makeshift dinner.

Mom was at the table, flipping through the mail. She paused when she saw me and forced a weary smile onto her mouth, which held the remnants of faded lipstick. Mom had a pretty face and was trim for her age, but it seemed that practically overnight, her brown hair had become lifeless and streaked with grey. She had soft brown eyes, almost like a deer, but there were many more wrinkles around them. This year had taken a huge toll on her. People always said Rachel and I looked like my mom. I assumed they meant when she was younger.

I went over and put my hands on her shoulders, and she put her hands on mine and patted them. It felt nice to be connecting. I missed having her around. A brown paper fast-food bag stood on the black granite island, calling to my hungry stomach. "That smells amazing," I said, and I squeezed her hands before I walked over to the bag and took a peek.

"I know it's just junk food, but at least there's something for dinner. The sushi place was closed, so burgers it is. Help yourself."

Mom picked up a large white envelope at the bottom of the mail pile. She pursed her lips and took a deep breath before she slowly opened it. The atmosphere in the kitchen changed on a dime. When she pulled out the contents, I could see that they were neatly typed legal-style documents. It was my turn to take a deep breath. Just as I prepared to take my first bite of my burger, I suddenly lost my appetite.

I didn't need to ask any questions. I knew these were the separation agreement documents, drafted by lawyers, outlining the financial and child-care arrangements between my dad and mom. By the looks of it, reconciliation wasn't in the works. And just when I thought the tension in the kitchen was pretty high, in waltzed Rachel, my older sister.

"So what do we have here?" said Rachel. I thought she meant the documents until she made a beeline for the food. We watched as she unwrapped a burger, lifted off the top, and examined the contents. "Let me see. Carbs, protein. The cheese slice is calcium. A pickle, so there's veggies. And last but not least, lots and lots of grease. *Im-pressive*!"

I felt my stomach sink. *So that's how Rachel's going to be.*

"It was the only place I could find open. At least it's hot food … for a change."

"You call this food?" Rachel said, flicking at the burger. The girl was clearly being dramatic; she had a known weakness for French fries.

"Uh, Mom just got a bit of news—" I piped up, gesturing toward the documents.

"As if, Dad's been gone forever." Did I mention that Rachel was usually oblivious to the suffering of others?

"But it's Mom who—"

"Should be doing something," Rachel interrupted. "And I don't mean playing Monopoly!"

"I am not playing Monopoly. It's called getting a real estate licence. And working full time. It's insane…"

"I mean about Dad." Rachel interrupted again

Mom sighed. "Look, I know it's hard to accept, but we have to. He's staying … in New York."

"It's not a done deal. Not yet. But you need to get going, before the bitch moves in…"

"What? How do you...?" Mom put her face in her hands for a minute while I glared at Rachel.

Rachel and I had been actually getting along a few days ago, and we had this idea to Skype Dad together. It was fun for the first few minutes, but then he got all serious and said he wanted to "come clean" with us. Then he spilled the beans about his girlfriend and their plans to start cohabitating. Soon.

It felt like a hard punch to the stomach. I conjured up an instant lie to my virtual father, immediately excusing myself to go study. Instead I sat on the window seat in my room and stared at listless grey clouds, wondering how they came to be the exact same colour as cement. And even with the room to my door closed, I could hear Rachel freaking out at him.

I never would have mentioned the girlfriend thing to Mom. While I was ninety-nine percent sure she knew, I was a hundred percent sure that she'd be real upset if I brought it up. But Rachel was different; she always putting the feelings of others after her own.

Mom paused to wipe away the moisture under her eyes with the back of her hand. A big, stubborn blob of mascara remained stuck under the left one, which just added to the indignity.

You had to admire her; she somehow kept it together. She took a deep breath and somehow soldiered on. "We've been over and over this. What happened was between him and me. I know it affects you both, and I'm sorry for that. You have to take my word that we did what we could. For your sakes, especially, we both tried..." said Mom, her voice cracking a little.

"You call that trying? Did you go to New York? Even once? This home is falling apart, and what are you doing? Selling other people houses? That doesn't make sense. This is your chance. Go sell Park Place. No one cares about London, Ontario!"

It was just a different version of the same old conversation, like hearing the same song put on infinite repeat. Rachel wouldn't let it go. I could see the future—both our parents in wheelchairs, living in an old age home, married to other people—and there would be Rachel, yelling into Mom's hearing aid, "There's still time to fix this!"

I wished I could have just crawled out of the kitchen unobserved at that point. I hated to take on Rachel. It never ended well, but I hated it even more when Mom got abused. I opened my mouth, but Mom took the lead.

"That's enough! I'm sick of this same old conversation. You need to accept it." She paused for a second, shut her eyes tight, and tried to compose herself. "Look, you've suffered, we've all suffered. Can we try to start moving forward? Can we sit down, the three of us for a change, and just eat? Together?"

Frustration and anger were etched on Rachel's face. "I won't listen to this garbage anymore," she said, picking up her burger. "And I won't eat this garbage!" And she tossed it into the kitchen sink and stormed out.

Mom closed her eyes for a minute. Then she looked up at me and slowly said, "I know that she's been really difficult. I keep reminding myself that she's hurting and she's angry. I hope you know we tried, that we never wanted this to happen?" She looked at me in a defeated sort of way, and I felt really bad for her.

"Of course, Mom." I went over to soothe her. "Rachel's really out of line."

"I guess she just needs more time to accept it. I know that she's really up and down emotionally. I want to be home more…to help get things under control. Soon." I nodded, but I wasn't hopeful. "I've lost my appetite. I'm going to turn in." Mom picked up Rachel's burger from the sink and chucked it into the garbage. She chucked in her own uneaten burger as well.

I knew Rachel was upset, but so was I, and so was Mom, and you didn't see either of us lashing out that way. The truth was that Rachel had acted this way before the separation, but it had gotten worse since Dad left—a lot worse. I seemed to be her favourite target these days, with Dad not here and Mom not usually around. That was fine by me—Mom had enough to deal with.

I knew exactly what to do when Rachel lashed out at me. It was all I could do not to react, but I had this whole routine going where I took cleansing breaths to stay calm. It's like what you do when you meditate. Most people use meditation to be transported to a nice tranquil state. I used it to prevent my picture from being splashed across the front page of the *London Free Press* under a caption that read, "YOUNGER SISTER SUFFOCATES OLDER SISTER WITH GREASY HAMBURGER."

CHAPTER 2

Even though it was a beautiful September day and pretty much everyone was outside for lunch, I went up to the library, again. As I pulled open the door, Mr. Khan smiled at me but I could see he was disappointed. I smiled back at him, but I sure didn't feel it.

As the steel door closed behind me, I was enveloped in a muddy beige; the carpet and walls were almost the exact same noise-cancelling hue.

Suddenly I felt desperate; I didn't want the dullness anymore. I wanted to be hopeful and positive. I focused on the sunny yellow polo shirt that Mr. Khan was wearing and tried to feel imaginary rays of sunshine on my face, but I couldn't quite make it happen. I had to do something, anything, other than just existing.

I was sick of sneaking lunch while pretending to study and was getting tired of feeling sorry for myself. I tried to figure out just how many lunches I had eaten here since I'd started at Elgin High over twelve months ago. Forty school weeks a year times five lunches. What was that? Two hundred lunches? Wow, that was a big chunk of my life wasted in the library that I would never get back. It made me feel even more depressed.

Well, I thought, *maybe I should get up and browse around.* What, it had only been, like, two hundred lunches? Had I made an effort? Here I was surrounded by all these amazing books. Maybe I could learn something, improve myself.

As I started wandering, I felt the watchful eyes of Mr. Khan tracking my progress. "So nice to see you browsing! Can I help you? Are you looking for an interesting book?"

"I'm not sure, I'm just seeing if something looks good." I did notice *The Book of Awesome.* I picked it up and leafed through it.

"A good choice," said Mr. Khan. "Everyone could use more awesome in their lives." I nodded but thought, *More awesome?* I had absolutely no awesome. Maybe this book was too advanced for me.

As I turned to respond, my eyes were inexplicably drawn to a display of pamphlets on the circulation desk. I'd seen the display a million times before, but it had barely registered with me. For some reason, though, I zeroed in on the one for Alcoholics Anonymous. No, no, it wasn't like that. I didn't drink. Well, once I'd split half a peach cooler with a friend, but that was ages ago, in eighth grade.

I remembered from health class last year that Mrs. Anthony had told us about Alcoholics Anonymous and how it helped desperate people turn their lives around. They had this twelve-step program that people could follow if they were ready to take the leap. Wasn't I a desperate person?

Like an alcoholic who was ready to seek treatment, I was at rock bottom. I was like a loser-aholic, and I needed to pull myself up. Find another way to live. My current path was lonely and bleak, and I needed to try something else. I could see myself at a meeting, standing in front of other friendless high school students from broken families, saying, "My name is Nadine, I'm fifteen, and my life completely sucks."

I passed by the pamphlet display, and as discreetly as I could, I grabbed the one for AA and hoofed it back to my study carrel. As I scanned the twelve-steps, I quickly realized that it was pretty specific and cloaked in religion, like Step Two: *(We) Came to believe that a Power greater than ourselves could restore us to sanity.*

Huh? Well, I actually did understand what it meant, but I'd never been religious, and if I needed to get religion first, that would really, really delay things. I had already wasted over a year of my life. I couldn't afford to lose more time.

Mr. Khan must have noticed that I swiped the pamphlet, since he appeared at my study carrel with a furrowed look of concern. "If there's a problem with a friend or a relative, you know you can talk to me or one of the guidance counsellors."

"Thanks, but … it's not that. I'm just, it's hard to explain. I'm wondering if you can follow a bunch of steps and … somehow … straighten out your life?"

"Oh, I see," said Mr. Khan. "You mean if your life's crooked?"

"Yes exactly. Crooked."

I quickly realized that the Twelve Steps to Sobriety were not easily transferable to a teenage girl looking for happiness in high school, but it gave me an idea. I needed to devise my own plan, to dig myself out of the hole I was in. I thought and thought for a few minutes. I wasn't sure how to begin. And then it hit me. My first step would be to figure out what I wanted to change.

Right away, I considered my disastrous home life. When I was a kid, I'd always thought of our family as a tree, with my parents as the trunk and Rachel and I as the branches. But lately our tree seemed sick, like the Asian beetle infestation we learned about in ecology. And Rachel seemed to think that spraying poison all around would somehow reverse the damage. But the truth was that it only made things worse; our tree was too far gone. It was rotten from within.

In the end, I decided that I couldn't change Mom or Rachel or Dad—I could only set goals for myself. And this is what I came up with:

Step One: Nadine's Goals for High School

To be a real part of the high school scene, not just some interloper who happens to have classes here.

To have a friends, or even just one good friend.

To have fun like any regular teenager.

To live, not just survive.

To have a boyfriend. Or even just the possibility of having a boyfriend.

I put down the pen and looked over the list, but I knew right away something was missing. So I picked it right back up and added one more goal:

To eat lunch in the caf.

But that seemed too simple. I needed to expand the dream. So I crossed that out and wrote this instead:

To walk into the cafeteria, look out over the sea of students chowing down on lunch, and see a hand up in the air. And to know that that hand is waving to me. And to make my way over to the hand (who is attached to a person who is my new BFF) and plunk myself down in one of those orange, greasy cafeteria chairs. And then, just like everyone else, eat lunch, far away from mice, grown men, and library books.

I put down the pen once again, and for the first time in a long while, I smiled. I felt that maybe it was a start, a new beginning. It was still September and I actually felt hopeful.

*

High school had seemed so appealing to me in eighth grade. I was reasonably popular, considered somewhat attractive, did well in school with little effort, and excelled at many sports, especially ice hockey. I assumed the transition from middle school to high school would be a breeze, and I couldn't wait to leave my PG-13 life behind and start life as a 14-A. But it definitely hadn't worked out that way.

Once I walked through the doors of Elgin High, all the old rules seemed to have instantly changed, and I'd obviously missed the memo. My former classmates got it, knew exactly what to do or say, and reinvented themselves in about three seconds. I had always been on the shy side, which didn't help, and I somehow lost all social traction. My old friends moved on, and I was unable to make even one new friend. I had nothing, no friends, no fun. Basically, I was an epic fail. Twelve steps probably wouldn't be enough.

Starting high school had also coincided with the meltdown of my family. In the end the drama at home was so bad — with my mom so miserable and my sister so apoplectic — that just showing up at school and functioning was about all I could muster. So when I should have been focused on ingratiating myself with at least one high school clique, I was focused on self-preservation. I had to admit to myself that my home life might not get any better. I had to stop wallowing in self-pity and get on with my life.

*

It was day two of my quest to fix my life, and here I was again, hiding out in the library during lunch hour. *Well,* I thought, *since I've figured out my goals, I've got to make a plan. To make it happen.* I knew that not hiding was an obvious one. But the library was like a security blanket that I wasn't quite ready to give up.

Once again, I was covertly eating my lunch in the carrel, and once again Felix came over to help with the crumbs. I watched him nibble while I tried to think of a small first step. I needed something concrete, something that would launch me to the first rung of the ladder so I could start climbing upward. How do you start the momentum?

But negative brain activity surged, overriding the hope. *Who am I kidding? My problems are too big.* It was too overwhelming. And it didn't help that Felix just took what he wanted from me and moved on. Some friend.

It was almost time for the lunch bell to ring, so I gathered my stuff and headed to the door, but Mr. Khan waved me over. "You know what's awesome? The Cooking Club! Our first meeting is tomorrow after school. You should come! We're making cookies!" He smiled kindly, but all I could focus on was his ample stomach. Today it was swathed in a shade of blue reminiscent of a perfect, cloudless day.

Cookies? Cooking? Didn't I have enough problems without turning to food for solace and the resulting weight gain? I pursed my lips for a second, trying to formulate an answer.

Every cell in my body wanted to shout *No*! I mean, the Cooking Club, seriously? But then again, hadn't I committed to doing things differently this year? Joining a club was a really good idea. Mr. Khan was nice, and my mother had pretty much abandoned cooking, so I should actually expand my repertoire past scrambled eggs, French toast, and grilled cheese. And hadn't I just read an article about how teens were at risk for scurvy? I definitely didn't want that.

What did I have to lose? Should I be worried that someone cool might shun me for belonging to the Cooking Club? Everyone had already shunned me.

"Maybe? I can't really cook but I guess I should learn?"

"It'll be awesome. You'll see!"

So there it was. The next step handed to me on a silver platter. Thank you, Mr. Khan!

Step Two: Try something new at school, even if it's the Cooking Club. You never know where you might find a friend.

As I opened the doors to leave the library, I noticed a girl quietly tidying up the remnants of her lunch in a study carrel tucked off to the side. *Huh*, I thought, *she must be new to the library lunch thing. Or maybe this is just a one-off.* She didn't look familiar, but it was hard to get a good look from my vantage point. I could tell she was petite, with short, shiny jet-black hair, and she looked relatively normal. From the back.

On the other hand, so did I. You wouldn't know to look at me that I was such a social reject. From the back, anyway.

I stopped myself and thought, *Why do I keep I dissing myself? Especially when I'm trying to turn things around?* Wasn't it a basic principle that opposite forces just cancel each other out? I needed to change the negative inner voice, or I'd never make any progress.

Hello, Step Three!

Step Three: Focus on building yourself up instead of putting yourself down.

CHAPTER 3

I took a bit of extra time getting ready for school the next day. I knew it was just the Cooking Club, not a party with the football team, but still, you never knew who was going to attend. Since Mr. Khan was famous for his love of sweets, I wondered who would sign up for such a club. Maybe children from organic granola-type families?

Making cookies would be an easy lure for kids whose parents banned white sugar and white flour. Or kids whose parents had put them on diets. But maybe, just maybe, some gorgeous, funny, athletic boys would be forced by their mothers to attend so they could survive college or university without subsisting on fast food.

I blow-dried my hair for a change, instead of just shoving it soaking wet into a ponytail. I had just finished dressing and thought I looked better than usual when Rachel appeared at my bedroom door. "So you *are* here. Didn't see you last night, Bean. Big test today or something?" I was taken aback both by her kind tone and the use of the name "Bean." Rachel used to call me that when she was very little and couldn't quite pronounce Nadine. It was a term of endearment she only used when she was in a good mood.

"Yeah," I lied. "Major math test. You know how I suck at math." The truth was that I wanted to avoid Rachel completely, since I had just vowed to improve my life.

"You blow-dried your hair?" I nodded as Rachel sat on my bed, cozying up for a sisterly talk. "What's up with that?"

"Nothing," I lied again. Like I would tell her that I made a special effort to look good for the Cooking Club. She would pee her pants laughing.

"Like that sweater." I nodded and she said, "The buttons are cool." Rachel flashed a beatific smile that made her look even more gorgeous. On the outside, anyway.

Teenage boys found Rachel ridiculously attractive, and she knew exactly how to work it. Interestingly, we had similar looks, but she came out on top in every direct physical comparison. Rachel had green eyes and shiny chestnut-brown hair with lots of natural red highlights. My eyes were basic brown, my hair was basic brown and unadorned with any natural highlights. Even though I did have some shine in my mane, it didn't stop there but spread forward to include my skin, and we all know what that means.

Sometimes skilled make-up application can compensate for mediocre looks, but my make-up skills were basic. Rachel, however, had a deft hand and could effortlessly enhance her features, especially her striking eyes, by adding just the right amount of pencil and shadow. The lucky girl didn't have shiny skin but rather one of those amazing, poreless complexions. On the other hand, she did have a slightly longer, pointier nose than me. But then again, maybe I just imagined that witch-like similarity.

"My silver ballet flats would tie it all together, just saying…"

Rachel was rarely nice without an ulterior motive, but you never said no to her, so I said, "Hmmm."

"Just a sec." She returned a minute later with her new silver shoes and presented them to me with a waiter-like flourish.

She paused and looked at me from head to toe. "Did I call it or what, perfection!" she said.

"Are you sure?" Her shoes were beautiful, but I worried about the consequences of accepting her kindness.

"Just don't trash them."

Maybe I needed to add another step?

Step Four: Take a chance with Rachel. She is being uncharacteristically nice. It will probably end badly, but I really want to wear the shoes!

"No probs," I said, still surprised. "Thanks." And I meant it.

*

When the lunch bell rang, I actually toyed with the idea of going to the cafeteria. I knew I looked okay, and I tried to talk myself into it. As I stood outside in the hallway contemplating, kids in groups and pairs headed inside. I visualized the moment when I stood pathetically holding my tray, and having no one acknowledge me. No one to sit with. I let out a deep sigh as I turned left up the stairs and went mouse-like back to the library. *Baby steps*, I thought. *Baby steps.*

I quickly scanned the room and noted that the girl from yesterday was sitting in the same study carrel. I mentally put a target on her head. I needed to get to know her. Maybe we had more things in common than just our sad hiding place. Here was a potential first friend. *You used to have friends, you know*, I reminded myself. Yes, I'd been shut out of the scene so far, but that was bad luck and bad timing mixed with an extra helping of shyness. It was fixable. I had to believe that. I decided to add another step to my multi-step plan of social rehabilitation.

Step Five: Get to know the other lunch loser who's also hiding out in the library. Maybe she should be on the program, too!

Wait, had I forgotten Step Three already? Let's reword that.

Step Five: Befriend the other person who shares your taste in unconventional lunch venues.

Instead of sitting at my usual place in the centre of the library, I went and plunked myself down near the other girl. Mr. Khan looked my way, immediately read my thoughts, and nodded his approval. Clearly he was rooting for me to expand my social circle. He would probably be happy to relinquish his lunchtime babysitting duties.

I started by checking her out with occasional glances. Not only was she normal-looking, but she was actually cute, with short, dark hair, and at one point I got a glimpse of her striking blue eyes. But she seemed intent on pretending to study her textbook and didn't acknowledge me. I even got up and walked past her toward the fiction collection, but she kept her eyes nervously focused downward at all times.

I tried to coax myself into just going over and saying hi. But I couldn't will myself to do it. And from what I could tell, she wasn't going to take the initiative either— she seemed even more timid than me.

My stomach was growling, so I decided just to go back and sit down. Halfway through my bagel, with several crumbs already under my chair, I could see Felix the mouse scurrying toward my new carrel. What a smart mouse! But as he got closer, I wondered what would happen if this new girl was actually afraid of mice.

If she started to scream or did something dramatic, Mr. Khan would have to bust us for eating, and we'd both be tossed out to avoid a complete infestation. I couldn't risk getting ejected. Plus, who knew what would happen to poor Felix.

I wanted to whisper a warning to her or toss a note her way, but I couldn't muster up the courage for even a small, pathetic attempt at communication. So instead I started kicking my legs a bit in the direction of the mouse, hoping to scare him back to his nest, but he kept his nose down and his pace steady. Just my luck that Felix, who was normally acutely aware of every movement, suddenly seemed to be one of those blind mice you read about.

My next tactic was to make a low hiss, you know, like a cat. Surely that would scare him away. I could see the new girl turn her head in confusion and give me a puzzled glance before she quickly averted her eyes. I felt ridiculous and embarrassed.

Great. My big goal is to make a friend, and here I am kicking and hissing. For sure she thinks I'm a freak. Surprisingly, Felix did not respond at all.

Frustrated with my efforts and anxious about the girl's reaction, I decided to take a more literal approach. "Psst, mouse, go away!" I whispered, but he kept coming. I tried one more time, a little louder, "Psst, mouse!"

In a flash, she looked directly at me, her blue eyes bugged wide, and the startled expression moved downward to her puzzled mouth. I nodded toward the mouse, which, I guess, made her even more confused. Oddly enough, she turned one hundred and eighty degrees the other way. Which meant, pretty much, that she was just staring at the wall.

She then quickly turned her head back to the middle and angled her face downward. From her profile, I could see she was biting her bottom lip. And that her cheeks had turned the same hue as the cherries at the bottom of my Greek yogurt. Now it was my turn to wonder who was the bigger real freak—her or me? I called it a tie.

Meanwhile, Felix was still zigzagging in her general direction. The mild commotion had no impact on his flight path. I took the decibel up a notch. "Psst, Fel, Uh … mouse!"

The girl looked over at me again, then retreated back to the same downward position. I tried not to look at her too obviously, but it was kind of impossible not to stare a bit when she opened and closed her mouth a couple of times. Like she was muttering to herself. It was most definitely a tiebreaking move. She had taken the lead in the freakshow contest.

Luckily, my friend Felix started loopily retreating from the danger zone, probably distracted by some tasty little morsel that would be invisible to the casual observer. The crisis ended, but it made me wonder how long it might take two shy people to actually meet.

A few minutes before the bell, she got up and started to pack up her "study props," you know, those textbooks that we kept open for show. I got up too. And for about a nanosecond, we exchanged a small smile. That would have been that, at least for the day, had Mr. Khan not appeared at my carrel, rocking a lime-green polo. It was amazing how those shirts stretched out just so to hug his stomach.

"So, Miss Nadine, I trust I will be seeing you after school today for the inaugural meeting of the Cooking Club?"

Great, I thought. *So the first thing this girl learns about me is that I go to the Cooking Club? Thanks a lot, Mr. Khan!*

"Yeah," I replied, less than enthusiastically.

"Where are my manners? Have you ladies been introduced?" We both shook our heads. "I was afraid not. Nadine, this is Miss Anne. Anne, Nadine." We nodded at each other. I'm sure we looked like bobbleheads.

"Miss Anne, have you an interest in the culinary arts as well? Did I mention that we're making cookies today?"

"I'm sorry, but I can't…." Anne began but then stopped abruptly. I waited in suspense, wondering if she was going to say anything else. It was a really awkward pause for sure. A few secs later she slowly continued, "I well, I sort of told my …um … brother I'd help him … you know … set up for the … the coffee house. T—tonight," Anne stammered, and then looked relieved as she finished speaking. And I couldn't help but think her red cheeks were a great combination with her blue eyes.

"He's performing?" Mr. Khan said. "Clap extra hard for me."

I was just going to ask about her brother, but the bell rang. Instead, we headed toward the door. I was in the lead but then slowed down. This was my chance to talk to her. And while I wanted to ask about her brother, I decided it was better to start by explaining my odd behaviour. "So … about the kicking and whispering. You see, there was this mouse…"

"I know," she said quietly. I was completely taken aback.

"You saw it?"

"I h-h-heard …" she stumbled and paused a bit. "You said mouse."

"I didn't think you did?"

"At first, I thought …you were … calling me."

"What?"

Anne stopped in front of a classroom, took a deep breath, and actually turned to look at me. "M-my nickname. My brothers, well, they call me 'Mouse.'"

"I sympathize. My family calls me 'Bean.'" She smiled at that, so I decided to launch into a question, you know, to keep the conversation going. "Soooo, your brother…?" I started but didn't even get a chance to complete the sentence before Anne pointed at the open door. I could see the teacher was already writing on the chalkboard, and kids were already taking notes.

"Okay, bye," I said, and she smiled apologetically before entering the classroom. I noticed her head was pointed downward as she scurried in. I continued down the hall, walking quickly. I felt hopeful. My friend count had stood at 0 since forever. Okay, maybe .25 if you counted Felix. But suddenly, for the first time in my high school career, it felt like there was a real possibly that it might actually hit a whole number. It wasn't like I had nailed Step Five or anything. Since Anne was even shyer than me, I needed to step up to the plate and take the lead.

Maybe it was going to be one for the books, the year I had two friends, one animal and one human. My Year of the Rodents.

*

"Welcome to the Cooking Club! We have so many wonderful things to make and enjoy this year," said Mr. Khan enthusiastically. As he spoke, he rested his hands on his ample stomach, as if it was a kitchen table.

"Today we are going to make the most delectable cookies for the teacher-parent tea this Friday. But don't worry," he said, lowering his voice a little and practically rubbing his hands with glee. "I promise we'll be able to sample our fair share of these sugary delights!"

I liked Mr. Khan, and I really liked how animated he was about food, but as I looked around the room I was quite disappointed. I knew it was superficial and shallow to judge people by how they looked, but the club members, who were all female with the exception of one kid whose gender I couldn't identify, looked to be, well, quirky. But maybe I just needed to embrace them. Maybe these really were my people now.

"Okay, everyone, find a cooking station—there are ten stations in all. You'll find the cookie recipe you're making on a recipe card, like so." Mr. Khan flashed a neatly printed card at us. "And all the ingredients, utensils and measures. I do have a central station in the middle for the flour and the sugar. We'll all be sharing those ingredients."

I went to a station titled "Aunt Ruth's Famous Oatmeal Chocolate Chip Cookies," where a serious-looking girl with thick glasses and frizzy hair was mouthing the words as she intently read the recipe. I tried to introduce myself, but she held up a hand.

When the serious girl finished reading, she looked me over and declared that she would measure, and I was to sift. I should have probed further at that point—you know, actually found out what sifting was—but I didn't want to look stupid, and she wasn't very approachable. I'm not quite sure how it happened, but it came as a complete surprise to me that flour could fly all around, except downward into the bowl.

I tried to crack a joke about dandruff shampoo to lighten the atmosphere, but the unnamed girl just wiped the white dust off her glasses and face and then glared at me. *Come on*, I thought, *any normal kid would see the humour here.*

Somehow, things deteriorated even further when I ditched the sifting and decided to work the beaters. I jumped the gun and starting beating before we added the liquid, and I shuddered at the awful grating of metal on metal.

I did notice one very small and very round student measuring out an extra cup of sugar. She had the foresight to bring a Ziploc bag with her, and she discreetly poured the sugar into the baggy then stashed it in her backpack like a contraband substance. While most parents who found a white, powdery substance in their kid's bag would think it was cocaine, I had a feeling that this kid's parents would know right away it was the other white death.

Our cookies turned out okay in the end, but the overall experience left me with a bad taste. Not only was I inept at baking, I instinctively knew I wouldn't find a friend at this club. After we'd washed and dried the dishes and did a bit of sampling, we each packed a small paper bag with our favourites. I said goodbye to Mr. Khan but decided to wait to tell him that it was my last as well as first meeting of the Cooking Club. I'd have to learn to expand my kitchen repertoire by watching YouTube or something.

As I walked to my locker clutching the greasy paper bag, I could see another person down the long corridor, leaning into theirs, grabbing some stuff. I thought it was a smallish male student, one of those poor suckers who starts high school before hitting puberty and looks about ten years old. He was sporting the standard issue dark hoodie. All the surreptitious library eating was giving me a complex about eating in public, but since the coast was pretty much clear, I jammed a lemon cookie in my mouth.

I located the books I needed for home, popped them into the backpack, and secured the lock. I started to turn to the left out of habit, since I normally ducked out one of the side doors. But I stopped myself mid-turn. I was feeling slightly more confident at having made some small strides toward my own personal rehabilitation. And so I thought, *What the hell, I'm just going to go right.* Head down the corridor and walk out the front door. Just like the regular people … even if they weren't there to see it. Well, probably *because* they weren't there to see it.

I passed by the prepubescent boy at his open locker and practically kept on going when I did a double take. The short hair had fooled me. So had the hoodie.

"Hey," I blurted out. Then belatedly tried to cover my mouth, which was half stuffed with a cookie.

When the recognition kicked in, a hint of a smile sneaked out around the edges of her mouth. Maybe it was the sugar talking, but I just thrust the bag toward Anne and said, "Cooking club eats, hungry?"

She seemed taken aback, but I could tell when her eyes lingered longingly on the bag for that extra second that she was probably half-starved. So I added, "You'd be doing me a favour, I've downed like three in three minutes…"

She swallowed but didn't avert her gaze. I pushed the bag slightly closer so she could take in the glorious smell of flour, butter, and sugar combined, then baked to semi-perfection. It proved irresistible. "Sure," she said tentatively. And then she added, "I'm starving."

She picked out one of my oatmeal ones and I cringed, but clearly she was famished as she munched it enthusiastically. I laughed a little, which was a complete mistake.

A pinkish hue began on her neck and spread to her cheeks. I knew I had to dig deep. I had to come up with something to say, and fast, before shyness enveloped us with the ice still not broken. I had to seize the moment before I lost my nerve, along with the sugar high.

She had just finished the last, controlled bites of the cookie and was using the back of her hand to daintily wipe away any remaining crumbs. In a moment we would mutter goodbyes … part awkwardly….

“So… setup’s done?” I finally mustered.

She looked up, a bit startled, but did her best to make eye contact with me before she began. Clearly she was trying, too. “Yeah, um, well, there was lots of stuff ….” She paused. I waited. And I was super glad that I decided to stay mum. “B-b-but yeah,” she finished. Phew!

“I almost walked right past you, didn’t recognize the hoodie.”

“I’ve been outside … unloading… So…” She finished the sentence by touching her hoodie sleeve.

We stared uncomfortably at each other for a second or two. I knew that I needed to keep this going… “Test today? You know, hanging out in the library … at lunch?”

“Uh, no.” She bit her lip like she wanted to elaborate but didn’t add anything.

“So, you just like … chilling with the mice?” Her mouth relaxed a bit. Her skin colour seemed to be normalizing, which I took as a good sign. “Let me guess,” I said. “You don’t want to sit by yourself in the caf?”

“Yes,” she said quickly, sounding surprised. And then for the first time, she asked me a question. “Not you?”

“Guilty,” I said.

“Are you new, too?” She was on a roll—two questions in a row.

“No, I just … fell into this stupid pattern of eating lunch there. You’re in nine, right?”

I offered her another cookie, which she quickly accepted. Another good sign.

“No, ten.”

It was my turn to be surprised, “Same,” I exclaimed. We both smiled. I grabbed another cookie as well, and we both took a minute to gorge.

Then she picked up the conversation thread. "I just transferred here from the Delaware Girls' School." And after a shy pause she added, "I, um … I well, I don't know anyone." It was amazing. She was like one of those old mercury thermometers we used in science class. As soon as she started feel the heat, the red just started rising,

"Tell me about it!" I then added with forced enthusiasm, "But you'll be fine, it's just me." I *so* didn't mean it. And by the way she sighed, skeptically, she knew it too.

I felt bad. We needed a new topic… Oh yeah, her brother, or was it brothers?

"So, your brother. Is he in some big band?"

"Not exactly."

"You're, like, a roadie?" I joked. She cringed a little, then I cringed.

Think, think, think… "When does the coffee house start?"

"At seven, but, well … I'm not staying."

"No?"

"I thought I could watch, you know, backstage. You can't, unless you're … performing. So I, well, I can't."

Then all the neurons fired in my brain simultaneously. I understood exactly what was holding her back. "Hey, I'm not doing anything. What if I stay? We can watch. Together?" *Two Step Twos in one day? That would be totally amazing. Oh, yeah, and of course so that Anne can watch her brother … sheesh.*

"You're staying? Sure, if you're staying…." A look of relief washed over Anne's face.

"Absolutely. Want another cookie?" I asked.

"Absolutely," Anne said and actually smiled.

*

Since I'd started at Elgin High last year, I hadn't been to a club meeting or a football game or a school dance or a team tryout or done anything at all, extracurricularly. So it was a total novelty to be at an actual school event, to be somewhat connected.

Anne wanted to practically sit in the back row of the auditorium. I dragged her to the middle, figuring that way her brother would be able to see her without binoculars.

"So what grade's your brother in?" I asked, discreetly sampling another cookie while eying the "no food in the auditorium" signs everywhere. What was with me and my illicit eating habits?

"Grade twelve. A senior. Both of them. They're twins." Her colour seemed to be normalizing again.

"Really? Huh. I'm sure I don't know them—like I said, I don't know anyone. What are their names?"

"Cameron, he's playing tonight. And my other brother is um, Matt."

"Not Matt Lavery?" I blurted out.

"Yeah," she said.

OMG! Her brother was Matt Lavery! Of course, she looked so much like him! She had the same gorgeous thick, shiny jet-black hair and stunning blue eyes. It was an unusual and appealing combination, for sure. Matt was like the god of Elgin High. He was the most popular, good-looking, athletic hottie around. Unless you were in a coma, every student knew Matt Lavery.

I took a deep breath and calmed myself. I didn't want to frighten her by overreacting to her connection with high school royalty. What was Anne Lavery doing eating her lunch in the library? She should be running the student council or the cheerleading squad. I couldn't panic here. I needed to say something neutral.

"So I bet you get this, but you look similar—Matt . . . a female version."

"Yeah, same colouring and stuff."

"So he has a twin brother. Cameron, right? He must do sports, I've heard his name on the announcements…" Anne nodded so I continued, "Does he, you know, look like you and Matt?"

"No, like the exact opposite."

I immediately pictured some white-haired, pink-eyed, three-foot-tall albino dwarf. *Poor Cameron*, I thought, *the black sheep of the family, or in this case, maybe the white one.*

Before I could respond, the music rep for the student council approached the microphone and welcomed us. It was an open mike event for which you didn't need to audition beforehand. One assumed that some amount of practice, or at least thought, had occurred before the acts took the stage.

There were a few okay covers of contemporary artists, like Usher and Jay-Z, and there was a moving a capella performance of Taylor Swift's "Shake it Off." One poor grade nine kid sang a really off-key version of "Hello" by Adele, and a gutsy female inexpertly attempted some of Beyoncé's dance moves, having more success with her lyrics.

When Cameron took the stage near the end, I swore I'd never seen him before. While he looked nothing like Anne or Matt, he was anything but a dwarf albino. Cameron was tall—really tall. Much taller than Matt. And in complete contrast, he had light hair and a fair complexion. I couldn't help myself. I leaned over and asked, "Are his eyes blue?"

She shook her head and said, "No, hazel."

Anne seemed real nervous for him, chewing on her finger as he assembled his eclectic collection of instruments. But Cameron didn't seem overly fazed. I knew even before he began that this performance was going to be different, a total contrast from the others. For starters, there was an accordion, a harmonica, and a cowbell. Even before he started to play, I just felt a crazy kind of electric energy run through my body. He adjusted the mike and began to talk a bit about the two songs he was going to perform. He provided some background while my heart started thumping wildly.

Cameron had written the songs himself. One was about time and used the metaphor of a rock slowly being weathered by the ocean, and the other was about his mother, who I assumed must have died. The songs were incredibly powerful, and I thought the performance was spellbinding.

And it wasn't just that he was totally gorgeous. Okay, so maybe that was part of it. But mostly, it was because he seemed so completely … well … himself. Free. Uninhibited. Nonchalant. Not self-conscious. Instead of … embarrassed. Awkward. Me.

It was obvious, though, that some members of the audience were unappreciative, since a few sniggered and shuffled noisily in their seats. Cameron could have cared less. He performed in the most unaffected way.

He spoke, he sang, he took a moment of silence, he played a long accordion solo, and at one point he simultaneously played the harmonica while he kicked the cowbell. In short, he did whatever the music wanted him to do. He played with passion and abandon. He gave absolutely no thought to being cool.

A feeling of overpowering infatuation hit me like a guitar slap to the head. Once I regained my equilibrium, I pondered this feeling of spontaneous attraction and realized it was like celestial gravity. Cameron was the sun, and I was this speck of intergalactic dust being pulled toward him, close enough to bask in the warmth of his rays but not so close as to get burned. I had it bad for him that day, but I also had this strong desire to keep a safe distance.

I sighed deeply when he left the stage. I didn't know what to say to Anne. I bit my tongue so I wouldn't automatically say something completely stupid like, "I've always wanted to play the accordion."

After we finished clapping, I took another deep breath. I needed to say something that was controlled. Respectful. "Wow, that was … good.… No, great. Different … but in a good way."

"Really?" Anne said slowly, happy with my reaction. "Not everyone, you know, gets him, gets his music."

"I sooo get it…" I said. "I sooo get him…" *Crap*, I thought, *what am I saying*? I had to get out of there before he came over. I was practically incoherent.

"OMG, look at the time.… Homework. And stuff. Got to run. See you tomorrow?" I definitely had to escape before Cameron emerged. What would you say to someone you'd instantaneously fallen in love with?

"Oh, okay!" And then Anne added shyly, "Library, right?"

I smiled, nodded, and waved goodbye. But just when I was about to turn to leave, I saw Cameron start to walk toward us from the front of the auditorium. For a split second our eyes locked. It was like a thousand beams of light being shot directly into my brain. I only had a moment to decide whether to stay and possibly go down in flames or just flee. I picked flight. So I just bolted out the door and disappeared from school as fast as I could.

As I walked home, I barely noticed the bit of chill in the air or that fall mums were making their seasonal appearance in porch planters. I crunched over a few dead leaves, not even thinking about the changing season or my own dying family tree. I was oblivious to everything; all my thoughts were of Cameron. And how he suddenly seemed to be the centre of my universe.

But when I rounded the corner of our street, I quickly got pulled back to life on Earth. I could see that Mom's car wasn't in the driveway, so it would just be Rachel at home. And before I turned the key in the lock, I took a good look at her shoes. There was some flour wedged into one toe seam, so I rubbed at it a bit until it was pristine. I opened the heavy wooden front door and removed her shoes, placing them carefully in the boot tray.

Since I'd eaten a whole bunch of cookies, I wasn't very hungry. I grabbed some cheese and crackers, a glass of water, and an apple from the fridge before I headed upstairs. I stopped by Rachel's door to say hi and to thank her for letting me borrow her shoes. But she was wearing headphones and a frown, so I just ended up giving a little wave. She ignored me, so I decided to hightail it to my room.

Of course, the first thing I did was log on to the computer and try to find Cameron. He wasn't on Twitter, Instagram, or Snapchat, but he did have a Facebook account. There were a few pictures and tons of friends. But I could tell by the old birthday wishes from months ago still populating his wall that he wasn't into it. His relationship status, if that was still current, said "single."

While I was disappointed that I couldn't find out more about him, it also sort of increased my respect for him. I admired people who didn't get completely sucked into living online. I thought about my own meagre Internet existence. How I was never tagged in stuff. Well, I thought, attempting to find a silver lining, at least if Cameron Lavery ever decided to find me, maybe he'd think I wasn't into social media. Not just completely friendless. I couldn't help but laugh. As if Cameron would ever be googling me.

I pushed him out of my head and settled back into my mundane reality. I did my homework, washed my face, and got ready for bed—all the usual stuff. But when I turned off the light and put my head on the pillow, I couldn't help but be transported back to the school auditorium. And it was a vivid image of gorgeous Cameron performing on the stage, subconsciously etched by my retina onto the brain, which lulled me off to sleep.

CHAPTER 4

I ended up having one of those super-realistic dreams that night. I was lying in bed but still awake when I heard someone calling my name. I knew I recognized the voice but couldn't place it. I got out of bed and stumbled around in the dark. It seemed like the voice was right next to me. I turned on the lamp and looked around all around my room, behind the bed, and desk and dresser, but no luck. As the sound got louder, I opened the closet and looked inside.

My search became more anxious, and I practically ran as I left my room. Making my way through the dark upstairs hall, the floorboards creaked noisily beneath me. Careening down the carpeted stairs, I got this sense that it was coming from right outside the front door. I glanced through the side window panels, but no one was in sight.

As I turned on the porch light, a light bulb simultaneously went off in my head. I knew whose voice it was. I grabbed the door handle, turned the knob, and swung the door wide open. A thick mist hung in the air, but the night was cool and pleasant. Initially, I saw only darkness, but then a pair of long legs in faded blue jeans became visible. My gaze followed the tall body upward. He was wearing a black nylon jacket, which I could clearly see, but I couldn't make out his face—it was blurry and indistinguishable.

But then the fuzziness parted and I could see his fair hair and the beautiful features of his kind face. He turned toward me, looking positively radiant, and I reflected the same emotion. He gave me a huge, beautiful smile, and his hazel eyes shone. At that moment we were the only two people in existence.

He was still smiling as he leaned down toward me. His lips met mine and we exchanged this amazing kiss. I practically floated. My subconscious knew I was dreaming, but somehow my heart was warm. There I was, lingering in this dream, this spectacular dream. I didn't ever want to wake up.

That's when the ice water hit me in the face and startled me awake. I sat up, sputtering, and mopped the water with my pyjama shirt. My cheeks stung, and my hair was cold and drenched. As the initial shock faded, anger swirled in my stomach and brain.

Rachel stood above me, empty glass in hand. She wore pale blue sleeping pants with fluffy white clouds, a sunny yellow t-shirt, and a brutal expression. Yesterday we were BFFs, but today I was somehow the enemy. Again. She glared at me with such venom, you would have thought she was the one who had just been jarred awake by the ice water.

Another person might have quickly exited after pulling such a cruel and unusual stunt. But not Rachel—she had all the time in the world, confident I would do nothing to retaliate. And she was right.

"Thanks a lot, bitch!" Rachel said as she tossed the glass on the floor. It landed on the white thick-pile area rug, and a few remaining droplets splashed out. She left the room nonchalantly, not even bothering to shut the door behind her. I remained seated on my bed, cold and wet, but inside, I was red-hot.

Instinctively, I started breathing in and out, slowly and rhythmically, a cleansing breath in and then stale air out, another cleansing breath in, more stale air out. I knew exactly what I needed to do. As the controlled breathing continued, some of my anger started to slip way, and I kept at it until I felt more or less in balance.

Cocooned in a plush pink bathrobe with a towel wrapped around my hair, I was standing at the bathroom sink when Rachel barged in. "Nice," I said sarcastically but calmly enough, despite feeling edgy.

She silently grabbed her big, round brush, elbowed me away from the mirror, and started stroking her thick, reddish brown mane until it cascaded smoothly down her shoulders. She then cleaned the hair out of her brush and put it back neatly on her shelf, exactly where it had been. I waited patiently for her to finish.

Before she left the bathroom, she turned to me, arching one of her eyebrows above her green eyes. "You so deserved it. Dog shit, on my new shoes!" she said coldly.

Not only could Rachel be cruel, she could also majorly paranoid. In her mind, I would have skipped along the sidewalk, spotted the dog poo, and then gleefully hopped right in, purposefully coating every inch. What a difference a day made. Today there was a dark cloud hanging over her, whereas yesterday she had been like a blue sky. I should have known better than to accept anything from her.

"Then use the water on your shoes. They'd be clean. I'd be dry… It was a chocolate chip or something. I was at the Cooking Club."

"The Cooking Club? What's wrong with you? At some loser club, stepping on chocolate chips with my shoes!" Rachel narrowed her eyes at me as my mother knocked on the bathroom door.

"Nadine, Rachel, is everything okay? What's taking you so long? I'm running late, I can give a lift to anyone who's ready."

"Be right out!" Rachel called out sweetly and exited the bathroom without a backward glance.

I kept my voice steady as I yelled my reply. "I'm good, just go."

When I heard the front door close, I collapsed onto the toilet seat. I was exhausted. Rachel exhausted me. It took every ounce of self-control not to reach over and slap her. Even though I was two years younger, I had two inches on her and was physically strong, where she was weak as a marshmallow.

Rachel used to be the person I always wanted to be around. I had worshipped her. For years. When she was on, she was the funniest, funnest person to be around. But even before Dad left, she had begun to change and her moods became more erratic. Darker. And I was an easy, obvious target.

For a long time, Mom could barely get out of bed, she had so many problems. She was so sad. I just decided to keep all the Rachel garbage to myself. Now that Mom was out of bed, she was pretty much never home.

So I still needed to deal with Rachel on my own. And my strategy for dealing with her was, well, doing everything in my power not to deal with her. I tried to stay calm while she tormented me. I just sat there and took it. I didn't react. The deep breathing helped, but I was close to losing it with her. And that would be bad for about a million reasons.

From experience, I knew that fighting back only made things worse. Much worse. Like Voldemort, Rachel was a master of the dark arts. Every time you lashed out at her, you would get it back fivefold plus. If you kept your cool and remained detached, you'd only have to deal with her ordinary, garden-variety psychopathy. If you retaliated, you risked penetrating deep enough into her psyche to initiate a full-blown apocalyptic attack. You would be at war and would have to watch yourself 24-7. I had been there and would not go back. Yes, she was a bully, and I passively took her crap. Maybe when Mom was stronger, I could enlist her support and move from man-to-man to at least a zone defence.

I remained seated on the toilet and resumed my breathing exercises. I counted as I breathed, trying not to think about anything, just as you would if you were meditating. But the breathing just didn't cut it this time. As her transgressions accumulated, practically filling a punching bag, my rage also deepened. It was pretty sure that someday soon, I would just erupt. And then it hit me. I needed a step here. I needed something more to keep from pummelling her.

What if I imagine her dead? I thought. *That could work*. I remembered my old hockey coaches talking about visualization. I could visualize Rachel permanently gone. I'd be free of her.

Step Six: Visualize Rachel's funeral instead of retaliating and being killed myself.

I turned my thoughts to Rachel's imaginary funeral. She would have to be old to be dead, so I would be old too. But I'd be so happy. I saw myself near the casket, my back hunched over, my hair white, my feet clad in black, sensible shoes. People all around were weeping, but I wasn't. Instead, I was biding my time.

When the service was near the end, I gently placed Rachel's beautiful silvery ballerina flats on her cold, dead feet. I then reached for a vase full of flowers, scattering the red roses over her dead body. And just as the casket was closing, I dumped the watery contents of the vase onto her still face. It splashed all around, running down her shoulders. It felt amazing just to imagine it, Rachel old and wet for all eternity. I bet there wasn't anything like that in *The Book of Awesome*, but there should be. Step Six rocked!!!

*

"So did you enjoy those delicious cookies? They were truly delectable," said Mr. Khan, half shutting his eyes, conjuring up the taste of butter and sugar.

"Absolutely. No question."

"So the Cooking Club? Is this type of thing to your liking?"

"The eating part was really good... But not so much the cooking part. I hope that's okay?"

"I understand. I really do. And between you, Anne, and myself, we seem to have our own little library club going, right?"

I laughed and said, "Yeah, I guess we do, but she's late! I'd like to join something but I need to find the right ... something."

"Another club, perhaps?"

"Maybe. Or a team. I sort of took the last year off from sports. But I like that stuff."

"What's your favourite? Are you a swimmer, a tennis player?" asked Mr. Khan as Anne walked through the door.

"My favourite was always ice hockey. I played it for years. What about you?" I asked Anne.

For a second I saw a "deer in the headlights" look in Anne's eyes, and I immediately regretted putting her on the spot. But she took a moment, composed herself, and said, "Well yeah, I play soccer, volleyball, basketball, softball." She hesitated a bit. "But, um, I like field hockey the best."

"Field hockey! Bravo! That's a wonderful sport!" exclaimed Mr. Khan. "I know it's not that popular in Canada, but where I grew up, the boys all played cricket and the girls all played field hockey. It's the national sport of India!"

"Really?" I said. "I've never played, but they have a team here at school."

Anne took a deep breath and nodded. "Yeah, we played them when I was at the Delaware Girls' School. I'm going to try out. I'm pretty sure Cameron and Matt would drag me out for it, anyway. My family is obsessed that way—about sports, I mean."

"Ahhh!" Mr. Khan shouted loudly, seemingly out of the blue. Sporting a look of sheer terror, he pointed at the floor. And there was my first friend at Elgin, slowly sniffing the carpet and making his way toward us.

What was wrong with Felix? He used to avoid people; we had that in common. Personally, I found the little rodent adorable, but Mr. Khan looked absolutely petrified. It was like Felix was packing heat, and his life was in danger. But unfortunately, I knew poor Felix's life was suddenly on the line.

"That phone?" I said, gesturing toward Anne. "It connects to the office. Maybe they could send a custodian? I think I know how to lure him away."

I retrieved a granola bar from my backpack and tore open the wrapper. I walked toward my regular carrel and dropped a few crumbs under the desk. Felix let his nose lead him to the crumbs. *Yup*, I thought, *full-blown rodent dementia.* He was still there, happily munching away under the carrel, when Tony the custodian arrived.

Tony nodded, and Mr. Khan, who had retreated behind one of those revolving bookcases full of paperbacks, reached out from behind and pointed at the mouse with a shaky index finger.

"Yup, I see it. And when there's one mouse, there's always a family and then some."

"You can just move them, right?" I said. "A family relocation?" Tony gave me a funny look. Mr. Khan tried to talk, but the words just didn't come out.

"Fresh air?" I said to Mr. Khan, who nodded.

So Anne and I each took an arm and helped steady Mr. Khan out the door and down the hall.

Tony came out of the library carrying my backpack and Mr. Khan's briefcase. He handed the items to us, pulled out his massive key ring, and locked the library door. "We need to close it for twenty-four hours, lay some bait, and get rid of that mice problem for you." I immediately envisioned poor Felix captured and lying dead in a trap. I blinked to get rid of the image but kept my mouth shut. Between Tony and Mr. Khan, saving Felix seemed like a pretty hopeless cause.

Mr. Khan cleared his throat and spoke for the first time since he'd seen the mouse. "I have a terrible phobia of rodents. It surely steams from my childhood." He paused for a moment to catch his breath before he continued. "We need to rid the library of them, and ban food. Completely." As Tony left, Mr. Khan turned to us and said, "I'm afraid our lunch club is going to disband. And by the way, all that coughing whilst eating didn't fool me one bit, Miss Nadine."

I nodded, trying to look contrite, and said, "I'm sorry. We understand."

"You two have each other now. You can start eating in the cafeteria together. No more hiding out anymore, sneaking lunch! I don't think my heart could take seeing another rodent!"

Which led me to Step Seven.

Step Seven: Eat in the cafeteria like a normal person.

This was actually less of a step than a direct order from Mr. Khan. I felt ready to comply, but Anne seemed more tentative. We exchanged cellphone numbers before we went to our afternoon classes so we could text about an exact time and meeting place.

When I arrived home, I made sure I didn't have any chocolate chips on the bottom of my shoes and was careful not to do anything else to ignite the combustible Rachel. The evening passed in relative calm as she and I just kind of ignored each other. I made some extra French toast, which I left on the kitchen island as a peace offering.

Rachel didn't acknowledge my efforts, but of course she ate the French toast. She probably didn't see it as a gesture but rather an expectation, and I didn't dwell on her non-reaction. I had the caf on my mind. A mundane prospect for most but a big nudge toward normalcy for me.

I knew that as long as Anne didn't turn absolute beet-red or that her knees didn't buckle, we would hopefully meld into the crowd. The odds were pretty good that we wouldn't spill on ourselves or do anything too embarrassing. What did have me panicked, though, was the possibility that Cameron might come over and talk to Anne. And what if she introduced us? Of course she would. She was a polite, after all. I honestly didn't know what I would do or say. I thought of the look of fear on Mr. Khan's face when he saw the mouse. I'm sure his look would be replicated if I ever met Cameron, and it wasn't pretty.

I texted Anne. *What r u up 2?*

She texted back. *Cant concentrate on hmwrk, 2 nervous!!*

It'll be fine ☺!!! I replied. Anne didn't respond, so I continued, *Where shld we meet 4 lunch?*

Anne replied, *???*

Water fountain outside caf doors 2 the left?

K, she texted back.

A few min after the bell?

K.

K, c u then.

CHAPTER 5

I clutched my lunch bag tightly to my body as I walked down the hall toward the cafeteria but then pulled it away again. *Crap*, I thought. *I probably squished those strawberries*. I checked my shirt, but it was fine. I wondered if anyone would notice my squished fruit, but then I thought, *Yeah, right.* So far no one at Elgin, with the exception of Anne, had even noticed that I existed.

As planned, Anne was standing by the water fountain. I could see her peering into the cafeteria, and she looked about as comfortable as if she was buying tampons with a hot boy behind her in line.

"Hey." I forced a smile, and Anne just gazed back at me, clearly uneasy. I noted that her knees looked solid, so I figured we were good to go. "Okay?"

She responded with a half nod, and I thought, *Good enough.*

Clearly, as a veteran of the school for over a year and practically outgoing in comparison, I needed to take the lead. I walked into the caf, tossing my head a bit to look casual while surreptitiously scouting for a couple of empty seats.

I wondered if there was any rhyme or reason as to who sat at what table. Did the stoners sit by the exit for a quick escape if the cops arrived? Perhaps the nerds were relegated to the corner so they wouldn't bother anyone? And the "It" girls and guys to the front and centre so people wouldn't need to strain their eyes or necks to worship them or diss their outfits?

I had no idea what the answers to these questions were but decided not to overthink. I spotted some empty seats partway down, and we plunked ourselves into the orange plastic chairs. It was all surprisingly uneventful.

No one threw us out or threw stuff at us or told us to go back to the library where we belonged. Anne tried to look straight ahead, but I could see her eyes darting around, taking in the people and smells and sounds. She was sufficiently distracted to ignore her lunch and offer little in the way of conversation.

It occurred to me that Felix was directly responsible for Anne and me being in the cafeteria. Maybe Felix's demise would be a turning point for me and signal the end of my mousey ways? He was most definitely a martyr for the cause, and it would only be appropriate to acknowledge the sacrifice he'd made at this important step in my social rehabilitation. I took a moment to remember Felix before I punctured my orange juice box with the straw.

As I took the first sip, Anne was still looking awkward and mute. It was up to me to make this transition. I took a deep breath then started talking to give her some time to acclimatize. I mentioned my family, but I decided to gloss over Rachel and the separation; I figured it was better that way. Anne just nodded at the beginning, but as I slowly turned the tables and started asking her a few questions, she opened up a bit. The way she spoke about her father made him seem nice but pretty strict. She talked a little about her brothers and how they looked out for her.

Her answers were kind of short, perfunctory. I knew she wasn't being rude or anything, it was just that she wasn't super comfortable talking about herself and seemed prone to undershare in a world of oversharing. She didn't bring up her mother's death, which I only knew about from Cameron's performance at the coffee house.

"So…" I said when there was a lull in the conversation. "Do your brothers eat lunch? Here?" Even as she responded, I was cleaning my teeth with my tongue to make sure there were no ugly bits. I was paranoid that Cameron would just appear out of nowhere to check in with his baby sis. If I was incapable of saying a word to him, if all I could do was smile, I didn't want any crud ruining the effect.

"Not usually," she said. I looked at her encouragingly, so she took the hint and continued after taking a big breath. "They share a car, they go out a lot … with friends. The seniors, they mostly leave."

My stress level immediately dropped. "Rachel's the same," I said. "She almost never stays."

"I wonder if my brothers know her?"

"Probably," I said. I was surprised this hadn't occurred to me. They were all pretty attractive seniors at the same school. One would think they might socialize. Or at the very least say "hi" to each other or something. I knew enough not to ask about "the girlfriend" situation with her brothers; surely that would raise some red flags.

"So, um, about tomorrow," Anne started hesitantly. "I, well, I heard on the morning announcements that there's a field hockey meeting at the start of lunch."

"Okay, cool. Well, maybe send me a text when it's done and we could meet up? I seriously can't see myself sitting here all alone waiting for you."

"Oh my god, I would die!" Anne blurted out, and we both laughed. "I'll text you." After a minute, she added, "So, what about coming, you know, to the meeting?"

"Me? No way! I've never played field hockey, not even in gym."

"You're probably busy with hockey…"

"No, that's on … ice." I didn't want to tell Anne I'd pretty much had to quit last year. Dad loved hockey as much as I did, and he'd driven me to almost every practice and game and all the out-of-town tournaments too. When he'd first gone to New York, it was just supposed to be for a month or so. Initially, other hockey families ferried me back and forth to the rink.

But when Dad started delaying his return by weeks and months, it got too embarrassing making up excuses for him and always depending on others for rides. Eventually, I just quit. It was the only sane decision. I'm not sure my mom ever even realized what happened.

"So you're not playing any sports?"

"Uh, no."

"Oh," said Anne, half-frowning. I could tell she wanted to encourage me, but the idea of playing field hockey seemed crazy to me. Just because both sports had the word "hockey" in their names wasn't a compelling enough reason. So I was happy when she didn't push it.

"Do you want to hit the washroom before class?" I asked.

"Sure," said Anne. We gathered up our stuff and headed out. It was actually anticlimactic. Step Seven had proved no big deal at all.

*

First on the announcements the next morning was the lunchtime field hockey meeting. I hadn't given it another thought after talking with Anne, but then I actually started pondering it. As a result, I was fidgety and distracted during the first few periods. The multistep plan was on track so far. I was making a new friend, and I was eating in the cafeteria.

Granted, I had taken a chance with Rachel by borrowing her shoes (Step Four) and ended up with ice water all over my face. But I should have known better—that relationship would never going to improve. Even with rehab.

I kept thinking about Step Two: Get involved with something new.

I had tried the Cooking Club, and that had definitely not worked out. But I'd pretty much known that. A sports team was more in my comfort zone. As for trying field hockey, the pros included: Anne was trying out and it would be nice to know someone on a team; I was reasonably athletic and had done pretty well at ice hockey; it would allow me to make an honest attempt at fulfilling Step Two.

The cons for trying out for field hockey were: I'd never ever played the sport and was terrified I'd fail and look like an idiot to Anne and others; and I would dread having to play if, say, Cameron was in the stands. Hadn't Anne said something about how supportive her brothers were? It was a sure bet they'd come to watch a few games. How did someone I'd only ever seen once and never spoken to have so much power over me? I was constantly scanning the halls but hadn't seen him since the coffee house. Argh! I was digressing from the cons.

I went over the mental list again, and something became clear. Every single con was about fear, about the unknown. I knew there were lots of reasons why grade nine sucked so badly, but one big reason was fear. I was shy and afraid of putting myself out there. Somehow I had to overcome all this fear if I was make a go at this personal improvement thingy.

Okay, I thought, *I've got to give this a shot. Literally.*

Her smile when she saw me at the field hockey meeting could have lit up the night sky. There were about a dozen or so girls in attendance. Aside from Anne, I only recognized an awful girl named Danielle from my grade nine gym class. She was always bragging about her great talent as a goalie and kept bugging Mrs. Anthony to do a field hockey unit so she could show off. I'm pretty sure that's why Mrs. Anthony never did a unit on the sport.

Danielle was tall, pretty, and blonde, but she came across as harsh. I swear she had taken courses in hair flicking and black eyeliner application. Her dad was like the president or CEO of some big insurance company, and she seemed to think she was presidential material as well.

The coach was a Ms. Davies, a small, efficient-looking middle-aged woman with short, spiky grey hair. Ms. Davies taught chemistry to the grade eleven and twelve students, so I had never had her as a teacher. She seemed pleasant, but she was also pretty brusque and didn't waste a lot of time. She circulated a sign-up list and passed out a schedule with dates and times for the practices and games.

"Look around, girls," she said. "There aren't that many of you. If you have any friends who might be interested in coming out, we'd love a few more players. I see some familiar faces out there, but it's encouraging to see some new ones too. Just a quick show of hands, is anyone well, a complete newbie here?"

I hesitated a second and then raised my hand, and so did a girl named Mei. "Oh, sure," she said in a jokey tone, "point us out for initiation!" Mei, who was medium in height and build, had gorgeous midlength black hair and a smattering of freckles on the bridge of her nose.

Ms. Davies half smiled and said, "So, girls, it's great to have you here. I'm looking forward to another exciting season. We haven't won the big one yet, but we've come real close and I have a good feeling this year. We'll work hard and have fun and make Elgin proud. I'll see you after school today. Drink lots of water, because you're going to be sweating a ton! See you at three thirty, sharp."

I waited for Anne outside. I'd never seen her so animated. She was like Tigger, practically bouncing with excitement. "Awesome that you came, I had to practically force myself to walk in there. It's going to be great having you!!"

"Chances are I won't even make the team. And please, don't feel like you have to babysit me, okay? I'm sure I'm going to completely suck." But I secretly prayed to the god of field hockey that it would go okay.

CHAPTER 6

When I opened the change room door after school later that day, I ran smack into Rachel. She'd had gym last period and was on her way out. A definite mellowing of her personality had happened since the ice water incident, but she surprised me by appearing almost happy.

"So you blow-dried your hair twice in a week?" said Rachel, pulling me over to the side to talk. I stared blankly at her. "What's up?" she continued.

"Nothing."

"Looks good."

"Thanks," I said, a bit taken aback.

"So why are you here? The library's upstairs, remember?" she joked but didn't wait for a response. "Want to grab a chai latte on the way home? Sound good?"

"Uh—" I tried to interject but she just continued talking right over me. She got into these moods where she talked a mile a minute; you could barely shut her up. When she was in a good mood she could be really wild and fun, even though it sometimes got a little out of hand. Remembering those good times helped me get through her bad days without killing her.

I could see some of the field hockey girls filing out of the change room, already dressed for practice. I had no choice but to interrupt. "Next time. I've got field hockey tryouts, I've got to get going."

"OMG, field hockey? Have you even played? Those sticks are lethal on the shins. And there's no skating. Like at all."

"Yeah, I know. See you later." I cut her off and ducked into the washroom. I waited a minute until I was confident she'd left and then practically raced out of the stall and quickly changed. Some coaches really loved to make an example of latecomers with lots of extra drills. I needed to blend in as best I could, because Rachel was right—I had no idea how to play field hockey. What was I doing?

"Go ahead, I'll just be a sec," I said as I was putting my hair into a ponytail. Anne was dressed and ready to go. Even though I appreciated having Anne around, it would be easier to fall flat on my face without her hovering too close.

Ms. Davies had us get right down to work with lots of calisthenics and running drills. Then we quickly moved into stickhandling, passing, shooting, and ended with a scrimmage. Ice hockey was lightning-fast, but I was surprised how quickly the ball moved in field hockey. I told myself to stop comparing the two games, since field hockey was the only type that mattered out here.

The field hockey ball was small and hard and the stick was short, with a curved bottom. Rachel was right—that stick did hurt when it made contact with unprotected flesh. And so did getting beaned with the ball. The shots on the field were quite powerful and difficult to stop, and only one player could fight for the ball with another player, or you got penalties.

I listened closely to all the instructions and tried my best to keep up with the other players. I definitely needed to wear my soccer cleats next time. Probably my biggest loser move was when I sprinted full-out after the ball, caught right up to it, and then instead of striking it, I started sliding. I tried to stop myself but ended up falling hard on my butt in front of everybody. I felt like a complete idiot.

At the end of practice, Ms. Davies pulled me over. *Here it comes! Let's pull the most pathetic player discreetly over to the side, tell her she's a hopeless cause, and send her packing.* So I was surprised when Ms. Davies didn't launch into some speech that began with, "Well, thanks for coming out" and ended with "Don't let the gym door hit you on the butt on your way out." Instead, she asked me what sort of sports I'd played before. She was actually encouraging. She told me that most of the errors I was making were due to inexperience and fatigue, which could both be overcome. In short, I was an out-of-shape field hockey neophyte, but I had potential. Ms. Davies suggested that I start doing some cardio to build up my endurance and perhaps borrow a stick and do a bit of shooting and handling practice on my own.

"Sure, I'll try to work on that. I'm just relieved you're not cutting me. Well, not yet."

"Cut! I can't afford to cut anyone. We have the bare minimum. We need eleven on the field at all times and at least a couple on the bench. So unless there's a sudden surge of interest in girl's field hockey, everyone's on the team."

Anne seemed like a different person on the field. She was amazing, coming alive during the scrimmage, playing really aggressively, never letting up. She reminded me of how I used to be when I played ice hockey. Maybe if I worked hard, I would become competitive at this, too.

As I sat in the locker room getting changed, I could already feel my muscles starting to ache. And I was so winded, it felt like all the air had been sucked right out of me. There was dirt and mud all over my shorts, socks, shoes, and legs, and my shirt was drenched. Lucky for me, someone had an extra pair of shin pads, or I would have had even more bruises and cuts.

Some of the girls had already showered, changed and left, but most of us were just finishing up when Danielle came into the change room. Her long blonde hair was out of the elastic and hanging straight down her back. "So you're Anne, Anne Lavery?" Danielle asked, her mouth kind of hanging open in suspense. When Anne nodded, Danielle smiled and then said in her phoniest voice, "I didn't know Matt had a sister. He's here to pick you up, and I for one would never make him wait!"

"Thanks," said Anne, blushing, uncomfortable with being the centre of attention, and possibly also uncomfortable with the reference to Matt, the God of Elgin High. She quickly mouthed "Goodbye" to me and made a hasty exit.

Then Danielle turned to the rest of us and started going on about Matt and how great it was for her that Anne was on the team. *What a piece of work*, I thought as I left the change room shortly afterward, deciding to walk home in my gym uniform and shower later.

As I started home, even walking was painful. I knew I would be practically crawling tomorrow; the next day always felt way worse. But it hadn't been too bad. Other than Danielle, most of the other girls seemed nice. I found myself gravitating toward Mei, who was super funny. Maybe being on the field hockey team would actually raise my friend count.

*

I was in the kitchen guzzling my second glass of ice water when Rachel walked in, took one look at me, and said, "Well, look what the cat dragged in," and started to laugh.

"It's not a good look, that's for sure," I said, surveying my filthy legs and arms. "But hey, why don't you toss some of this at me." I pretended to hand her my ice water. "It'll clean me up, and the ice would be good for my sore muscles."

"I would lose the crucial element of surprise," Rachel shot back with a smile.

She watched me drink for another minute and then said, "I have an idea. Come with me." She grabbed my hand and pulled me out of the kitchen. I followed her up the stairs to the bathroom. "Wait here," she said. I peered in the mirror at my dusty face before she returned with an armful of stuff, including a fresh towel, bath salts, candles, and a lighter.

"What, are you operating an illicit spa?" I sputtered, secretly pleased that she was carrying objects of pleasure and not torture.

"Ask me no secrets, and however else that stupid saying goes," Rachel said as she hung up the towel, turned on the tap, and sprinkled in the salts. She then arranged the candles around the bathtub perimeter and lit them. "Sorry, all out of rose petals today."

"Wow, thanks. This is really amazing, Rach." I was practically speechless. I couldn't help but remember that the last time she was nice to me, I'd ended up with ice water in the face. But I was too exhausted to refuse her ministrations. She put her finger to her lips, gave me a quick smile, and was gone. The bath felt so heavenly on my sore butt and achy muscles, I practically fell asleep.

Before I turned out the light that night, I sent Anne a quick text: *R u sore?*

She replied: *Yup! 4 sure. So glad u came u did good 2.*

Clumsy is good? least I only hurt myself! gnite.

Gnite.

CHAPTER 7

Anne and I sat in pretty much the same spot in the caf most days. As I pulled out my chair, I couldn't help but notice an unappetizing sight. Sitting nearby was a girl from my science class nicknamed named Mad Monica. A frayed thong protruded out over her exposed lower back. The way some girls wore their thongs just wasn't attractive, and this one was ready for the trash bin. With her back to me I thankfully couldn't see her front. She usually sported low-cut tops, letting the boys get a preview of her girls.

I knew part of it was jealousy because I had a boyish body, and boobs were a status item in high school. If you had them, you didn't need anything else to be noticed. I didn't possess much cleavage, but even if I did, I told myself I'd never flaunt it as overtly as some of the girls did. At least that was what I told myself.

"So … I need to see that old purple thong thingy when I'm trying to eat?" I grumbled to Anne, nodding toward Monica. "It's way overdue for the itty-bitty rag pile." I scrunched my nose as I took a bite of my sandwich.

"Maybe she doesn't realize it's … showing," said Anne. The first field hockey practice seemed to have been a real turning point for us. Anne seemed pretty much over her shyness with me.

"You're new, so you're allowed to be naïve. She's in my science class. They call her Mad Monica. I don't think we're talking wardrobe malfunction. It's more like bragging rights 'this thong has seen definite action.'"

I took another bite and started wondering if maybe some of Rachel's nastiness was starting to rub off on me. Or perhaps it was genetic? Did being mean make Rachel feel good somehow? For some reason, badmouthing Monica behind her back was really raising my spirits at the moment.

"So by action, are you talking washing machine?" said Anne. I knew there was a reason I liked her.

I laughed out loud and said, "Agitation cycle?" And Anne laughed at that.

"Hey, you were awesome at practice," she said. "You've got good game sense."

"So it was my game sense? When I ran over the ball and fell on my butt??"

"Seriously, we've all done that, still do."

For a second I envisioned Cameron and Matt in the bleachers watching me land on my ass. Then I thought about Danielle and what she'd said about Matt, and I decided it best to give Anne a heads-up. "Just so you know," I said, "Danielle kind of made a comment about Matt after you left. You know, lots of girls are totally into him? He's a real big deal."

"Yeah," said Anne evenly. "I'm starting to get that impression." She swallowed hard and then said, "I hope that, like, you're not one of them?"

"Me? Noooo! I am absolutely not!" *Phew*, I thought. Technically I wasn't lying—we were talking about Matt. "But don't take that the wrong way—I don't dislike him or anything. I'm flying so far under the radar that I'm practically invisible."

"Thanks for the warning. Being at the same school with him—with them—it's well, new."

"It's not all bad. So they're really popular—it should make things easier for you, right? It's not like you want to avoid them or anything," I said, thinking of my sister.

"What about Rachel?" Anne asked, reading my thoughts. "You don't talk much about her. Are you guys close?"

"Um, not really," I said. "We just sort of live in two different worlds." *I live on planet Earth,* I thought, *and she pretty much lives on Jupiter, the one with all those moons revolving around it. 'Cause doesn't everything revolve around her?*

*

Something was killing my nose. I could barely breathe. I woke up from a dead sleep, and it wasn't pleasant. The first thing I saw was the early morning sky peeking through my white and purple paisley curtains. But then my eyes were drawn to the centre of my vision, which was partially obstructed by something. And it was painful. I touched it. It was a clothespin, and not just any clothespin. My mother had favoured these heavy-duty stainless steel ones from some crazy mail order place. She loved the smell of sheets and towels that dried in the open air, and these suckers kept the laundry on the line even during a tornado.

They were not made for use on humans. I plucked it from my nose and hurled it across my room. It hit the wall, denting the pale lilac paint and then fell to the ground with a substantial thud. *My sister is insane*, I thought.

As I slumped back on my pillow, I could see a piece of paper propped up on my window seat. I sighed as I picked it up and read the message in red letters. *Stop snoring, BITCH!*

When I was young, Rachel had purposely lost me in the forest, which was terrifying. I had also been hung by my coat hood on a low tree branch for quite a long time and been tied securely with a skipping rope to the backyard fence while Rachel fired the water hose on me. On the jet setting. At close range.

And those were just the tortures I suffered as a child. Some of the more imaginative ones from later times included the anchovy paste she smeared on the bottom of my shoe insole and the maple syrup she dumped onto my Bristol board project the morning it was due. All of these were in revenge for some "wrong" I'd committed against her.

I hadn't always just taken her abuse; in the past I'd told my parents, but that only fixed the immediate problem and was never a real solution. And right now, there was only Mom, and she was barely holding on. How could she help me with Rachel when she was just learning to help herself? If I retaliated, I knew from experience that Rachel would go into overdrive.

My nose throbbed, and I knew I'd have a bruise. But the greater my reaction, the greater her triumph, and the more inventive and twisted her next attack would be. So I took my cleansing breath, again and again. And I started counting. I counted the days until I was due to go to summer camp and wouldn't have to see her for a month, and then I counted the days until Rachel would hopefully leave home to go to university.

And if it was really bad, I could now embrace Step Six. I counted the years until she was an old lady and died. I saw myself at the funeral, my back hunched, my hair white, my feet clad in sensible black shoes. This time, as I placed the last red rose in the casket, I clamped a hard steel clothespin on her cold, dead nose and watched it practically collapse with the weight. I then slammed the casket closed with a big smile.

I inspected my nose in the mirror, and I was able, with some strategically placed makeup, to minimize the discoloured indentation. I got out of the house as quickly as possible without seeing Rachel. As I walked to school I tried to think of a workable step to improve things with her. But everything I came up with was just a fanciful daydream.

Choose one of the following for Step Eight:

a) Convince a doctor to perform an emergency lobotomy on Rachel.

b) Have Rachel declared criminally insane and then locked away in a padded cell, like forever.

c) But hey, let's go even further! Why not send Rachel to NYC, and then she could be Dad's problem?

And just like with Step Six, imagining Rachel out of my life was good for my mental health.

CHAPTER 8

"Okay, girls, we're going to start off this practice with some running drills. You can be amazing at passing and stickhandling and even getting past the goalie. But if you can't get to the ball first on a consistent basis, then everything else is a waste of time." Ms. Davies blew her whistle and we set out to run the perimeter of the field, five times. I was huffing and puffing by the time we finished the first lap and had to fall behind most of the others to continue.

"Good plan," Mei said. "Draft off the speed bunnies!" I grinned. Not only was Mei irreverent, but unlike me, she was also both loud and bold. But when it came to field hockey, we were similarly awful. We started running in tandem. Sometimes running with a partner can help you find a faster pace, but compared with the others, our pace was practically backward.

Danielle lapped us with her long, powerful legs and made a point of sneering at us. "The sculpted look is so last year, don't you think?" said Mei, almost wheezing.

"Yeah," I gasped. "I'm going for rolls."

Anne came up behind us and tempered her pace so as not to further embarrass us. "Almost halfway there!"

"Okay," I said, huffing for both of us. Mei was panting, so I was pretty sure she couldn't speak. Anne passed us gradually but then as she increased her speed to her natural pace, she moved further away real quickly. "It's like we're running in slow motion!"

"Or reverse," gasped Mei, who suddenly clutched her stomach and doubled over, stopping. "Why did I shotgun that protein bar? If I puke, I'll die," she gasped as I jogged on the spot.

"I tossed my sandwich — mould." I struggled to talk. "My stomach's empty. So dry heaves," I said, and we both cringed as we imagined these grim scenarios. "Real slow?" Mei nodded and we started again at a speed that was probably not far from regular walking.

Danielle lapped us again and couldn't resist taunting us as she ran by. "You suck! You can't even keep up with the goalie. It's all in the glutes! Glutes, gotta get them!"

"Gross," Mei sputtered, her anger greater than her breathlessness. "That's a 'g' word for you. Looking at your butt, it's gross!" Danielle paused to wiggle her butt for effect and took off.

We had reached the stage where even just the act of speaking was becoming too much, so we trotted along in silence at the end of pack. Anne, whose shyness seemed to go into remission on the field, clapped and cheered when we finally finished the last lap, way behind everyone else.

Despite my embarrassingly poor fitness level and some of the liberties I took with the rules, Ms. Davies was encouraging, which really went a long way to help convince me to keep trying. At the end of the practice she asked us to stay for a short meeting. "We have some seasoned talent on the team," said Ms. Davies, "and for those players like Anne, Danielle, Kathleen, Alana, and Carly, we really need to fine-tune your skills so we can count on consistently solid play from you. You people are the backbone of the team, and we need you to help push forward the talent of the more intermediate players—people like Nakeisha, Estella, and Jesse—to play at a higher level." Ms. Davies paused for a minute to shake her head at Carly, who was whispering to Kathleen.

"And then we have our new players, Mei and Nadine," Ms. Davies continued. "Thanks for coming out. All of us have been there before, right? Stepping on the field and being an absolute newbie to the game. We need every single one of you. I've tried recruiting, but the reality is that we have thirteen players. You are all officially on the team. Oh, and some good news, we get new uniforms this year."

"Yes! Those polyester ones were a nightmare!" cried Nakeisha.

"Thank you, Nakeisha," said Ms. Davies, cutting off the others, who were also trying to interrupt. "Let me just finish so we can all go home. My point is that we need all of you for every practice and for sure for every game. We all know how exhausting it is to run up and down and up and down the field while fighting for the ball, blocking shots, and trying to find a break to score. Except for Danielle, everyone needs time off the field. Our starters will play the most, but every member will get a chance to play each game. We need all of you there. No excuses unless you are in the hospital. And if you're not in the hospital and you miss a game, that's where you are going to end up, okay? Got it? Good!"

Coach Davies then called Mei and me over for a short conference. "You two girls are coming along nicely. Nadine, I heard that you used to play ice hockey. I can tell. You're picking up the stick skills real fast. What's holding the both of you back, though, is your fitness level. You two should partner up and do some extra running, work on that cardio, okay? I'm serious here."

I nodded and looked at Mei, who nodded too.

"Doing anything this weekend?" Mei asked me as we were changing.

"Not much. You?" I pulled my hair out of the ponytail, brushed it out, and put the elastic back in again.

"Nothing special," said Mei as she pulled on her socks. "Well, I know it's, like, masochistic, but the coach is right. We're going die if we don't get in some extra running."

"Agreed. I'll find you on Facebook, we can make a plan?" I said as I put on some chapstick. "Does Sunday work, maybe afternoon?"

"Perfect. Painful but perfect," Mei said as she repositioned her backpack, waved goodbye, and left.

Anne came up to me just as I heading for the door. "Cameron's picking me up. Want a lift?"

"Oh, um, thanks. I'm … walking."

"Really? Why? We can drop you, it's on the way."

"Uh, well, the coach, uh, she just came and busted us about our cardio. So I figure, um, I'll power walk home. For the extra workout." I wasn't proud of it, but for some reason I was a really good liar.

Danielle, who seemed to circle Anne frequently in the hopes of dive-bombing Matt, was hovering nearby. "I'll take that ride," she said brazenly.

Anne stood tongue-tied, not sure how to swat Danielle away, so I spoke up. "That's … not on the table." Less was more here, so I grabbed Anne's arm and we walked out into the hall together to get away.

A ride in a car with Cameron? I would go surely into cardiac arrest, especially after all that stress I'd put on my heart at practice! I had caught the odd glimpse of him lately, and it was all I could do to keep it together. And that was from a distance. I didn't want to make a fool of myself. Up close.

"That girl is persistent!" said Anne, far too politely.

I just shook my head in disgust and said, "You're way too nice. That's not the word I'd use—more like obnoxious.

Anne smiled and changed the subject. "Well, I'm impressed you're walking. And if you want, we could practice shooting and passing and stuff. This weekend even…"

"Yeah, um, I've, well, got some stuff happening. But another time, for sure." It wasn't that I was trying to steer clear of Anne—she was awesome. But how could I invite her over with the unpredictable Rachel around? Who knew when her evilness would emerge? And clearly I wasn't up to going to Anne's house.

I didn't want to hurt Anne's feelings, but if I kept avoiding her after school, I probably would. I knew I needed to address my Cam-a-phobia as part of my multistep plan, but I just wasn't ready for that. Maybe I needed an interim step. I pondered the possibilities after I said goodbye to Anne. This is what I came up with:

Step Nine. Again, multiple choice:

a) Hire a hypnotist to overcome my phobia.

b) Undergo electric shock therapy to burn away all traces of shyness and cowardice from my brain.

c) Schedule frontal lobe surgery on a two-for-one deal with Rachel. *Remove and dispose of her psychotic sweet spot, then scoop out some of her excess self-confidence and insert that grey matter directly into me.*

Was it just a coincidence that Step Eight was a mental health plan for Rachel and that Step Nine was a mental health plan for me? I wondered if Rachel might have fewer issues if I had fewer issues too. There was a pattern of avoidance here: I avoided Cameron, I avoided the whole school by hiding in the library, and I just generally avoided Rachel. Were we a bad combination, Rachel and me? The bully and the bully enabler? I had learned about "enabling" when I looked through the Alcoholics Anonymous pamphlet. Maybe I should have read that bit more closely.

CHAPTER 9

It might sound weird, but I was truly happy as I walked over to Mei's house. So far I had 1.0 friends, not that I was counting or anything. But Mei was completely different from Anne, and yes, I was gunning for 2.0.

As I'd found out during field hockey practice, if you had to do something painful like running, at least Mei would make it almost fun. She had read on some website about a run-walk training technique in which you ran for five minutes and then walked for five. We covered more than three kilometres with the run-walk method, which wasn't too bad for two out-of-shape fifteen-year-olds. She had me laughing so hard at one point, imitating one of those "official" power walkers, that I got a stomach cramp.

After we finished our cardio, we sat on the grass in Oakridge Park under a maple tree, huffing and puffing. "I could so go for a cigarette!" said Mei, which surprised me.

"What? Are you serious? That's, like, the last thing you should be inhaling when you can barely breathe as it is," I said and then reached for my water bottle and started chugging away.

"For some reason, whenever I work out, I just seem to really crave a smoke. Stupid, isn't it? Maybe it's my body's way of telling me 'don't bother.' It's pointless because I'm going to light up. So, zero health benefits."

The dangers of smoking had been drilled into my head since I was a preschooler, so I totally didn't get why you would want one at all, especially after a run. But I didn't want to seem too uptight, so I decided to ask the most obvious question. "So you're a smoker, for real?" I offered the water to Mei, but she shook her head, so I finished it off.

"I'm not, like, addicted or anything. My mom is this closet smoker. She has maybe two or three a day. I found her hiding spot ages ago, so I tried a couple. And it was calming. I just have a the odd one now and then."

"Do you think your mom knows? Like, does she notice any missing?"

"And what could she say? She'd be a complete hypocrite, right? So who knows," Mei said as she massaged her calves. "They're seizing up. Why we are torturing ourselves? Let's just quit, pretend it was a bad dream. Field hockey sucks." She stood up and brushed herself off.

"So why'd you try out?"

"I was on the team last year, for a total of one pathetic game. I broke my wrist. This huge player, I think her name was Helen something, she fell on me, and it snapped in half. Danielle told me she did it on purpose, that the girl overheard me call her 'Sasquatch,' but you know Danielle—she's full of it...."

"So did you?"

"What?"

"Call her 'Sasquatch?'"

"Yeah," Mei said sheepishly.

"That's not cool."

"I know. And being an Asian kid, I can relate when people call you names. I don't know why I said it, I was just mad. It was my first game and she was so big, it was hard to get at the ball. I just blurted it out. I didn't think she heard me. I guess that's not really an excuse? Anyway, Danielle got a hold of this picture of her when she fell on me, and she posted it everywhere. It was totally embarrassing."

"Yeah?" I said.

"Luckily, you couldn't really see me, just my arm and this huge player landing on my wrist. Danielle added this stupid hashtag, #Sasquatchsnapswrist. Thank God she didn't tag me in it."

"I think I saw that picture."

"Everyone did. It got reposted like a million times. That Danielle. Anyway, maybe I got what I deserved, even if I didn't mean to start the name. But it was kind of a lucky break. I got to sit out for the season," said Mei.

"So why try out again?"

"My parents. They say you need to be on one school team every year. That it looks good on your university application and that you'll meet new people and get fitter, blah, blah, blah. My older sister Lian was a star field hockey player at Elgin. She promised to practice with me, but that was a load of crap. She's away at McGill, so you're stuck with me."

Now that a few minutes had passed since we'd stopped running, my body was luxuriating in the endorphins. I had forgotten how much I loved the feeling after really exerting myself at hockey—all warm and fuzzy.

Still on the runner's high, we made plans to do it again the next weekend, which morphed into the idea of also seeing a movie or something. As I walked home, it occurred to me why the plan was called "steps." It seemed that once it started, one led to another. I would never have gotten to know Mei if I hadn't tried out for the team. I was about a block from home and swigging from the water bottle, lost in thought. And I almost missed Cameron driving by me in the red Jeep that he and Matt shared. We made direct eye contact, just like at the coffee house.

Fortunately, my mouth was empty at that exact moment, or I would have been sputtering. I smiled, reflexively. Like some dope. I brought my hand up to cover up my stupid grin, but Cameron must have assumed I was about to wave. So he waved and smiled back at me, so then I really waved. It was all kind of awkward.

As his car drove past, I was torn between whether I should be mortified because I was so socially inept or pumped because Cameron had waved at me. I opted for pumped. What the hell! He'd remembered me somehow, and I had managed to wave and hadn't sprayed water out or anything. *Huh,* I thought, *does that count as Step Nine*? If so, I managed that without any intervention by a hypnotist or neurosurgeon! Did I have it in me to take this one step further…?

Step 10: Utter a real live word to Cameron, ideally without any crud in my teeth.

CHAPTER 10

With a bit of a nudge on my part during field hockey practice, Mei and Anne started hitting it off, and Mei often ate lunch with us. The three of us were sitting in the cafeteria when I spied Rachel. She went out of her way to give me a quick wave. For some reason her mood had seemed to be on an upswing lately.

"That sister of yours is hot," Mei said. "Does she, like, invite you to parties and stuff?"

I shook my head and could sense Mei's disappointment. For sure, if I'd answered otherwise she would have immediately started lobbying to be included.

"She's definitely pretty," said Anne. "You two look alike in some ways—you both have that classic thing going on. But there's something different about her eyes, though, right?"

"Yeah, she wears the best eye makeup. No offense," said Mei. "And her eyes are a cool colour but not crazy blue like Anne's."

"No, they're green, light green."

"She totally nails it," said Mei. "They look, like, twice their size." She turned to me. "Do you know how to do that?'

"No clue," I said.

"You have nice eyes too, different … they're warm, soft," said Anne.

"Boring," I added. Anne shook her head in disagreement.

"Hate to eat and run," said Mei. "But I'm meeting with Mr. B. *and* my Mom. Apparently I didn't do the last lab, and I got like zero or something on the quiz. So I suck at science! *Quelle surprise*!"

"Good luck with that," I said.

"See you at practice?" asked Anne.

"Yeah, unless I get stuck with extra help after school because I'm so stupid!" Mei grabbed her stuff, said goodbye, and left.

"So I hear you saw my brother Cameron," said Anne after Mei was out of earshot.

"Sort of, yeah," I said, purposely checking my lunch bag to avoid looking Anne directly in the eyes.

"I hope it's not weird to say this, but I've talked about you at home, you know. You being my only friend and all. I guess there's Mei now. Anyway, Cameron keeps teasing me that you are this 'imaginary friend' because he's never met you."

I continued the laser focus on my lunch bag so that Anne wouldn't notice how flustered I was becoming.

"He thought it was you. He remembers seeing you at the coffee house." I nodded. "He said that you waved, so maybe you were real after all. He asked me some questions, about you..."

OMG. OMG. OMG. Time to stop paying attention to the lunch bag and start paying attention to this conversation. Cameron. Cameron Lavery. Was. Asking. About. About me? For sure this is the most major thing that's happened since, since ... forever!!! Okay, stop freaking out, I thought. *Maybe he was wondering why his sister would hang out with me. Wait... Enough with the negative thoughts!*

I was trying to process all this when I saw Cameron coming our way. There was no escape. Unless I was a superhero and could really make myself invisible, I was going to meet him in real life. Face-to-face. My tongue went into overtime, trying to make sure there was nothing stuck between my teeth. *Stay cool, stay calm, and try not to talk, just smile. And remember, the school has a defibrillator if it comes to that.*

Anne greeted him excitedly. "We were just talking about you!"

Really? Did she have to lead with that?

Somehow I opened my mouth and words just flew out. "Hi, I'm Nadine, you know, Anne's invisible friend?" *Really? Did I have to lead with that?*

"Huh, and for some reason I can see you!"

"Uh, well, maybe … it's this Gatorade. There's some, uh, pretty powerful dye, that might, well, counteract the invisibility."

"So it's like a cloak, you know … Harry Potter?"

"I didn't say that," I said and smiled.

He laughed. "I'm Cameron," he said.

"Yes. Hi," I said, forcing myself to look right into those amazing hazel eyes. Up close. It was a good thing I hadn't looked directly at them earlier. I would have been Anne's mute friend instead of her invisible one. His eyes were dazzling … everything about him was … dazzling.

I remembered learning about Helen Keller and how some of her senses became heightened to make up for the others. And even though I had all my faculties, it seemed like his presence caused my entire circuitry to overcompensate, causing full-on sensory overload. He turned to talk to Anne and I focused my thoughts on breathing, and then reminded myself not to stare. I can't tell you how relieved I was when the lunch bell rang. And I could escape. Before my brain short-circuited, causing my head to explode.

CHAPTER 11

Rachel was not a morning person, so getting out of bed early was not her favourite thing. The only time she was normally up before me was when she was planning to inflict torture. Her tactics were quite effective when the victim (me) was asleep. As she said, the element of surprise was crucial. So it was unusual to wake up the next morning and find her in the shower, and to find myself unscathed. Of course, that also meant she would use most of the hot water.

Just when I started to weigh the pros and cons of a cold shower versus no shower, the water turned off and the bathroom door opened. "Hey, can I dry my hair with the door open when you're in the shower?"

"Sure," I responded, then wondered why she was being so nice all of the sudden, actually considerate. Was she medicated? Or maybe it was a time of the month when the hormones are happy?

"So," Rachel said super casually, "who's that girl you're hanging out with all the time? Not the Asian girl. The one with dark hair?"

"That's Anne," I said. "She plays field hockey, too."

"And her last name?" she asked. Nonchalantly.

"Lavery," I said. Rachel smirked but didn't respond, and then she started carefully blow-drying her tresses. She had amazing hair, and it looked great with very little attention, but when she took extra care, she looked like one of those hair models who must get whiplash whipping their heads around to let their shiny locks waterfall over their shoulders for the camera.

I pulled off my sleeping pants and t-shirt and stepped into the shower. By the time I was getting dressed, she had expertly applied makeup to her whole face, which again was not the norm for her, either. She usually just focused on her eyes and then applied a bit of lip gloss. Anne was right—we did have a similar look, but Rachel was definitely much prettier.

"Anything special going on? Got a photo shoot booked?" I joked.

Rachel just smiled vaguely, not giving anything away, and exited the bathroom. I heard her on the stairs moments later. She was way ahead of her usual schedule. Once the front door slammed, I knew I should hurry up myself. It would be smart for me to get to school a little earlier. That way I could attempt to figure out what Rachel was up to. She wasn't much of a joiner, and most detentions were served after school, so it was a bit of a puzzle.

Trying to stay on Rachel's good side was important for my sanity; you couldn't let your guard down, even during a happy phase. And that meant constant but unobvious vigilance. "Trying" being the operative word. I didn't hack into her Snapchat account or read her texts when she was in the shower. If chocolate chips on shoes translated into a glass of ice water in the face, cellphone hacking might inspire her to up the evilness and, say, set my mattress on fire? While I was in bed.

Then my head started spinning at the implications. Fire? Ice? Was Rachel really the devil, or was that just my unconscious association?

As I approached the school, I did a reality check. It was unlikely that I would complete my morning's mission. Although ours wasn't a huge school, there were well over a thousand kids, so my chances of seeing Rachel in action before class were pretty slim. I did a quick tour around the outside. It was a nice day, and there were lots of kids loitering pretty much everywhere. But not my sister. And true confession, I was secretly hoping to catch a glimpse of Cameron, but I struck out there too.

The bell started chiming and everyone started moving. I went in the nearest side door. Bull's-eye. My target was halfway down the hall, leaning on a locker, smiling beatifically, deep in conversation with … drum roll here … Matt. Lavery. That girl was a master when she wanted to be. I watched her touch his arm and flick her beautiful hair, all in one seamless motion. She then turned away, moving in my direction.

I hid amongst the bustling students. And probably because I'd made a mini-science of studying her every nuance, I couldn't help but detect the subtle lift of her left eyebrow. And noted the tiniest, smuggest smile at the edges of her glossy mouth. As Rachel made her way down the hall, I remained invisible. My go-to state.

I held my breath as she passed by me but then exhaled deeply the second she was gone. Holy crap. Matt Lavery. I thought he was too big and too obvious to be on her radar. She was usually more intrigued by the "bad boy" or the "sensitive" type. This was an interesting development—very interesting. We both seemed to have eyes for a Lavery brother. For the tiniest second I wondered if Rachel could be an ally for me. *Yeah. Right,* I thought. *When was the last time she had my back?*

And in any case, while it was nice to daydream about Cameron, I knew I had zero chance with him. So daydreaming was definitely the way to go. No pressure. No disappointment. He could always just be perfect.

*

The lunchtime hum was at full volume. I leaned in as Mei prattled on about this stoner kid in her drama class. "Then the bell goes, and he's still on the floor, doesn't even move, like totally unconscious. Everyone practically steps on top of him—" When out of the corner of my eye I saw Matt and Rachel huddled together, just inside the cafeteria door.

Rachel was gesturing toward us, fake smiling. She whispered something into his ear, and I saw Matt look our way, nodding approvingly. I instantly suspected she was taking all the credit for my friendship with Anne. I could almost hear her say, in a completely understated way, of course, "Oh, it's nothing. You would have done the same! Any sister of yours must be amazing. I just hinted to Nadine, and blah blah blah—*lies*..."

But then a thought popped into my brain. With Rachel so seemingly into Matt, then maybe *she* was the vulnerable one now, meaning that *I* could take control. Just suppose I happened to mention ... super casually of course ... maybe one or two *True Stories About Rachel.* To Anne, for instance.

How long would it take Matt to run for cover? About a nanosecond. And it wouldn't be a stretch to come up with material.

On the flip side, Rachel was a lot of things, including a master strategist. She'd likely already thought of that possibility and was betting against me. But there had to be this *little doubt* in her mind that I just might *spill the beans.* I needed to plant a seed.

Looking directly at Rachel and Matt, it was my turn to fake the smile. Catching the attention of Mei and Anne, I waved right at them, pointing out my *wonderful* sister. Rachel, sensing the threat, shot dagger eyes my way. I couldn't help but smile for real. It was a rush. Maybe two could play this game?

*

As I would have predicted, life at home became much less dramatic—Rachel was on her best behaviour. Initially, I cynically assumed she didn't want to give me any more ammunition. But what can I say, I'm a romantic at heart. She seemed to be happy, and I had to credit that she was really and truly into Matt.

Having her balanced reminded me of the good old times. Despite her ups and downs, and especially before Dad left, Rachel and I did have some fun. Even though I was two years younger, she would happily go to Masonville Mall with me. We would pick out clothes together, and sometimes, if she had extra babysitting money, she bought some sushi or green bubble tea or greasy French fries for us, and we lingered in the food court. Interesting things always seemed to happen with her—or rather, Rachel always seemed to make interesting things happen.

For instance, one day she spotted a cute security guard, struck up a conversation with him, and suddenly we were behind the scenes, monitoring the hidden mall camera, giggling at people who were discreetly trying to pick their noses. We even witnessed a guy shoplifting and kept tabs on his movements while we waited for the police to show up.

Or there was the time when Rachel had fake ID and we went to one of those piercing parlours. She was probably fifteen or so, but the ID said she was eighteen. She insisted I was her twin sister, and we both left with pierced belly buttons—even though I was only thirteen. Needless to say, Mom and Dad went ballistic. But we stuck together, denying in unison that we had ever been asked our ages. And together, we put it back to them—how were we supposed to know they'd flip out? It's not like they'd ever said *specifically* never to get our belly buttons pierced.

Our parents dragged us back to the store and chewed out the manager, who was completely apathetic. Eventually the storm passed, our bond was that much stronger, and our belly buttons that much cuter. But that was then and this was now. Even though she *seemed* different, I knew that I could never fully let my guard down.

Rachel posed innocent-type questions about Anne. All the while, I could tell that she was trying to figure out our friendship and her own vulnerability. To keep her wondering, I kept things superficial, ambiguous. I gave her just enough info to keep her on an even keel. The truth was that I had no motive to trash her to Anne.

In the end, that would sabotage my current peaceful domestic situation. It was nice to not sleep with one eye open, to wake up and not have cold spaghetti in my hair. But I wasn't going to be blind, dumb, and mute. I knew that Rachel could change on a dime. Even though it was a period of relative calm, I needed to maintain the usual hyper-vigilance.

CHAPTER 12

I had a bad case of nerves; my stomach lurched with every bounce. I had not been on an old, rickety yellow school bus since our awful trip last year to a farm near St. Thomas with the Grade Nine geography class. From the looks of the wads of hardened gum stuck in pretty much every crevice, that was probably about the last time this bus was cleaned. I made a mental note to check my backside as we disembarked. It would be horrible to run around with gum on my butt; Danielle would never let me live that down.

Gum was a good idea, though. I found some in my bag and started chewing a minty stick. I always used to do this before hockey games, since mint was calming. I didn't remember ever being so nervous, but this was the first game of my new field hockey career. I hoped I could keep all the rules straight and not be completely clumsy.

As I chewed, I picked a bit of lint off my uniform skirt. I will say that it was love at first sight. I used to be a huge tomboy, but that phase was clearly history, since the uniform was super girly. It consisted of a crisp white and ocean-blue fitted athletic shirt, a matching cute light blue woven skirt, and light blue socks with a white band at the top. The exception to the rule, of course, was Danielle. As the goalie she was the only one allowed to don a non-team shirt, and I couldn't imagine another goalie choosing such an over-the-top shiny gold-and-brown leopard-print one.

I offered a stick of gum to Anne, who was sitting wordlessly next to me. We were an oasis of silence surrounded by a constant hum of nervous chatter. As the bus pulled into the parking lot of Sydenham High School, the chatter stopped abruptly. Ms. Davies, who was standing at the front, lurched forward for a second but then grabbed on to a steel pole and managed to right herself. As everyone scrambled to grab their belongings, Ms. Davies signalled for us to stay put and listen up.

"Okay, girls, this is our first game of the season, the first time we're going to try to work together as a team. I know you're ready for this. Just remember, sometimes we're our own worst enemies, so don't let your nerves get the better of you. It's important to stay calm, remember what we've talked about so far, what we've learned. If they get a goal on us or whatever, don't panic, okay? That will lead to sloppy playing and more goals, or even penalties."

Ms. Davies paused for a minute to make sure she still had our full attention. "I know this might sound silly, but when you're feeling nervous or uptight or whatever you want to call it, just smile, okay? That's what I always do, and trust me, it works, even though I've developed terrible wrinkles right here." She touched the sides of her mouth. "So if you're fighting for the ball, or running like a banshee down the field, it's okay to flash that grin. I know everyone is feeling some nerves, so let's start right now and break out into big smiles as we exit the bus. At the very least, if it doesn't make you feel any calmer, it will freak the hell out of the other team."

And so that was how we looked as we exited the bus—not like Elgin Eagles, but like grinning Cheshire Cats. The Elgin High Cheshire Cats. That my mouth was killing me by the end of the game gives you an idea of my mental state. The game was a bit of a disaster since the score ended up being 5–2 for Sydenham.

It was hard to pinpoint exactly why we lost, but I think it was a combination of first-game jitters (including my own), inexperienced players (such as, um, *moi*), and the inability to capitalize on opportunities (*moi encore*).

As new players, Mei and I manned the bench most of the time, but we did get substituted in now and then to give the other players a rest. I didn't make any huge mistakes, but I also didn't distinguish myself in any way. I guess that like in any sport, the more exposure you got to different situations, the more you learned, and ultimately the better player you became. Since I had never played a real game before, getting the first match under my belt was huge in terms of learning and building confidence. I had few expectations, and to have simply completed the first game was a minor victory, despite the score. I was hopeful that if we played this team later in the season, we would end up on top.

As we loaded back into the bus, the smiles had been wiped from our faces and were replaced by fatigue and disappointment. Many were still jostling for seats when Anne's cellphone began to ring next to me. I could overhear her conversation despite the noise. "No, we lost. Yeah, it's too bad. No, well, I played okay. Uh-huh, yup, okay. Oh, but we're just about to … Cam? Cam? Argh! My cell just ran out of juice!" Anne jumped up from her seat and went to the front of the bus. "Ms. Davies, excuse me, but um, my brother is on his way to pick me up. I need to get off the bus." Anne gestured to the front door.

"Why don't you save him the trouble? We'll be back to the school in fifteen minutes."

"My battery is out, I can't call him back. He's on his way…" Anne was getting flustered.

"Just borrow someone's phone," said Ms. Davies calmly.

"But I don't know his number… I have to get off, he'll get here and not know where I am." Anne was visibly upset.

"I don't like you being here by yourself without a cellphone. Someone should stay and catch a ride with you. Is there anyone who'd like to volunteer?"

Danielle stood up, gave Anne a friendly, fake smile and said, "I'd be happy to, it's no problem whatsoever."

Ms. Davies looked at Anne, who looked pleadingly back at her. It was pretty obvious, even to the coach, that Danielle saw Anne as an easy "in" with her brother Matt. Danielle was anything but subtle.

"Thanks, but I think Nadine might be the best candidate here," said Ms. Davies. She then looked at me directly and said, "Is that okay? You live in Oakridge too, right? Does your cell phone actually work? Do you mind being the buddy?"

I didn't want to wait with Anne. I didn't want to be the buddy. I would have happily crawled home on my hands and knees instead. But I couldn't subject Anne to Danielle, so I nodded. Ms. Davies continued, "So here's the deal. Make sure your brother drives Nadine home, too. It's settled then—you two grab your stuff." I nodded again. "Okay, you're good to go. We'll see you both on Friday after school for practice. "

Anne and I disembarked. My last glimpse as the bus pulled away was of Danielle glaring at me out the window and using her thumb and index finger to crush my skull.

"Thanks," said Anne.

"No problem," I lied. My mouth hurt as I tried to force a smile. I really had overexerted those muscles. But this was even more nerve-wracking than playing the game, and that said something. Anne tried to smile back at me and then cringed. I instinctively laughed but had to grab my mouth, too. "My mouth is killing me!" I said as we both tried not to smile. "Nervous?"

Anne nodded, so I continued, "That forward I was covering when I subbed in for Carly, number 22? She was really good. I had no idea what she was going to do next. I tried my best, and when she assisted on that first goal, I was, like, 'Ahhh!' Thank God Danielle was wearing a mask and I couldn't see her eyes too clearly. If looks could kill, dead!" I grabbed my water bottle and drained the last inch.

"You're being way too hard on yourself. She was crazy fast. It was a tough game. They're a pretty good team, but I think we played all right. The last goal was pure luck. I would never say this to Danielle, but that should have been an easy save. We definitely had first-game jitters … nerves can really cost you."

When she spoke, I saw an expression on her face that was pure Cameron. Physically, she looked much more like Matt, with her dark hair and blue eyes. But her eyes were kind, like Cameron's.

It was impossible to believe Matt and Cam were twins; they were as different as night and day. Matt was average height but very muscular, with hair so dark and eyes that were so startling a blue, you could tell what colour they were from far away. And according to the type of girl who liked to write on bathroom walls, Matt had an AMAZING body.

Matt was the football quarterback and was on all the other important teams and seemed to be the star of most of them. His athletic prowess *du jour* was regularly applauded during the morning announcements. I think it would be tough for anyone who was worshipped that much to still be a nice person. I was under the impression that he was a bit full of himself, but almost anyone would be. He definitely had a Romeo rep, but who knew? High school was full of rumours, and it seemed like it was about 50-50 for the false vs. true ratio. Having a crush on Matt would just have been too depressing since you would never, ever have any hope unless you were beautiful, or a rock star, or, like Rachel, attractive and cunning, or perhaps just a huge slut.

"That's him, thanks again." Anne got up off the bench and grabbed her stick and bag as my heart started to uptick. I pursed my parched lips and shook my water bottle nervously, as if I could somehow conjure up water by agitating an empty bottle. Of maybe it was just my hand that was a little shaky. After being hopelessly devoted to Cameron Lavery from afar, I was about to get into his car. Even though I had purposely tried to stay away, I was once again being pulled toward him. I really wished I had that *Harry Potter* invisibility cloak now.

As the Jeep pulled up, I tried to at least smile a bit to make a good impression, but the pain returned and I ended up clenching my jaw instead. And I'm sure my next expression—shock, perhaps—was also equally unattractive. As I gazed through the windshield, I audibly gasped as the deep blue eyes of Matt Lavery stared back at me.

He was talking on the phone and gave us a curt nod as he unlocked the doors, all while remaining fixed in the driver's seat. I hopped into the back seat, barely getting my seat belt secured before he reversed out quickly, not pausing his conversation. For the first few blocks, I had the privilege of eavesdropping, but the talk was about some football play, so it wasn't exactly riveting. "Got it, later," he barked into the phone, ending the call abruptly.

"I thought Cameron was coming?" asked Anne.

"No, I used his phone. Hey, how was the game, Mouse? Did you crush 'em?" As he turned to look at Anne in the passenger's seat, he must have caught a glimpse of me in his peripheral vision. He craned his neck around to get a better look. I did manage a weak, painful smile, and was rewarded with one in return. Satisfied, he turned back to Anne.

She started to explain the progression of the game, the frayed nerves, and the disappointing end results, but suddenly Matt cut her off. As he stared at me in the rear-view mirror he said, "You look familiar."

I almost choked on my saliva. Was this guy for real? I had on the Elgin team uniform. "Well," I said as tactfully as I could, "I go to your school."

"Oh yeah, of course," he said. He shook his head and then a few moments later said, "I know you from somewhere else. What's your name?"

"Sorry, Matt, this is Nadine," said Anne, noticeably blushing as she looked at me apologetically. "She's on the team. Nadine, this is Matt, my brother."

"What's your last name?" asked Matt as he squinted—I could see his eyes in the rear-view mirror.

"It's Stewart, Nadine Stewart," I said and decided that any further elaboration might confuse him.

"Uh-huh." He thrust his hand off the wheel and up in the air. "You have a sister—Chelsea, right?"

"No, but I do have a sister, Rachel," and I added slowly, just to help him out. "She's in your grade."

"Right, you're Rachel's sister." He turned to look back at me again with a victorious smile, and I nodded lest there be any further confusion.

"Yeah, she pointed you out. She told me you were on the team. That you were playing with Mouse here." Matt again made eye contact in the mirror. "She's nice, your sister."

Anne turned and gave me a big smile. She was clearly happy that our family had her brother's seal of approval.

I wasn't surprised that Rachel was described as "nice." And I wouldn't have been shocked to hear she was into say, Quantum Chemistry. Rachel could be whoever she wanted to be. It was pretty obvious, though, that she'd used my spot on the team to ingratiate herself with Matt. Like I said, she was cunning.

"Does Rachel play? It's a great sport..." Matt fondly put his arm on Anne's shoulder. "She's only played for a couple of seasons, but you'd never know, she's a pro!"

"Uh, no actually. Rachel doesn't play field hockey. I'd never played it either. I thought playing ice hockey might help, you know, but it turns out, not too much." I looked at the mirror and smiled. Although I was on the verge of saying that Rachel sucked at sports and hated doing anything that made her sweat, I held my tongue. The last thing I needed was for Rachel to hear that I said anything remotely negative to dreamy Matt.

"I know where you live, then," said Matt, to my surprise. That Rachel was cool as a cucumber. She had never ever mentioned Matt's name at home, but clearly there was something potentially happening. *I am going to have to watch that girl more closely*, I thought as we spun around the last curb and screeched up the driveway.

"Thanks for the ride," I said, slamming the door.

Matt nodded and called out, "Say hi to Rach."

"Will do," I replied before he backed up and sped off.

I dropped my stick and bag in the front hall, kicked off my cleats, and hightailed it to the fridge. All I could think of was drinking a big glass of orange juice. I took out the container. Yes, just enough for one decent glass of hydration. And I'd use the ice machine to make it super cold.

I was in my field hockey uniform and standing by the fridge, filling up the OJ with ice when Rachel burst into the kitchen. "Matt dropped you off? And you didn't text me a heads up!"

"I didn't think of it," I started, taken aback.

"Yeah, you didn't think! By the time I got his text it was too late."

"He was just doing a favour—"

"Duh! It's called an opportunity lost. I would have made up an excuse to see him. I like the guy, don't you get that? Or are you up to something? Like trying to keep him for yourself?"

"What? That's ridiculous!"

"Is it?" Rachel pulled a face and glared at me for a sec, considering. Then she arched her left eyebrow and started coughing a bit, you know, like she was clearing her throat. "Ew, there's something really gross in the glass, hand it over," she said as she grabbed it out of my hand. To my horror, she then proceeded to hork a huge, disgusting phlegm blob into the OJ. The blob landed on top of an ice cube and twirled around the glass like polar bear snot on an ice floe.

"Drink up, it's brain food," she said with a fake sweet smile as she thrust the glass toward me. I refused to take it back. "Your call, but you better think harder next time," said Rachel. She shrugged and slammed the glass down with a whack on the granite countertop, causing the OJ to overflow a bit, and sauntered out of the kitchen.

Focus on the breathing, cleansing breath in, stale air out. I dumped the glass out and watched the blob swirl around the drain before it disappeared. I wiped down the counter before I ransacked the fridge but couldn't find anything else to drink, so I poured myself tap water—in a different glass. I stood sipping while my mind immediately wandered to Step Six. Again, Rachel was old and dead and laid out in her casket. I leaned over her, and everyone would assume that I was going to give her my final sisterly kiss. But instead, just before the casket lid fell shut, I horked a huge one onto her face. Man, I was getting really good at Step Six.

CHAPTER 13

It was over a week since that first field hockey game, and I was lacing up my shoes at the front door. "Going for a run with Mei," I yelled up to Rachel, who was in her room.

"*Quelle* devotion," Rachel said, coming down the stairs. Her tone was mocking, but she seemed a bit.... Impressed. She'd never been very coordinated, but the Lavery siblings were all really into sports. Maybe Matt's enthusiasm had rubbed off on her.

"Just trying to keep up with the goalie."

"Don't trip," Rachel called as I left the house. Her relationship with Matt must be progressing, I thought. She was much more even-tempered again, and we'd been getting along since the OJ incident. Whatever crazy suspicions she had about me seemed to have evaporated. She was like a polished rock with all the sharp edges smoothed away. For now.

Mei and I had been meeting at least once, often twice a week for a run, and we had both come a long way since those first painful shorter run-walks. Now we were mostly running and going much farther. We were doing way better with our stamina, each taking turns talking so we could have breaks to breathe.

"So, Rachel and Matt...? True or false?" Mei asked, delving right into the hottest school gossip as we began our run.

"Yeah, that sounds about right."

Mei hooted so loudly that I almost did trip.

"Volume control!" I commanded, eyeballing the sidewalk.

Mei kept probing. "So their status? Are they friends, friends with benefits, hooking up, what?"

"Try sister wife," I said sarcastically, but then added, "I don't ask, they don't tell, but they're together, like, a lot." Mei nodded, huffing a bit, so I continued. "I've only met him once with Anne. I'm not sure what to think. The only stuff I know about him comes from the bathroom wall." I gave Mei a knowing look and matched my stride to hers. She'd started slowing her pace a little.

"Well, I know him … kind of," Mei said while she gasped fairly substantially. "He used to be really good friends with our next door neighbours before they moved to Waterloo."

"So he's like—brainless mega-jock/stud or what?"

"For sure the mega-jock/stud thing, but why do you say brainless?" We slowed down as we approached a traffic light.

"I don't know," I lied, "maybe just a stereotype."

"I don't think he's Einstein, maybe average. If he comes off that way, it's probably on purpose. Cameron's … like brilliant, so he might not want to compete. Then again, I'm not exactly a brainiac, so how would I know?" said Mei, and I shrugged.

"He's hot, so who cares what's upstairs?" she continued. "If we were hanging out, just the two of us, we wouldn't be talking about, like, black holes."

I pretended she wasn't making overtly lustful comments about Rachel's boyfriend and tried to wrap up the conversation diplomatically. "I guess I shouldn't make assumptions."

"So they're what, dating?"

"Possibly. A relationship, perhaps," I said. "My sister is private about these things, so I'm not sure what to call it."

"Hmmm, even with my sister Lian away at McGill, we know everything about each other, lots of FaceTime. But I guess everyone's different," said Mei. "Private sounds right. I usually know the dirt, but I've got no intel on her. Danielle will be pissed. She's always going on about Matt…."

I suddenly had this vision of Danielle trying to bite me through her goalie mask, like Hannibal Lecter. I forced the image out of my brain and said, "Or she might get into position for the rebound."

"Hey, that's my position!" said Mei. "But seriously, I will say, your sister must be something to get Matt."

"Oh yeah, trust me, she's something," I said without lying.

"Is your watch broken? I'm dying over here." Mei didn't wait for my response, just abruptly stopped running.

"So, promise," she continued. "If Rachel invites you to parties, you'll *extend* the invite. But I bet you'd ask Anne instead. She's practically family, right? What a waste..."

"Hey, not nice," I said defensively.

"Kidding!" said Mei but not quite convincingly. "You know, I like her and everything, but there's a reason they call her Mouse. I'm much more party-friendly, trust me."

"Yeah, I get that. It's a bit weird, you know." I added, "My sister, Anne's brother. At least she has us as real friends, not the Danielle type. Who just want access..."

"Poor Anne, with those gorgeous brothers. Bringing home all their hot friends, day and night, night and day... Taking off their shirts..." She pulled a face at me, and I pulled one back ... at her.

Mei had given me an opening, and even though I hesitated to raise the subject, curiosity prevailed. "So ... what do you think? About Cameron? He seems a bit ... different. But hot too, no?" My heart started racing as his name rolled off my tongue.

"Yes, definitely. And underrated," she said firmly before pausing. "Okay, so Matt's more my type, but true confessions, I used to have a super-huge crush on Cameron. So, like, ages ago, I got myself invited to their neighbour's house and managed some alone time with Cam. I practically threw myself at him. Turns out, he wasn't interested ... at all." Mei shuddered a little bit. "But he was, like, a gentleman. And didn't go around blabbing about me being some idiotic slut." Then Mei looked directly at me. "Cone of silence, okay? Especially with Anne."

"No probs. I think we've all been there, right?" Of course, I was referring to my own unrequited crush on Cameron. *Take a number*, I thought…

CHAPTER 14

My body was practically drenched in sweat, but the air was cool. Once I stopped, goose bumps fought for real estate on my dirty arms and legs. It was the Friday before the Thanksgiving long weekend. We had just finished our early-morning field hockey practice.

It was tougher than usual since Ms. Davies said we had to kick it up a notch to be ready for our next game, and afterward she asked me to stay behind to help clean up the equipment. I knew she often did this when she wanted a few private minutes to talk to a player.

"So how are you feeling about our game next week?" Ms. Davies was carrying a stack of pylons we'd used for a weaving and dribbling drill.

"Nervous. I always feel nervous, but not so bad as the first one. I thought my mouth would crack from the smiling." Ms. Davies chuckled while I continued. "I love playing. That is, when the starters need a rest..." I trailed off and focused on repositioning the nets I was carrying so I could hold open the gym door for Ms. Davies.

"Well, I think we need to shake things up a little. Nakeisha is a good player, but she's missed a few practices, and we all know what that means. I've been very clear about the consequences. You've been here for every practice, and I've heard that you and Mei have been running on off days. It's really paid off. Your stamina has increased by leaps and bounds, so to speak—you're right where you need to be."

I nodded appreciatively. Ms. Davies went on. "Let's see, your dribbling has really improved, passing is getting sharper, you get yourself open. So ... this is a roundabout way of saying it, but you're starting next game." As we put the equipment down in the storage room, she made direct eye contact. "Ready?"

"Absolutely! Totally! But Nakeisha's a forward, and I usually play midfield, so where am I playing?"

"Forward, definitely a forward. I think you and Anne will work really well together. We'll keep Estella as the striker. Anne's experienced, so you need to follow her lead. I'll be counting on you to get us into that shooting circle and on the scoreboard. Are you sure you're up for this?"

"Yeah!" I couldn't quash the huge smile that spread across my face. "Yes, I'm ready—for sure."

"Great, and hey, a little favour? Can you just tidy up our equipment for a minute? I've got to get to a staff meeting before first period … well, right now." Ms. Davies checked her watch and frowned. "Mr. Parker, you know, the soccer coach, has been making cracks about our equipment being sprawled everywhere."

"No problem, I'll straighten up." I quickly started rearranging our sticks as she grabbed her clipboard and exited the storage room.

As soon as I knew she was out of hearing range, I grabbed a stick in each hand and pounded them on the floor to mask my cry of glee. And it was at that precise moment, when I was standing in my sweaty clothes, covered in dirt, pounding field hockey sticks on the floor while screaming, that Cameron poked his head into the storage room. I stopped. And stared. For a second we were both so surprised that we stood there eyeballing each other, uncertain. I felt my cheeks get hot, and the smell of my gym clothes became even more disgusting as my body temperature soared.

"Ummm … new team cheer?" I blurted out as soon as I was able to form words.

"Sure?" he said, looking embarrassed for me while I just stood there looking well, embarrassed. *Please leave*, I prayed, *please, just turn around and leave.*

He did turn partway around but then rotated back. "I play … music. Sometimes. It kind of sounds like that … noise," Cameron said in a deadpan voice. "You know, anything goes, right?"

"Right," I said, relieved. "So, if I practice, can I join the band?" *Okay, that was forward.*

Cameron laughed. "No, no. No practicing—that's the only way to get in. But hey, I'm, um, looking for Anne? She's not doing the cheer?"

"Uh, well no. She's probably in the change room. I can get her. I'm on equipment clean-up." I started to feel a bit less paralyzed and was able to put some sticks in the pile.

"Don't worry. If you see her, though, can you tell her that I can't watch the game today? There's a football practice, mandatory." Cameron glanced at his watch, and I realized I'd better get hustling or I would either be late or forced to spend the morning in a stinky, unshowered state.

"The game's on Tuesday. I think it was supposed to be today, but it got changed because of the holiday. So yeah, Tuesday, right here, after school." *Crap. I really did say Tuesday twice, didn't I?*

"Then I'm good." He smiled at me—such a lovely, dreamy smile. I forced myself not to look too closely at his hazel eyes, lest I become mute again. "So I guess I'll see you then? You're playing?"

"Yeah," I said, and despite clenching my jaw to keep the words from being spoken out loud, I said, "I'm starting, as a forward." *Argh, I sound like an idiot.*

"Starting as a forward, eh? That's great. I'll see you starting, uh, Tuesday. Happy Thanksgiving."

"You too," I said and then cleared my throat to increase the likelihood of getting the last word out. "Cameron."

I practically collapsed on the floor after he left. It was only eight thirty, and I was exhausted. So it could have gone worse with Cameron, but it could've gone better.

I needed a Step Eleven, something like, *Stop blurting out random, embarrassing crap.* Really, my autobiography could be called *Eat (your words), Pray (for laryngitis), Love (in silence).*

Step Eleven: Actually engage your brain before you open your mouth and talk to Cameron. Circle one (1) selection from below:

a) Pre-plan safe topics of conversation.

b) Just stay mute. All those years of not talking to boys can finally help you.

d) Don't change a thing! You'll have more material for a book. Potential titles: The Book of Awful or The Book of Awkward. Better yet, The Book of Awfully Awkward.

CHAPTER 15

Anne, Mei, and I went to see a movie that night. We made an interesting trio. Anne was the angel, Mei was the devil, and I was somewhere in the wishy-washy middle.

As for Rachel and Matt's relationship (I mentally dubbed the pairing "Rat," you know, like "Brangelina"), Anne and I were clearly on the same page. We had an unspoken agreement never to discuss them as a couple. I had a feeling that, just like me, she suspected it was not exactly true love. We wanted to distance ourselves from any future fireworks that were bound to erupt between them, protecting our friendship from potential implosion. I still didn't have the nerve to go to Anne's house, and I wanted her as far away from Rachel as possible, so we decided to meet at Mei's house since it was neutral territory. Switzerland.

The theatre employee gave Anne an extra hard look before taking her ticket for the 14-A movie; I exhaled with relief as she was spared the embarrassment of having to produce ID. The theatre was packed with other teens, mostly females, since the film *Ghost Dances* was of the chick-flick genre. We ended up craning our necks in the third row, and the movie was definitely not worth the strain. The junk food we shared—popcorn, Swedish Berries, Cokes, and M&Ms—turned out to be the highlight.

"I have to pee!" Mei announced loudly as we left the theatre and then started walking like a penguin down the corridor to the huge washroom. It was pretty busy, not surprising with all those jumbo drinks consumed in a venue where bathroom breaks meant missing the entire point of attending.

So we let Mei take the first available stall. I was starting to wash up when Mei came over and whispered, “Psst, see that girl with the green coat at the sink behind us? That’s Helen. The Highbury Hawk.” I shrugged my shoulders to indicate that I didn’t know who she was talking about as I turned slowly to check her out. Mei said, in a voice that was just in the audible range, “Sasquatch.”

“Don’t say that!” I hissed.

“I didn’t mean, I was just … helping you remember … sheesh!” said Mei.

The Highbury Hawk player recognized Mei and sauntered over. She was really tall, with big hair that was dark and wavy. She had a large head and large facial features. Everything about her was just, huge. “How’s the hand?” she asked.

“The wrist! It’s fine, thanks,” said Mei uncertainly.

“It was an accident, you know.”

“Okay,” said Mei.

“I should have done it on purpose.”

“What? Why?”

“I heard what you called me … that was harsh.”

“Harsh, okay, yes, I was out of line, I admit. But to hurt me on purpose, that’s like, way harsh…” Mei was trying to be cool, but I could tell she was a little freaked out.

“So you admit it. Okay, just so you know, it may not be an accident next game.”

“You’re threatening me? Over a stupid name…” Mei began. But as the Hawk player closed in on her personal space, she quickly backed down. “Sorry. And I mean it. Are we good?”

“It’s way too late for that,” Helen said calmly. “You started something … big with that name. It was all over Instagram, retweeted everywhere. That bitch of a goalie, she posted it a thousand times. That picture of me when I fell on top of you. And the hashtag, what you called me. It stuck. People heard you. I still hear it, walking down the halls.”

Mei stood there, speechless.

"Fair warning. Watch your back at the game. I'd go after that goalie if I could, but that's way too obvious," said Helen, jutting out her chin. She gave Mei one last angry look and turned and walked out of the washroom.

"How was I supposed to know?" Mei said, distraught, twisting her hair. "I didn't mean for all that to happen. I just blurted out 'Sasquatch' … Danielle sent it viral… Did you hear her? She's going to take me out. At the next game. I'm completely screwed."

"What. Just. Happened?" Anne said as she came out of stall.

She had overheard some of it, but I filled in the blanks while Mei just stood there incredulously.

"Did you know about the posts?" asked Anne.

"Of course, everyone knew about them. That stupid cow, Danielle. I didn't mean to start anything. I just blurted out a dumb name."

"You're sure?"

"Honestly, I had nothing to do with it. And the wrist was an accident, the name was an accident, it was all an accident. I didn't start any like, cyberbullying."

"You never reposted it?"

"No," Mei said firmly. "Never. I felt badly but then I forgot. We all make mistakes."

"Yeah it's just that that one is … hard to take back," I said.

"You need to talk to Coach Davies, immediately. Like after the weekend," Anne said. "She doesn't have the right to threaten you. The coach will help us figure it out."

Mei's eyes darkened and she replied, "That's so naïve. Oh, let's tell Mommy and Daddy about the big, bad wolf. And that way, next time when I run into her, like in some dark alley, she can she break both my wrists. And then maybe she'll break my legs too, just for good measure, because I told on her."

As the Hawk player had just done a few minutes earlier, Mei quickly turned on her heels and walked determinedly out of the washroom. Anne and I followed and soon caught up with her amidst the thick crowd, bustling in all directions on the blue-carpeted theatre hallway. I squeezed her hand when I got close enough, and when she turned my way, I could see her trying to blink back tears. Mei was a tough cookie, but she was clearly shaken up by this encounter. Who wouldn't have been?

I know it wasn't like Mei was blameless at all, but it somehow reminded me of, well, Rachel and me. She always accused me of doing things purposefully that had been innocent. Or at the most, inconsiderate. Yes, Mei had called her an awful name, but she hadn't taken the picture or written the hashtag or posted or reposted.

I knew I had to say something to Mei, but I also didn't know what. It wasn't like I had some stellar antibullying record. Rachel bullied me all the time, and there was no point trying to involve anyone else. It always made the situation worse, especially when we ended up alone. So Mei was right. If we told, Mei might run into her again and without any teammates by her side. And for sure, Danielle would be no help at all.

I took a deep breath and spoke up as we piled onto the escalator. "We'll have your back on the field. If you rat her out, you're totally right, she may not get you at the game. But at another place, and you could be all alone. Anyway, the game against Highbury isn't for, like, another two weeks, so we've got some time."

Anne shook her head firmly, but Mei looked at me, sniffled, and nodded. I could tell her mind was churning, that she was weighing the best options. "Look," Mei said, "just drop it, okay?"

"Okay," said Anne, walking out the theatre into the mall. But I could tell by her determined expression that while she might agree to "drop it" for now, she wasn't about to let this go.

I spied The Marble Creamery, a hot spot for dessert. Comfort food sounded like a good idea after such a bizarre encounter. I pointed to the restaurant and said "Nightcap?"

Mei wiped at her eyes but forced a smile. And not missing a beat, she said, "I could really go for a shot of tequila, but I'll settle for some rum and raisin!"

CHAPTER 16

When I woke up in the morning, I could already detect the subtle scent of turkey wafting up the stairs. Since my mom was in charge, it would cook at a low temperature all day, nice and slow, until the meat practically fell off the bone. I immediately felt depressed. I couldn't say that I had great memories of Thanksgiving dinners from years past. Even in the happy times, Mom and Dad each wanted to be in charge of that holiday signature dish, the roasted, stuffed turkey. Yet they had very different ideas about how it should be prepared and cooked and presented.

Just as you could count on cranberry sauce and gravy at Thanksgiving dinner, you could also count on one good, drag-'em-out shouting match between Mom and Dad before we got to the pumpkin pie. Dad was convinced that we would all get food poisoning, since the salmonella bacteria would not be killed by Mom's low, slow cooking technique. My father's preferred method was the blast-and-burn type, which ensured, said Mom, that the turkey would be dark brown and dry—safe to eat but practically inedible.

Usually neither Mom nor Dad's method won out. Instead, my parents would each constantly sneak into the kitchen and either crank the oven up or down. If someone was not caught red-handed, that person would be blamed if the bird was deemed too dry or too undercooked.

At our last Thanksgiving as a foursome, only Rachel and I were left at the table to finish the meal at the end. Although at that point they were not just fighting about the turkey. Dad was going back and forth a lot to New York, but we just thought it was temporary. Even though I was pretty sure there would be fewer fireworks this year, I knew the hole in our family would feel larger than ever. It would be our first Thanksgiving without Dad.

By the time I eventually made my way downstairs, it was almost eleven. Mom gave me a hug, and I nodded when she asked if I would like some tea. She poured boiling water into her favourite white enamel teapot that was sprinkled with colourful flowers and added some teabags. It was nice to have Mom at home, taking care of me. I was practically never fussed-over any more, and I missed it. Luckily, even real estate took a holiday for Thanksgiving.

"So, does it smell nice?" asked my apron-clad mom as she cracked open the oven door to do some basting, allowing the roasting turkey scent to waft out. I nodded appreciatively. It was during this postcard-worthy moment that Rachel stormed into the kitchen. She was dressed up in black pants, a crisp white blouse, and high heels. Her hair was twisted and pinned into a beautifully executed messy up-do and her makeup was applied flawlessly. She looked gorgeous. This was not her usual holiday morning look; it was more like cocktail party glam.

"Shut the oven! We're going to get poisoned without Dad to protect us," Rachel barked at Mom. The incongruence between her outward beauty and her inward anger was startling. "If I wasn't going out, I'd crank it up high!" Rachel then grabbed the cup of tea that was poured for me and spooned about two tablespoons of sugar into the steaming cup with a slightly shaky hand.

I knew I should have said something to Rachel by way of warning about the hot drink, but I pretended not to notice. Instead I thought, *Wait for it*, as she started to chug. A second later she sputtered up the scalding tea, spilling a few drops of the brown liquid onto her white blouse.

"Goddammit! You scalded my tongue! And my blouse!!" I could tell by the crazy look in her eyes and the scrunched expression of her mouth that she was on the verge of a full nuclear meltdown.

Thank god Mom was in the room, or I would have had the steaming tea thrown in my face or poured down my sleeping pants, or something even worse. I turned to Mom to see whether she was going to crumble, which had been her tendency over the past year, but she seemed surprisingly stoic. Within a minute she had wordlessly but successfully rummaged through our kitchen junk drawer to produce a stain removal pen.

Mom dabbed at the spot while cooing at Rachel, whose face was softening. Her hysteria had peaked and she was in deceleration mode. *Wow*, I thought. Even though Dad wasn't here, it almost seemed like old times. I had forgotten what a calming effect Mom had on Rachel—that was when Mom was in control of her own emotions.

Rachel muttered an insincere "thanks" and promptly left the kitchen to blow-dry her blouse. A few minutes later we heard a car pull up in front of the house and the honk of a car horn, clearly Matt was not bothering to get out of the car and knock on our door. Mom left the kitchen to get Rachel, and moments later I saw her breeze down the steps, and out she went. I snuck up to the front window, curious to get an up-close look at this couple, as Rachel stepped onto the driveway,

With the stain fixed, Rachel looked totally put-together and gorgeous once again. Matt smiled up at her from the driver's seat, and when she pivoted at the car door, I saw Rachel smile back. It was subtle, but there was hardness around her mouth. She was forcing the smile, not feeling it. Maybe her dark side, which had been lying dormant for the last month or so, was making a comeback. That certainly seemed like a distinct possibility based on her recent mood. *Crap,* I thought, *I hope she's just nervous or something.* I'd really been enjoying my calm home life.

"Where are they off to?" I poured myself a fresh cup of tea from the slightly cooled pot and sat down at the table with Mom.

"She's going to Matt's for Thanksgiving lunch. I don't think she slept well. I could hear her pacing around her room in the middle of the night. She's just nervous or tired is all, maybe both. She'll be fine." Mom took a sip of her tea, and I could tell she was trying to convince herself that what she just said about Rachel was actually true.

"Fine? You really think so?" I said, challenging her. I know I fantasized about her getting a lobotomy, but maybe she really had a mental illness?

Her behaviour was pretty unpredictable, and it seemed more than typical teenage moodiness. Mom wasn't around much, but was she really that oblivious?

"I know I should come down harder on her; she bullies us both sometimes, doesn't she? And maybe I've created a bit of a monster, you know, blaming it all on the separation. Just excusing it?"

"I hate to say so, but yes. I agree. And even though she's been much better than usual overall, she still seems pretty much out of the normal range."

Mom gave me a weak smile, and I gave her one back. She said, "I hear you, okay? I'll try to be more on top of it. It's Thanksgiving, though, so let's try to enjoy."

Maybe someday Mom might be strong enough to deal with Rachel, but she wasn't there yet. And it wasn't like Rachel would willingly seek psychiatric help at The Parkwood Institute or that I could drag here there by myself. So instead I decided to look on the bright side. It was unexpected to have this day with my mom all to myself. She was right—we should make the most of it.

"I have an important question for you, and I want you to think about your answer very carefully." Mom brightened up as I continued. "If you could have your choice between French toast with maple syrup and icing sugar or pancakes with maple syrup and icing sugar or porridge with maple syrup and icing sugar, which one would you choose? Again, take your time, choose wisely." I sipped my tea as Mom contemplated the culinary nuances of each possible dish.

"Hmmm. That's difficult. I'll rule out porridge because I was force-fed that as a child." I smiled a little as Mom shuddered. "And your dad used to make pancakes every Sunday even though he knew I was a French toast fan, so I guess that's my final answer: French toast."

"Good choice," I said. "I'm going to have a shower. Call me when the French toast is ready?" My mom, always quick to the draw, tried to launch the Tide pen at my backside, but it fell short and hit the floor as I scurried out of the kitchen.

After breakfast we spent the day companionably preparing our Thanksgiving dinner, boiling and mashing potatoes, making bean casserole, caramelized carrots, and even "homemade" pumpkin pie using a tin of pumpkin and an instant pie crust.

We had all the food prepared before Rachel was due back from Matt's, and we even had time for a brisk walk through the ravine a few blocks away. And while the leaves were mostly gone, I refused to see the symbolism between their lifelessness and my own family tree, which between Dad and Rachel was on life support. Instead, as Mom and I crunched over the dead leaves on the dirt path, I was happy that she was with me and that we were enjoying a Thanksgiving walk, together.

*

"I'm sorry, but did the pilgrims really eat bean casserole with canned fried onions on top?" Rachel said, making a playful face as we sat together later at the dining room table. She tried a bite, smiled, and said, "Okay, they may be bad for you, but they taste pretty good. And by the way, the turkey is amazing! I was out of line this morning. Please forgive."

"Of course. So how did it go at Matt's?" asked Mom.

"Good." Rachel was still smiling. "Really good."

"Uh-huh?" Mom smiled again.

"So, there's not much to tell. Well, Matt's mom is dead, did you know that? I won't try to set you up with his dad or anything. That would be weird and well, he's just okay. You deserve someone really good this time."

"Well, thank you, Rachel. So how was the food?" Mom said.

"Not bad, but there just wasn't like a woman's touch, you know? No centrepiece or nice napkins, that stuff. Anne's a bit on the butch side, so she's no help there."

I almost inhaled my water. Gentle Anne was hardly butch.

I held my tongue and Rachel continued. "They had this buffet. Heavy on, you know, dude food—meat and pickles. I was the only guest, and they all went out of their way to be nice." Rachel readjusted her messy do then picked up her fork and put it down again.

"There was a comment that sort of bugged me, though. Matt's dad, Glenn, he asked me what sports I played at school. I don't 'play' anything, and I told him that and he started going on about Anne and the boys, and how important sport is in everyone's life and that even if you're not a natural, you can work hard and still be part of a team. Blah, blah, blah." Rachel's face started to cloud over a bit.

"Oh well," I said, trying to head off what I suspected was coming, "if he saw how lousy I was at field hockey, he might change his mind."

Rachel raised her eyebrows at me. "That little mouse, Anne, of all people, tried to get him to drop it, but he kept circling back. And your name even came up. I think it was Matt who said you'd never played field hockey before, and Anne had told him how great you are and about the running stuff. You should have seen Glenn nodding up and down. I hate to admit, I felt totally jealous—" Rachel's demeanour started to darken again, and I knew I needed to get her back on course. I didn't want this dinner spoiled.

"So, you were the only guest? Matt must think you're pretty special, meeting his family?" I said this both to flatter Rachel and to double-check that Cameron didn't have a "special friend" in attendee.

"I guess," said Rachel, brightening. "You're right." And then she added, "Wait a sec, we've forgotten the tradition. You know what we're thankful for this year?"

"You're right. We need to do that," Mom began in a really excited way. "I'll start, okay? Give me your hands, just like always. Well, I am truly thankful for my two beautiful daughters who helped me get through his awful year. What did the Queen say, 'annus horribilis?' I am so glad we made it, together. Things are definitely looking brighter. And I'm so thankful for your company and this wonderful meal. What about you?" Mom asked me.

"I'm thankful for this turkey … so moist, yet salmonella-free!" I quipped as Mom and Rachel laughed, and then we both turned to Rachel.

"I am also thankful that this crap of a year is behind us. So I was a doubter about the turkey and other stuff, but when people stop putting you down, Mom, not mentioning any names, your true talents and beauty ... they shine," said Rachel. I could tell that she sincerely meant every word. And just when I thought she had her head completely up her anus, Rachel had shown real awareness.

"Amen to that!" I cried, and Mom squeezed our hands tight. Moments like these were few and far between, but at times we three felt like family. "All those battles every year over the oven. I wish he was here to see this, to see how right you got it, the turkey is perfect!" I said, cutting up another mouthful.

"Let's show him," said Rachel. She arranged the turkey platter just so, took a photo, and uploaded it, totally breaking the "no cellphone at the table rule."

And she narrated her message out loud as she typed away, *"Dearest, farthest-away Dad, You missed the bestest, most perfectly cooked turkey this year, prepared by Chef Mom. She was right all along, slow and steady all the way! xo Your Former Family."*

"Don't send that," Mom said, grabbing for her phone.

"Done," said Rachel.

I retrieved my phone and sent another message to Dad. *Joking! Miss you ☺ xoxo.*

*

Many thoughts were racing around my head as I tried to fall asleep that night. Not only was I terrified about starting the game, but I was also extra uneasy that Cameron would be there. And I kept thinking about the encounter with the Hawk player and how it sucked for Mei having a bully hassling her.

As I got up to go to the washroom, it was almost 1:00 a.m. However exhausted my body was, my mind was running a marathon. As I walked past Rachel's room, her door was open and I saw her silhouette in the darkness. She was sitting on her window bench, looking past her curtain into the night sky.

"Hey," I spoke softly. "Everything okay?"

She turned toward me slowly and sighed. "Yeah, insomnia. Again. Sometimes I just stare at the stars. It reminds me I'm just this insignificant … speck. Compared to the universe, my life isn't even like an eye blink. It's a bit of a downer, but it makes me feel sleepy."

"Well," I said, "it must be contagious. I'm wide awake too but am just lying around like a lump while you're here being all soulful. True confessions, whenever I see you awake at night … it makes me wonder, is she scheming, dreaming up a new torture?"

"Should I be? You were nice at Thanksgiving dinner. I guess we all made an effort, didn't we?" She yawned.

"Yeah. Something on your mind?" I took a seat next to hear on her window bench. I worried about her not sleeping, but maybe that was the pot calling the kettle black.

"Oh, you know … not sure how things are really going with Matt. Maybe you need to be a super jock just to hang with that family. You'd fit right in. It's funny, because I didn't really like him that much before. I just you know, thought, well, it would be a good challenge—to try to see if I could snag him…" She trailed off.

"But now you like him?" I offered.

"Guilty, it totally sucks. There's more to him than you'd think. And if he dumps me, I'll freak." Rachel turned back to staring out the window.

"I don't see that happening. It sounds like it went well today. Well, I hope the star thing works and that you get some sleep," I offered as I left the room.

"Same," she said. "Thanks for checking in." And I could hear her sigh again deeply as I closed my bedroom door.

CHAPTER 17

I walked into the school library at the beginning of English to retrieve the DVD of Leonardo DiCaprio in *Romeo and Juliet* for our class. The supply teacher must have decided I looked trustworthy enough not to bolt from school, so I got selected for the errand.

There was Mr. Khan, holding court in the library, attired in another tight polo shirt, this time in fluorescent orange. He was half turned away from me, and I could see he was talking to someone in the study carrels. But it wasn't until Mr. Khan swerved around, changing from profile to the less obtrusive frontal view, that I realized he was talking to Cameron.

"Hi," I said simultaneously to Mr. Khan and Cameron, and they both smiled at me.

"Well, Miss Nadine, how nice to see you. It's been too long. I assume you're here to inquire about the mice infestation?" Mr. Khan threw me completely for a loop raising this long-forgotten and embarrassing topic. I couldn't even stammer out an incoherent response. I just stood there paralyzed for a second as Mr. Khan continued, "Don't worry, the exterminator was successful. So let's just forget about it, okay?"

I could see Cameron trying to keep a straight face behind Mr. Khan, and I averted my eyes. I knew at any moment I might just lose it. I never imagined that I'd been discussing pest control with Cameron in the library. Here I was with him for the second time in what, five days? And once again it was in the midst of a bizarre situation. And Cameron seemed be enjoying it, and I started to find it funny, too. Mr. Khan was being so sincere that I would have felt really bad and even more embarrassed if I had started giggling.

I swallowed hard and looked directly at Mr. Khan before I spoke. "Deal," I said and forced my mind away from the image of Felix caught in a mousetrap. "But I'm actually here to pick up the *Romeo and Juliet* video. The English supply teacher, Ms. Castelli, she sent me up."

"Yes, yes, of course, it's a popular one this week. It was just returned the other day. Hmm, where did it end up? I need a moment."

As Mr. Khan started rooting through a mound of returned material, I took a deep breath and strode a few steps to stand directly beside Cameron in the study carrel. I knew we needed a change of topic, so I jumped right in. "Are you on spare?" From the few times I had spotted him in the hall, along with a few comments made by Anne, I had pretty much figured out his schedule, that he didn't have class this period. I just assumed he hung out at Fireroasted Cafe with the other seniors, not that he'd be holed up in the library.

"Yeah. I'm trying to break the Fireroasted habit. I might be on spare again next year too, you know, if I have to come back to upgrade." I smiled and he continued. "But I can't say I'm being productive. Sometimes Mr. Khan and I get talking, and well, the period is over and I haven't even cracked a book."

"Soooo," I racked my brain for something to say, "are you two, like, talking about cooking and stuff for next year? You know, if you go away to school." It was Cameron's turn to look puzzled, so I continued. "Mr. Khan runs the Cooking Club and, well, I hear there's, like, a high incidence of scurvy during first year." I cringed as soon as I stopped talking. It had been meant as a funny comment, but Cameron looked a little disturbed.

"Scurvy? Really? Huh, well, maybe I should ask him about that stuff. We usually talk about music, older stuff. I've learned a lot about The Smiths but unfortunately not about physics."

"Aren't universities looking for well-rounded students, not just the brainiacs?"

"True. So maybe instead of looking at my marks, I could just answer some random music questions?"

"Or what about a multimedia type of application?" I ventured. "Like play your favourite songs, mash them together … with a recipe, something with vitamin C? They might prefer students who actually live long enough to graduate." My face was practically on fire. What was I saying? And why did I keep talking?

"So like the Smashing Pumpkins and pumpkin pie? Too obvious maybe?" said Cameron. I tried to look pensive but was desperate to extract myself from the conversation. From the corner of my eye I could see that Mr. Khan had sifted through the mound of material and was holding the DVD.

"Here it is," Mr. Khan said waving it victoriously. "Personally, I think DiCaprio was much better in *What's Eating Gilbert Grape*, but he's not bad in this one, and Claire Danes is always fabulous. Enjoy."

"Thanks, I will. Bye," I said.

"Bye," Cameron and Mr. Kahn said simultaneously. And I couldn't help but smile as I left the library clutching the movie.

Forget Step Eleven. I couldn't pre-plan my conversations with Cameron—I only seemed to run into him when I was least expecting to, and I always got so flustered. On the bright side, at least I was collecting more material for *The Book of Awfully Awkward*. But on the other hand, it was almost as if he had enjoyed talking to me… Nah, who was I kidding? He was probably nice to me because I was Anne's friend. And Rachel's sister. I could still dream, though, couldn't I?

CHAPTER 18

"I can't believe this—you promised me you'd talk to her!" I was walking toward them and could hear Anne practically yelling at Mei. It was definitely a first to see Anne so revved, off the field, anyways. Mei was struggling with her lock and didn't respond to Anne.

Anne turned to me and said to me in a calmer tone, "Mei hasn't even talked to Coach Davies or anyone else about what happened in the washroom. And we play them, like, next week."

Mei continued to ignore Anne, but from the downward curve of her mouth, it was clear that Mei was radiating a negative vibe. So I chimed in with my two cents. "I know you think she should tell someone, but I don't. I disagree. And I've had lots of experience with bullies. What happens," I continued, "is that you just make things worse for yourself. Imagine how extra mad she'd be at the game? And then if Mei just runs into her when she's all alone? She'd get slaughtered. Mei's way better off if she's chill about it. It'll probably blow over, anyway...."

Anne tried to interrupt, but Mei nodded at me, slightly defused, before continuing to fumble with the stubborn lock. I just kept talking. "I think she's safer on the field with us and her teammates, all around."

"That's *not* good enough! We just can't count on that. We all get distracted during a game."

"Then maybe you could talk to Danielle—you know, she likes you," I interjected, putting the ball in her court. "It's a long shot, but she might apologize for the posts."

"I could try, but what if she won't? And even if she does, I doubt she'd come across as ... really sorry. Sincere. Like I've said all along, we need to talk to Coach Davies," said Anne firmly.

It was like Anne and I were opponents on the field, fighting over the ball, and Mei was the referee. We both turned to her for the ruling. But there was silence and then the tell-tale click of Mei's lock, victory over her combination. She savoured the moment before inching her locker open just a crack to ensure that the contents weren't going to explode. Reassured, she opened it fully, retrieving her uniform and muddy cleats. She then impressively crammed everything back and closed the door in one quick motion. Anne and I stood wordlessly nearby, waiting for her decision.

"Yeah, I'm so not talking to the coach," Mei said. "I may not get killed during the game, but then she'd find me and, like, drown me in the toilet. That's such a better way to die. Let's do that. *Not!*" she said simply. "End of discussion."

As Mei walked authoritatively to the change room, Anne and I followed behind like two coaches, one hopeful and one not that the ref might change her ruling. In a frustrated way, Mei threw her stuff down, dry bits of mud from her cleats scattering on the floor. "I don't need bodyguards just to get changed..." she said, kicking at the dirt.

"I don't agree, we should tell Coach Davies..." Anne started to protest again.

"It's my decision, it's final," Mei exploded, her words as shrill as a loud whistle. She pushed away from us and took refuge in a bathroom stall, slamming the door so hard, it rebounded back and she had to close it again.

Mei obviously wanted space, so I signalled to Anne and we moved away, farther down the locker room. "Let's just get through this game today, okay?" I said, trying to broker a deal. "We don't even play Helen and the Hawk team till next week. We have some time. Maybe she'll be more open and you could try talking to Danielle."

Anne seemed placated, which was a relief. Having to deal with me as a new forward was going to be enough of a distraction. Especially since I was exhausted from lack of sleep and extremely nervousness knowing Cameron would be there, watching me.

"So, did Ms. Davies say anything to you about this game?" I asked, fishing around.

Anne had discreetly started changing into her uniform but turned her head back to me and smiled. "I heard it first from Cameron. Congrats about starting. He thinks you're really funny, you know. We'll be an awesome duo."

Any other sane person would have been excited to hear that the love of her life, or at least the love of her life to date, thought she was funny. Perhaps if I hadn't been feeling so stressed, I would have enjoyed the moment. Instead, it just seemed that the stakes kept getting higher, since I really, really didn't want to screw things up, either with field hockey or Cameron.

"Don't look so nervous! You're ready for this. You'll see."

"Easy for you to say! I'm a wreck! I think it's going to be worse than that first game. With all that smiling, my face will be permanently paralyzed, like with lockjaw!"

"You played competitive hockey, right?" I nodded, all the while trying to regulate my breathing, which had suddenly become much quicker. "Then you remember that once your feet get going, your head starts to follow. Before you know it, you'll get completely lost in the game. Of course, you'll mess up, a bit, but it will be okay. You'll get into the rhythm, you'll be good." I nodded again, but my hands started quivering as I tried to apply some chapstick.

I needed a step here, something to deal with my nerves. No, I thought, I already had too much to think about. I'd have to leave that for another day, another time. As we started walking to the field, I thought about how different Anne now seemed to me from the "mouse" I'd first met in the library. I didn't agree with her about solving the Helen problem, but she was comfortable enough with Mei and me to speak her mind. If Anne continued along this vein, pretty soon we would be calling her Lion...

"Do you still get nervous? I know you were, that first game," I said to Anne as my shaking hands fumbled with my ponytail.

"I was a mess. I've been a lot better. But then you told me that Cameron was coming to watch, so that makes me stress… And then I got a text from Matt. He's coming, too. I'd hate to play badly, disappoint them. So much for the pep talk. Looks like both of us will be grinning like idiots out there."

I made Anne laugh as I pulled a stupid, oversized grin, but then thought, *Crap, Matt's coming too.* I couldn't even go there. There was no room left on my stress-o-meter. Since Mei was still locked in the bathroom stall, Anne and I walked out of the change room, out the side door toward the field together, happy that we were once again on the same team.

I decided to try to tune out all other thoughts and just concentrate on the drills. I was having some success until the opposing team's bus pulled into the parking lot.

"Let's gather together, girls. The other team is just arriving, but this game is going to start real soon," Coach Davies began. She went over strategy as our opponents walked down the short path to the field. I listened and glanced up occasionally as the girls passed by.

Wow, I thought. *Most of these girls seem to have two inches and twenty pounds on us.* And just when I thought I'd seen the last of them and was focusing on the coach's words instead of sizing up the opponents, I caught a glimpse of a larger shadow moving on the ground. I couldn't help but look up. As if on cue, she shook her long, dark hair from side to side and I could tell, even from behind, that it was none other than Helen herself.

OMG! How was she here? She wasn't a Westminster Warrior; she was a Highbury Hawk! Had she switched schools? She must have, or this didn't make any sense. Anne and Mei didn't see her. Their backs were facing the opposing players in the huddle circle.

Helen stopped and turned, making direct eye contact with me, but the menacing look she gave Mei temporarily took my breath away. *Damn*, I thought, having a quick change of heart. *Mei should have ruled on Anne's side, not mine*! I let Rachel abuse me. I'd given up trying to stop her. But that didn't mean Mei had to accept whatever Helen might have in store for her. I knew I'd screwed up, big time.

"Like I just said, girls—earth to Nadine, let's listen here." Coach Davies continued, "We've got to really move fast out there. That's what all the running drills have been for, and speed is our strength as a team. The Warriors here, well, look at them, their strength is their strength. They are powerful in the way they shoot the ball, and they are powerful in the way they pass the ball. But none of that can beat speed. We will win because we are fast. We will get to the ball first, and we will steal the ball from them."

She stared at me and then continued. "This needs to be an offensive game for us. Nadine, Anne, that means you. You two need to stay near the goal, in the shooting circle, and be aggressive about taking shots when you get the ball. And Estella, as striker, you stay in the centre. You need to get open. You feed balls to each other, but stay in position. Let the midfielders feed you the ball. You three must be ready at any moment, so stay deep in the scoring circle. Girls, are we clear here? Okay, let's play a good game. Starters off to the field, everyone else onto the bench, please."

Crap, crap, double crap. I thought at the very least Anne and I could protect Mei on the field. But how were we going to be able to protect her if we had to stay deep? We were out of time for a plan B, since we were going right into play after the huddle. So unless we could somehow change our positions or change Helen's mind, there was a strong possibility that Mei would get hurt. What had I been thinking?

"She's here," I said to Anne as we walked onto the field, "Helen's here. Playing. In this game."

Anne turned to me, her eyes wide with panic, and we both looked to Mei on the sidelines. Mei was staring directly at Helen with a grim expression. Her bravado in the locker room just a short while ago had vanished. And just when I thought things couldn't get much worse, Matt and Cameron came down the path and took seats in the front row of the bleachers as Anne and I took our positions.

Unexpectedly, on the way to her offensive post, Helen made a sudden beeline way over to Danielle. I could hear volume and see the body language of hotly exchanged words before the Warrior coach yelled for Helen to get back to her half of the field.

The ref then called a last-minute conference with both coaches, and as we stood around waiting, I was struck by a brilliant idea. Running a few metres over to Anne, I whispered, "Go tell Danielle that Matt is here to watch her. But he didn't like all those postings, that picture with the Sasquatch hashtag. He thought it was mean. Tell Danielle she needs to somehow apologize to Helen during the game, to take the blame, get the heat off of Mei." Anne raised her eyebrows and hesitated for a second, but then quickly nodded and ran like a bat out of hell directly to Danielle on the other side of the field. The ref took off his cap to signal to Anne to get back into place.

After a brief exchange with Danielle, Anne hurried back as Ms. Davies gesticulated in surprise. Anne played dumb, resuming her position as if nothing happened. She then gave me a brief nod, all businesslike, but then an angelic Anne smile burst forth, so all was okay, for now at least. I breathed a sigh of relief as the game began, with the Warriors taking the ball at the centre line.

The first half went surprisingly well. At one point I saw Danielle come out of the goal and speak to Helen, and I was pretty hopeful that she was apologizing, but Helen kind of brushed her off. Danielle seemed to think all was good, since more than once she waved her stick flirtatiously toward the spectators. Helen played aggressively and incurred more penalties than anyone else in the first half, but the times Mei subbed into the game, Helen didn't go after her. I breathed a huge sigh of relief.

Coach Davies was right about the Warriors. They were a powerful team of forceful stickers and talented dribblers but struggled to take command since we could outrun them in every position. Danielle's goaltending was awesome. She was able to save two particularly tricky shots that could have easily gone into the net. It probably worked to my benefit that we were thrown such a big loop at the start of the game. I completely forgot all my nervousness and focused on making sure Helen behaved and Mei was okay, and then on playing my best. Anne was right—we worked well together as forwards, and by halftime we were up 2–0. We had each scored a goal.

"What did Anne say to Danielle?" Mei practically skipped as we left the field. I whispered to her that Danielle was supposed to apologize and that she thought Matt might be interested in her. We both turned to watch Danielle walk slowly toward our bench, her hips swivelling as she flicked her shirt up and down as if to air herself out.

"Ouch," said Mei, rolling her eyes at Danielle, "she's hurting my eyes. I hope it works! But seriously, it means a lot that you two are looking out for me. And keep working it, starter!"

"Mei, listen carefully." I took a swig from my water bottle at the half time. "Don't let your guard down out there, okay? Remember, we still have a whole other half to play. I gave you bad advice, so let's keep paying attention."

I was breathing a little easier. Mei was fine and with any luck would stay that way. The score was 2–1 for us. The Warriors made it on to the scoreboard at the beginning of the second half when they managed to sneak a shot to the lower left-hand corner of our net that went right past Danielle. And while Helen didn't interfere with goal itself, she pretty much slid over the goal line.

Danielle started kicking up a fuss, complaining that the goal shouldn't have been allowed because of Helen, but the ref disagreed. And when he gave Danielle a warning, she totally lost it and cried out loud enough that practically everyone could hear, "She fouled me, ref!" Helen started to get pretty agitated. And I started to really worry. But Danielle backed down and things started to settle down, and I took a deep breath and got refocused on the game.

It was disappointing that the Warriors had scored, but we were still outplaying them, and I was confident we would be able to hold our lead. I had just received a pass from Claire when a commotion occurred downfield. It was Danielle, waving her hands as if she was drumming and then intermittently pointing toward the bleachers. Thankfully, the ball stay stalled at midfield or the Warriors would have scored on us, for sure. Both Anne and I completely lost focus with this theatrical display.

I panned the bleachers, trying to figure out what was upsetting Danielle and was taken aback by the sight of Matt and my sister Rachel locked in a passionate kiss. Cameron was sitting next to them, trying discreetly to look away. And there was Danielle, flailing about the field as if her fiancé was making out with some other chick at the altar.

Double crap! Anne and I exchanged looks of Holy S#$t and in the process completely missed a scoring opportunity. Coach Davies yelled at me, I yelled at Anne not to panic, and suddenly all our yelling to each other was drowned out by Danielle—she was spitting mad. Even though she was a bit of a distance from me, I could see her fierce gaze still directed at the PDA happening in the bleachers.

I didn't really see exactly what happened but for sure Helen said or did something that further inflamed the already apoplectic Danielle. And it was like lighting a firecracker. Danielle seemed to sizzle with rage for a few seconds, and then she full-on exploded. Setting the decibel level to loud, she shouted, "Shut up … SASQUATCH."

While the ref went over to eject Danielle from the game, it was Helen's turn to lose it, stomping her feet in anger. She looked around the field, finally resting her outraged gaze on Mei, who was cowering on the bench. She hadn't played a lot in this game, just a bit here and there, but now we were down a player, so that might change things. Luckily, there were only a few more minutes left.

Danielle didn't go quietly but made a spectacle of herself vacating the field. As the ref called a time-out for us to substitute in another goalie, Coach Davies did her best to ignore Danielle, summoning everyone over to the bench. But before she spoke, she paused for a moment and rubbed her hand over her eyes as if she could erase all she had just witnessed.

"Does anyone know what's going on with Danielle?" Coach Davies asked, looking around hopefully to all the players who had gathered into a huddle. "I know she was upset about the goal, but that was a total freakout."

Mei kept silent, so Anne and I did likewise. The coach continued, "This game isn't over yet, and we suddenly need a goalie. Claire, you're Danielle's backup, so you're on, okay? Get suited up. And Mei, this is what all that practicing and extra running stuff has been all about. You're replacing Claire in midfield. Go."

When I look back to that day and to that game, I realize this was the time I should have spoken up. Come clean. Told the coach about the situation. I could blame Rachel's incessant bullying of me for my lack of action, but the truth was I could only blame myself.

The Warriors had already assumed their positions and were waiting to start up again when the ref blew his whistle and motioned impatiently for the Elgin Eagles to hurry it up. Mei sat on the bench, paralyzed for a second, but then Coach Davies hollered, "EVERYONE OUT ON THE FIELD, NOW!" and Mei swung into action.

Anne squeezed Mei's arm as she walked resignedly to the midfield, carrying her stick with one hand while she wiped at her eyes. I came over and hissed loudly, "Mei, hold on, it's almost over. We've got your back." But the truth was I wasn't really sure about that at all.

As Mei took to the midfield, Helen came right up glaring at her and purposely bumped right into her. After Danielle's spectacle, the truce was over and the battle was on. My stomach was tied in a knot as I contemplated the physical disparity between the two opponents. And to think my greatest worry an hour ago had been starting this game and having Cameron in attendance. Oh, how I longed for that simpler time!

The Warriors smelled opportunity with the arrival of a new, unproven goalie. Suddenly the momentum changed and Anne and I, who had listened to Coach Davies and stayed deep in the field thus far, started to move toward the midfield. We needed both to protect Mei and to help our defence.

We ignored the coach as she tried to reposition us and flanked Helen instead. She wasn't intimidated by our presence and kept the press on Mei. Anne and I were thinking the same thing; we could stay and guard Mei at midfield for the rest of the game as long as we could hold the score at 2–1.

But the Warriors' defensive players repositioned themselves and stole the ball from me as I tried to pass it to Anne. After a pretty impressive charge, the Warriors scored fairly easily on Claire, and the game was tied. I refused to even look at Coach Davies, who was wildly signalling to me from the sidelines.

The Warriors got another ball from a faulty pass and the play moved again in front of the Warriors' goal. Instinctively, we followed the ball and went deep again to get into scoring position, momentarily abandoning Mei. Out of the corner of my eye I could see Helen bullying her, bumping into her and even sneakily whacking Mei's shin with her stick.

Mei remained stoic and did her best not to react. I forced the play out of scoring range and went back into midfield. When I got a pass from Nakeisha, I made a split-second decision and fired the ball to Mei. My thinking was that it would get all eyes on Helen, and she might just go into autopilot and start playing. It was faulty logic that backfired. Helen viciously fought Mei for possession of the ball.

I'm still not sure exactly how the accident happened—it was too shocking at the time for me to feel confident that my eyes had not betrayed me somehow. But if I was asked in a court of law, I'd say that the attack was completely premeditated and this is how it went down: while crazily battling with Mei for the ball, Helen stuck out her foot to flip Mei, and while Mei was falling to the ground, Helen thrust her stick to inflict a powerful blow on Mei's hand.

Helen mistimed it a bit and almost failed to make contact. Instead of hitting Mei directly on the hand, the full force of the blow hit Mei directly on her left pinky finger, causing the finger to separate from the hand and fly up into the air.

The ref called an immediate time-out, and if we thought the field was chaotic when Danielle was ejected, the chaos that ensued after the finger amputation was insane. Mei lay on the ground, clutching her hand to stop the bleeding, but with blood squirting everywhere nonetheless. Someone cried out, "Her finger, it fell off!"

And then people were suddenly everywhere too, milling about in groups, screaming, yelling at Helen. Anne, Coach Davies, and I hurried to Mei and then started to look around for the digit.

The ref blew the whistle again and yelled in a loud, clear voice, "Everyone stop. We need to find the finger, now. Don't move unless I tell you, we don't want it stepped on." He pointed to Anne and me. "You and you, keep doing what you're doing, find that finger. Everyone else stay put. Warriors coach, get 911 on the line. We need an ambulance! Coach Davies, attend to your injured player!"

Anne and I crawled around the field, immediately surrounding Mei. We searched every blade of grass for the sign of a four-inch, pink, bloody, fleshy thing which I assumed was sporting Mei's signature black nail polish.

"Anything, Anne?" I called out as we both combed the vicinity.

"No, nothing," said Anne.

Mei was intermittently sobbing and moaning while Coach Davies talked in a soft and reassuring tone. I looked up from the search and could see that a crowd had formed on the sidelines. While the ref talked to the 911 operator on a cell phone, the other players ignored his instructions and tiptoed off the field.

"OMG! It's just so gross!" shrieked Rachel, who was standing near Helen and was frantically pointing toward the back of the girl's shirt.

"What is it? Oh, eww! But stop acting like a baby," Matt reprimanded as Rachel covered her eyes, but continued pointing and shrieking.

Cameron walked quickly over to Helen. A tiny black fingernail poked out of a fold in the back of her team jersey. He grabbed a Kleenex from his coat pocket, extracted the finger from the jersey, and held the bloodied, swaddled finger.

At that second, the sound of the approaching siren permeated the air, and Ms. Davies assumed the role of drill sergeant and began shouting out orders. "You," she pointed at Cameron, "give Nadine the finger, she's going to ride in the ambulance with Mei. Anne, if you can get to the hospital, I know Mei would appreciate it. Ref Smith, you need to write a report. This is unbelievable. Such an injury, playing this game..."

Then Ms. Davies turned to Mei and gently said, “Help is here. We’re going to move you into the ambulance, and we’ll get that finger back on in no time, okay, honey?” When Mei nodded the slightest bit, Coach Davies gestured to Matt, and the two of them assisted her off the field and into the ambulance, which had pulled up onto the field.

Cameron turned to me and carefully placed the Kleenex with the severed finger in my hand. Under other circumstances I would have been thrilled to be touching him, but this was surreal. “It’ll be okay,” he offered. “I’ll see you at the hospital.” I turned to walk away, and he called after, “Hey, you did good out there. That was bizarre, but Mei’ll be all right, you’ll see.”

Cameron was wrong. I had done “bad” out there, very bad. I’d never felt so low in my entire life as I had when I walked to the ambulance. I felt directly responsible for Mei’s injury.

I could still hear Rachel carrying on—I knew she was squeamish and detested blood and gore, but her behaviour was over the top. Anyone who passed by would have thought Rachel was the one who’d lost her finger.

CHAPTER 19

The attendant helped me into the back of the ambulance. I cradled the Kleenex with the black fingernail of the gruesome specimen poking out at the top. She then took the finger from me and placed it in a ready container of ice. I kneeled by Mei's stretcher. Ms. Davies was perched beside her, pressing on the injured left hand that was already wrapped in bloody white gauze.

The reality of what happened descended on me like a sudden storm. A tornado of emotion swirled in my stomach, making me feel nauseous. I chocked back bile and blinked back tears as the attendant checked Mei's vital signs. Red hot and lightning-quick, the words *mea culpa* flashed around my brain. If I had opened my mouth, at any time during the game—or beforehand—Mei would not be here.

From the back window of the ambulance, I saw Helen standing by herself, looking downcast. Her jersey was stained with blood and dirt. The much shorter referee had his head tilted upward to hers, asking her questions, I assumed. Helen shook her head but stayed mute, looking silently defeated. And while I had felt sorry for her after I heard the cyberbullying story, I didn't feel sorry for her now. I only felt sorry for Mei and shame for myself.

And if it was possible for the situation to get any worse, Mei started sobbing as the initial shock wore off. The perky blonde ambulance attendant instinctively knew what to say. "Mei, my name's Paula, and that's Bill up front driving. We'll be at University Hospital in just a couple of secs, okay? Can you hold on till then?" Mei nodded weakly and quieted down for a moment.

Paula smiled. "And once we get to the hospital, the doctors and nurses will take over, but don't you worry, they'll get it back on and have all your ten fingers working again real soon. Trust me, they've had lots of practice. It's a real specialty when you have a train running through the middle of town, right next to the Ceeps Bar. All those drunken college kids."

Oh, thank God, I thought. *Everything's going to be all right. I hope she's not lying.* A surge of relief spilled over me, and I quickly made a decision to be strong. Wallowing in my own wretched state would not be helpful. Not at all.

"You've got this Mei," I said encouragingly. "You'll be good as new, and next year, I bet we'll still both be tapped for cardio training." Mei, who must also have been channelling inner strength, forced the tiniest smile.

Ms. Davies piped up. "Excuse me, Paula, in all this, we've forgotten to contact Mei's parents. Is it okay to use a cellphone here?" Paula nodded, and Mei recited her mom's number while Ms. Davies called Mrs. Chen.

Mei's mom was in nearby Stratford seeing a play but said she would leave right away and meet us at the hospital. Even though it wasn't on speaker, I could hear the panicked tone in her voice as they spoke, and it was like a fresh storm of violent weather literally twisting inside of me. I willed myself not to cry.

Ms. Davies passed the phone to Paula the paramedic, who reassured Mrs. Chen that Mei would be all right and that Mrs. Chen should take her time and drive carefully. Ms. Davies held the phone for Mei, who weakly said, "I'm okay, Mom. Love you too."

Once Ms. Davies had hung up, Mei turned to Paula, cleared her throat and said, "I want drugs!"

"In a few minutes you'll get some painkillers. Don't worry, Mei, we'll be there in just a sec."

After we arrived, Mei's stretcher was lowered out of the ambulance and she was immediately wheeled into surgery. And from the number of nurses and doctors who trailed after her, I felt reassured that they would do everything possible to make her whole again. Ms. Davies and I sat in the waiting room, and I had the awful task of telling her about the encounter with Helen after the movie, and my rotten advice to Mei, leading up to the terrible current situation.

"I'm sorry, but you blew it big-time. I'm simply stunned that you'd put your friend in danger after such a threat, that you didn't come to me."

A few tears slowly trickled down my face. I discreetly wiped them away and reprimanded myself. *I have to be strong for Mei. And anyway, what right do I have for self-pity?*

"I still don't quite get it," Coach Davies said. "Why, if Helen didn't like Danielle's posts, did she go after Mei? It doesn't make sense to me. It's just so, what do you kids always say, random? But this really is random. Mei's not a star player, so why take her out?"

"At the game last year, the one where Mei broke her wrist, Mei called Helen a 'Sasquatch.' And then Danielle posted the picture, using that name, and it just stuck. Mei just blurted it out; she had no idea what she'd started. Helen couldn't easily go after Danielle, being the goalie, and then once she got ejected, she went after Mei."

Coach Davies shook her head, and I couldn't tell if it was disgust or disappointment. Probably both. The only good thing I could do at that point was own my inaction. I swallowed but my throat felt bone-dry, so I spoke with a croaky voice. "It's totally my fault. One hundred percent. Anne wanted to tell you, but I thought it would be too risky if Mei ran into Helen again, like, off the field."

Coach Davies nodded stoically, and we sat quietly for a minute. "I didn't want to say anything in front of Mei," she said, breaking the silence, "but I still can't figure out how Helen managed to take off a finger. I've been coaching this game for over ten years, and I've never heard of such an injury, much less seen it with my own eyes."

"I was right there just before it happened. She was really knocking Mei around good, and that last hit was totally intentional. Maybe she fixed her stick—you know, doctored it?"

The glass doors opened. I could see Anne, Rachel, Cameron, and Matt coming toward us. Anne hurried ahead of the others, carrying my backpack and Mei's.

I must have looked puzzled, because Anne said, "The janitors got them out of your lockers. They have this master list of all the combinations." Then she sat on the other side of me and said, "What am I saying? How's Mei?" Then she leaned in closer to me and whispered, "Don't stress, I won't tell anyone, promise."

"I already told the coach it was all my fault."

Ms. Davies motioned for the approaching trio to give us some privacy, and Cameron, Matt, and Rachel all sat a short distance away from us.

"How's Mei?" Anne asked again. I could tell from her glassy expression how upset she was.

"She'll be fine." Coach Davies went and put her arms around Anne's shoulders. "The paramedics said they can reattach the finger. It will need to heal, which will take a while, but she'll have a full recovery, and her hand will function just like new."

"Mei wouldn't be here if I had spoken up. And I regret tricking Danielle," Anne started.

"You tricked Danielle?" Coach Davies furrowed her brow.

"Don't go there. Like I said, mea culpa—" But Ms. Davies interrupted me.

"Girls, I've heard enough for today. Yes, we do need to talk about this further, but now isn't the time. And I want you both to keep absolutely mum about this situation with Helen. For Mei's sake, I don't want gossip flying all over the school. Based on what you've said, we're going to have to get others involved, so don't breathe a word about this for now. And I don't want to hear that awful name again!"

We nodded and Ms. Davies continued, "Let's just focus on being positive and seeing Mei through this."

I hated to admit it, but I was momentarily relieved that the team, Cameron, and everybody else for that matter, wouldn't find out about my part in this awful situation. For now, at least.

Coach Davies gestured for the others to come and sit with us, and I could tell by the look on Rachel's face that she wanted to be anywhere else but the hospital. I was sure Matt hadn't offered to drive her home first, or she would have jumped at that option.

Cameron sat across from me, gently touched my bloodied arm, and with a very concerned expression softly asked, "Doing okay?"

"Yeah," I lied.

Then he said, "Well, if I can do anything, let me know." I nodded again and was caught off-guard when he tenderly squeezed my hand for a second. I noticed both our hands were stained with blood. "Mei, she's going to be all right?" he asked.

This time I found my voice and said, "Yeah, eventually, she should be fine. She's in surgery right now." I managed a weak smile and thought, *If he knew what I did, he wouldn't be so nice to me.*

Rachel sauntered over to me and practically hissed, "That blood on you, it's totally gross. Why haven't you washed?" She shook her head. "Trying to steal attention, much? Do us a favour and get cleaned up!"

Suddenly, I was hyper-aware that if Rachel hadn't worn me down, I would have given Mei different advice. I needed to do more. I needed to start standing up to Rachel. So, right in front of Cameron and Anne and Matt, I completely forgot about the breathing exercises and Step Six. Something inside me snapped.

"Do you hear even yourself? You sound like one of the Kardashians or something! Don't you get it, she lost her finger! She's in surgery! I couldn't care less how I look! I only care about Mei. We're all here for her. Well, we're supposed to be, anyway. I don't care what you think. It's not about you, Rachel. For once, it is not about YOU!"

I immediately regretted what I said. Why, in front of Cameron and everybody else, had I given Rachel a reason to humiliate me? Why hadn't I just used my Rachel coping techniques instead of taking her on?

She opened her mouth to lash back at me, hesitated, then took a quick look around. From everyone's expression, she knew she didn't have any support. Even Matt was looking pissed at her. He said, "Maybe you should go home. I know you'd rather be anywhere else." Softening for a moment, he added, "Call me later, okay?" I could see Rachel's jaw tighten as he spoke, and while the rest of her face remained stoic, her piercing eyes spoke volumes.

She turned back to stare me down. I returned her gaze without blinking, but inside I wasn't feeling so brave anymore. I was lucky she hadn't killed me right there. Thank God for Matt's presence. I could just imagine what would be in store for me when I got home.

Soon Rachel was walking away, her shoes clacking angrily on the tile floor. When I heard the whoosh of the sliding glass door, I knew she was gone. I audibly exhaled. And while everyone around me probably thought I'd "won," I knew I hadn't. Winning this battle only meant that the war would get bloodier, and we both knew who would ultimately "win."

I excused myself, went to the washroom, and splashed cold water on my face to keep from crying. Then I grabbed the soap and started to scrub. I scrubbed my hands, and scrubbed my arms, and I tried to scrub the blood off my uniform too.

I stopped scrubbing once again to splash cold water on my face, but I couldn't hold it together. I willed myself to be strong, but strength eluded me, and I started sobbing. I felt so guilty about Mei getting hurt, and standing up to Rachel had just made me feel worse. And who knew what she would do to me, especially if I'd wrecked everything with Matt.

Anne came into the bathroom in the midst of my crying fit, saw me and hesitated. I was ashamed for being so weak. I turned, grabbed some paper towels, and attempted to dry myself off. I examined my reflection in the mirror while Anne watched with concern. My eyes were red and puffy, and my skin was blotchy. I took a deep breath and managed to pull it together. A few secs later I attempted a small joke. "Please don't post this on Instagram."

Anne gave me a hug, and I leaned in. "It's been the worst day. And Rachel's probably just upset. She was pretty awful, but well, I'm sure that's not normal. It's good to cry, but you need to stop beating yourself up. Mei's going to be fine, you meant well with Helen and everything. And you and Rachel will sort it out, you'll see," she said with a confident smile.

I wished I could tell her the truth about Rachel, but I knew that would be a huge mistake. I had so much bottled up inside me, but at least Matt had gotten a glimpse of Rachel's true colours before I'd exploded. It was unfortunate in some ways. Things at home had been almost normal recently. Rachel really liked Matt and was behaving like a happy person for a change.

Mrs. Chen arrived while we were in the bathroom, and she was absorbed in conversation with Coach Davies when we emerged. "Let's just focus on Mei's recovery today, okay, Eleanor? I promise I'll look into the situation in good time."

With a Kleenex clutched tightly in her hand, Mrs. Chen wiped away a tear and nodded. And when she turned to glance at Anne and me, even though she gave us a weak smile, it was just like another punch to my stomach.

Clearly concerned, Cameron offered to drive me home. On any other day that would have been the highlight of my life. Instead I said, "Thanks, but I'm going to wait until I hear how the surgery went. I can't leave until I know she's okay." I took a seat in the waiting room, my arms wrapped tight around myself for protection. I assumed Cameron, Anne, and Matt would leave at that point and was surprised when the Lavery siblings came and sat down, waiting out the storm with me.

There was very little conversation, and every minute just seemed to drag on and on. It was pure agony. When the doctor returned, I felt like I had aged a year. He smiled, which instantly made me feel much better, before he privately conferred with Mrs. Chen. I could tell things were good when the tension lines around her mouth smoothed out, and then she enthusiastically shook both of his hands in thanks.

Once the doctor left, she turned to us and said, "It is very good news. The surgery was successful. Mei just woke up, and she swore at a nurse in the recovery room. So she's almost back to her old self."

It was as if the clouds parted to reveal all sunshine and blue sky. My body actually felt lighter. I never knew that relief could be so physical.

"Thanks all of you for being here, everyone. I'll tell her you were here, rooting for her. But it's time to go home and rest. She's going to need you a lot. There'll be pain and lots of rehab until she's fully recovered." Then Mrs. Chen dabbed at her eyes.

Ms. Davies jumped up and they hugged each other, with Mei's mother resting her head on Ms. Davies' shoulders, shedding happy tears for a minute. She then gathered her coat and purse and walked to the elevator to see Mei.

"Can we give you a lift back to school to get your car, Coach?" offered Anne.

"No, no thanks, honey. I normally never tell students where I live, for obvious reasons, but I will tell you that I live very close by. I could use a bit of fresh air, so I'm going to walk. It feels like the calm after the storm. I'll get my car later. Rest up, kids." She grabbed both Anne and me by the hand. "It's good news. I'll see you tomorrow. We're going to need to talk to you further. Say a little prayer of thanks!" With that she turned and walked out the sliding glass doors.

CHAPTER 20

We were a pretty quiet foursome as we left the hospital and walked toward the car. Anne tried hard not to look surprised when Cameron threw the keys to Matt and then slid into the back seat next to me. The radio was about the only sound for most of the trip. When we got closer to my house, Cameron whispered, "Can I get your number?" I nodded and he passed me his phone. I typed in my number but wondered if I would be alive later if he actually texted me.

He squeezed my hand as we pulled into my driveway and asked if I was going to be okay, and of course he meant with Rachel. I told him I'd be fine, which was a huge lie. Even though it was almost 10:00 p.m., our driveway sat empty, so my mom still wasn't home. I was kind of hoping Matt might at least come to the door to talk to Rachel, but he didn't say anything other than a polite goodbye, which Anne echoed.

I wasn't worried as I entered the house, knowing how Rachel operated. She would be watching for our arrival and would wait until Matt was a safe distance away before springing into action. I went into the kitchen and poured myself a glass of orange juice. My stomach growled, and it occurred to me I hadn't eaten anything in hours. I heard the shower start and felt instant relief. So Rachel wasn't in any big hurry. Good, I'd have time for a last supper. I found some leftover pasta in the fridge and put it in the microwave. The message alert on my phone dinged twice.

The first message was from Mei: *Txting on drgs is fun.* I laughed out loud. I started to reply with a "thumbs-up" sign but remembered her pinky finger just in time and instead sent her back a bunch of smiley faces.

The next message was from Cameron (!): *Crazy day, sleep well, c u 2morrow.*

My hand was shaking as I typed my reply, *k, u 2*, and my first thought was that I did live to receive a text from Cameron. My second thought was that if I continued to live I would never, ever delete that message.

I ate my pasta ravenously, periodically listening for the water to stop, but it kept running. Rachel loved long showers. I had the phone hidden under the serviette in my lap, but I picked it up again and again, rereading Cameron's message between bites. Hiding the phone under the serviette was an automatic habit. Cellphones had always been banned at the kitchen table because Mom thought we'd be so engrossed with texting that we'd forget to swallow and would choke to death on our food or something.

It was a rookie mistake to be so distracted. Rachel had obviously left the shower on when she made her approach. I had just finished my last mouthful and was probably smiling stupidly at the phone message when I was startled by Rachel's sudden appearance. I quickly tried to stash the phone back in the serviette, but I was too slow and she snatched it from me in one fluid gesture.

She showed no emotion as she read the text, but then she jutted out her chin and raised her left eyebrow. "What a performance you put on. And it wasn't for my boyfriend and his stupid sister after all. I didn't realize you had your claws into Cammie. What a *complete* bitch. You humiliated me! I underestimated you."

"*I* humiliated *you*? Well, only after..." I started to defend myself, but then Rachel nailed me with one of her piercing looks. *She is holding my phone*, I thought. *I'd better shut up.* So I held my tongue while Rachel took a minute to flip though my other texts. I started the breathing exercises, stale air in, cleansing breath out.

Satisfied, she refocused her steely gaze and resumed her rant. "Wasn't it just yesterday that you were all holed up in the library, like, all alone? And now—you're this field hockey star, and you have all these little friends. And Cameron. Trust me, it's not going to last. Unless of course you turn things around with Matt and me."

I opened my mouth to reply. But then I just shut it once again. I knew that whatever I said would only further inflame her. And man, she was pissed already. Still holding the phone, Rachel paused for dramatic effect.

"Rachel, don't..." I started to say, but with Cameron acting like he almost cared about me, there was so much more at stake now. I had everything to lose. I instinctively resumed my fallback position. I stopped talking and focused on cleansing breath in, stale air out, repeat.

"And here's a hint to help you out, Jelly Bean. Since you made me look like a witch at the hospital, you better work the PR for me to Anne and Cam. I just don't get that family, so freakishly tight. Anyway, if you pull it off, you can start planning the double wedding. And if you don't, kiss it all goodbye, just like the phone!"

Rachel held my phone out and stared straight at me, the slightest hint of a smile at the edge of her lips. She then stretched her arm up as high as she could and used every ounce of her 115-pound body to slam it into the granite island. The glass cracked, parts of the plastic cover shattered, and pieces went flying everywhere like shrapnel.

"You better keep this one in the vault. Too bad Dad's preoccupied. You always had him in your back pocket. You were his little ice princess. It was so nauseating, but you know the saying, the higher you rise..."

Rachel examined the remains of the phone with a fake smile plastered on her face. I knew that this was my chance to engage in a counterattack; the enemy was standing right before me in clear view. But the moment came and went. Instead I focused on my breathing. I just kept breathing, breath in, air out, breath in, air out. Satisfied with the level of destruction, she made a face at me, blew a phony kiss, and then was gone without a backward glance.

As she left, that same image of an old, dead Rachel lying in her casket popped into my head. And she was sporting that same fake smile on her embalmed face. This time I held her cell phone up high in the air and then used all my strength to smash it down on the hard wooden coffin. I then dumped all the pieces on top of her dead body. And just before I pulled the casket lid shut, I leaned over her and whispered, "Matt just called, he said to rot in hell."

It helped. I felt a bit better. I'm not sure that I could have survived without Step Six.

I picked up some of the larger phone bits and examined them. Not only had Rachel completely screwed me over again, but she was also severely deranged if she thought I could somehow help mend her relationship with Matt. Anne was obviously put off by her behaviour at the hospital, and I barely knew Cameron, so what influence did I have with him? I probably would have been more impressed with her strategizing if she hadn't destroyed my major tool for communication with Matt's siblings. Clearly, she'd improvised.

It was dangerous having a sister who was not only unbalanced, but also had a flair for drama and loved the grand finale. And it didn't help that Mom had given us her sales pitch about the benefits of rock-solid granite countertops in the kitchen.

I sighed deeply as I tried to remove the SIM card from my mutilated phone, but the casing was so damaged, I couldn't get it out. I wasn't sure it could be extricated successfully, but I sure wasn't going to give up without trying. I rummaged around the kitchen and tried to use the tip of a steak knife to dislodge the card, to no avail. I then grabbed a Ziploc bag, placed the smashed phone and all the remnants inside, and stashed it in my backpack. I would try again once I figured out the best way.

I thought back to Mei and bullying and hospital beds. Rachel needed to be stopped, but when and how? Would I just crack one day, murder her, and spend the rest of my life in jail? I wished I had someone to talk to, to get some advice about dealing with Rachel, but I definitely couldn't talk to Anne. Mei was clearly indisposed, but even if she wasn't, I didn't know if she could really be trusted with this type of stuff.

Maybe I really did need to look elsewhere for help, or at least devise some steps to help me fix things, once and for all.

Possible Choices for Step Twelve:

a) Crush Prozac into her daily smoothie in the hopes her mood might improve.

b) Crush rat poison into her daily smoothie. Rachel might die but then my mood would certainly improve.

c) Say goodbye to Cameron, my friends, and my former life. Secretly record Rachel in action, broadcast it on YouTube and go into hiding like the other whistle-blowers. Forever.

The phone looked really bad, but you never knew. I had another cellphone that had fallen into the toilet and had somehow survived. I'd taken it apart to let it dry and put it in rice. A few days later it was as good as new. A few months later I got a new phone for my birthday. My mom couldn't understand why I'd wanted a replacement, since the "pee-pee" phone worked perfectly well. I still had the old pee-pee phone stashed away in my closet in case of emergency, and I might be desperate enough to use it again.

Aside from the phone, I had other big problems to consider, the most immediate being Rachel. How was I going to make her look good to Anne and Cameron? I didn't want to con my friends, but I also wanted to continue my life. I thought some more, and a plan popped into my head. I wouldn't have to lie or say anything that wasn't true. I'd just focus on Rachel's good qualities and stonewall like a politician if they asked any questions. Besides, did I really want Anne and Cameron knowing how demented my sister was?

I thought of a few truthful lines I could use as well, like: "It's been hard for her since Dad left for New York" or "She really feels it when Mom's at work all the time" or even "Rachel's not good in emergency situations." I could also add things like, "Isn't she beautiful?" Which would be completely true if I was referring to her superficial outward appearance.

Step Twelve: Engage in conversational subterfuge with the Laverys to start the myth of an angelic Rachel, replete with a halo and possibly wings!

I knew I was being Rachel's "enabler," and deep inside my brain, I could hear a voice saying, "Coward, chicken!" But then a louder voice drowned it out with, "Survivor!"

CHAPTER 21

As I walked to school, I quickly decided I needed a step to help me make amends with Mei for my role in her injury. It was an easy one. *Step Thirteen: Be the best friend to Mei I can possibly be.*

I knew visiting her would be important, since she was easily bored and might emotionally crash once she came off the drugs. I couldn't text her, which sucked, and I wondered what texts I had already missed in the last twelve hours since my phone was destroyed. I was pretty sure I wouldn't have heard from Cameron again. I would have texted Anne last night to make a plan to visit Mei today, but that hadn't happened.

I had found and charged the pee-pee phone before bed, but I still couldn't get out the old SIM card. It would be really annoying if I lost all my contact info, like Cameron's phone number. I would need to get a new card and start all over again.

As expected, the school was abuzz with news of Mei and the field hockey incident. Some girls and even some guys who would never normally give me the time of day were suddenly acting all buddy-buddy with me to get the deets. But I refused to cash in on my friend's misery to climb the social ladder, especially since I'd played a significant part in her injury. I was thankful for the vow of silence that Ms. Davies had imposed on Anne and me.

Rarely was I lucky enough to score a Cameron sighting in the halls during a normal school day; our paths didn't cross at all. We were on different floors and used different stairwells most of the day. So I was surprised to see him in the upper hallway after my second period geography class. He gave me a bit of a questioning look, so I just walked over, and said "Hi."

"Is everything okay? You only replied to the first text. I thought I better track you down, after yesterday." I was so distracted by his big, beautiful hazel eyes that I didn't quite catch everything he said but I did get the gist of it.

"Yeah, sorry. I misplaced my phone." I instinctively touched my mouth as I spoke, even though I knew touching your face is a dead giveaway when you're lying.

"I hate when that happens." His expression softened. Obviously he hadn't read *Style* magazine's "How to Spot Your Cheating Man: Learn to Read the 10 Easy Signals." Cameron continued, "Did you leave it somewhere?"

"No, no, I didn't really lose it. Well, actually, to tell the truth, it kind of fell in the toilet," I lied. Cameron raised his eyebrows, but I decided to continue in the same vein. "But you never know, it might work maybe when it dries out…?" I felt myself grimace.

Curse you, Rachel, for putting me in this stupid situation! I ended up looking like a complete dork to protect you, to not expose your diabolical ways.

"You just … you don't hold back." Cameron smiled and shook his head.

"I'm sorry, I'm not sure what comes over me. My mouth gets ahead of my brain, I forget to pause … edit, sometimes." I could feel my cheeks colouring in embarrassment, but he seemed to have found my story more entertaining than revolting.

"I like that…" he said as I half-smiled in a self-conscious kind of way. But I stayed mute; I didn't trust myself.

"So moving away from toilet talk," Cameron said, looking directly into my eyes with a semi-serious, semi-amused expression, "I was wondering if you might want to grab a coffee after school? But maybe you have to meet a plumber, you know, the phone?"

"No, no, absolutely—I mean, yes." I decided to take a second and inhale deeply. "Okay, rewind…. Yes, I'd love that and no, the plumbing's all good."

"So, we could meet at Fireroasted Cafe say, four?"

"Perfect, yes, see you then." I smiled but quickly ducked away to escape before I said anything else that might give Cameron second thoughts.

A hex on you, Rachel! How can I possibly talk her up to Cameron? I need all the help I can get for myself! As I walked down the hallway on my way to the cafeteria, I told my jittery brain that meeting Cameron after school could hardly be construed as a date. Maybe he just found unusual conversation topics intriguing somehow, similar to how people were attracted to freakshows at the circus.

But—holy crap, it finally hit me. He wanted to have coffee with me! The awfulness of yesterday took a back seat for the first time since Mei's injury. I was dying to tell someone—anyone—the news. But it was like last night. I couldn't very well tell Anne, and I definitely could not tell Mei.

As I sat with Anne at lunch, my mind started churning. I needed to get on with implementing Step Twelve and float the myth of Rachel the Good. I managed to drop her name in casually during the conversation, steering away from Mei and her predicament. I recounted a humorous family story about Rachel faking a British accent with a waiter and ended with, "That Rachel, you gotta love her, she is too funny!" Unlike Rachel, I wasn't naturally good at drama, but I would have given myself an A for that lunchtime performance.

"I'm going to see Mei today. Are you in? Maybe five-ish?"

"Yeah, definitely," said Anne.

I did see Rachel and Matt briefly in the hallway, but it was hard to know what was going on between them. And Rachel, who had never been known for subtlety, made eye contact letting me know she was watching. I sweetly smiled and waved, and she did the same back to me. I saw Anne take note.

Even though I had a great teacher and loved English class, I tuned out the discussion and started to tackle Step Eleven. I needed to come up with some intelligent and appropriate topics of conversation with Cameron. It was too bad I didn't know more about music, but I could talk a bit about sports. Cameron was on a lot of teams. Hmmm, what else—what else? I was lost in thought.

"Nadine! Earth to Nadine!" said my English teacher, Mr. Werstine, cupping his hands. He pointed to Mrs. Chow, the principal's assistant, who was standing outside the classroom and motioning for me to come.

"You're Nadine Stewart, right?" she said as I went into the hall. "Funny, I've never had to speak to you. You must be much better behaved than Rachel. Anyway, Principal Hayes needs to see you after school. Come directly to the office, okay? It's urgent. Got it?"

"I can't. I have plans … important plans. And I, I lost my phone … so I can't let, um, him, I mean the person, well … know that I'm busy, so…" I struggled to try to convince her to give me some leeway.

Mrs. Chow looked at me directly, unsympathetically and unblinkingly. "Do not keep Principal Hayes waiting, do you understand? Come immediately after the bell."

"Yes, of course," I said, sucking in some air.

I'd spent the entire class tuning out *Romeo and Juliet* to mentally rehearse conversation, and now how I was going to let Cameron know I couldn't make it? And why was I being summoned to the principal's office anyway? When the dismissal bell rang, I searched the hallways for Cameron but didn't have any luck finding him. I then walked quickly to the Ms. Hayes' office, cursing Rachel for the millionth time that day. He would be at Fireroasted Cafe wondering where I was, and it was probably the last time he'd ever talk to me.

When I finally arrived, I saw Anne waiting outside the door, and I figured it out pretty quickly. Clearly this meeting was about Mei. I thought about my idiocy, and then about Cameron and the cafe. I wanted to burst into tears right then and there.

"OMG, I was praying you'd be here," Anne said, jumping up out of the chair.

"Same." I tried to smile, but it didn't happen. Anne looked distraught at the prospect of seeing the principal but was trying to put up a brave front. I knew this was going to be a very awkward question, but I needed to ask anyway. "So, this might sound weird, but can I borrow your phone for a sec? Remember, I dropped mine…."

"Sure." Her hands were shaking as she unzipped a pocket of her backpack and handed her phone to me.

"Could you find Cameron's number? So I can send a text."

I tried to be nonchalant, but I could feel my body temperature soar about twelve degrees. I tried to swallow but my throat felt dry. Anne's demeanour softened a bit, and she bit her lip so as not to smile. "No probs," she said finding the number and handing it back to me.

I quickly sent off a message: *Hey this is Nadine, @ school office with A, got called 2 a m8ting with principal, about Mei? can we do Fireroasted nother time? sorry, had to use A's phone. N.*

A few seconds later, I received a response: *K, good luck, another time 4 sure, didn't want it 2 b weird 4 her so I told A.*

I smiled at Anne and handed the phone back to her. "Thanks," I said, and she managed a smile in return. I felt good that Anne wasn't upset by whatever was maybe starting to happen.

The principal's door opened, and we were ushered into her office. I had never been inside before, and it was exactly how I would have envisioned it, with a fake brown leather couch and chairs and a large wooden desk. I had occasionally seen Principal Hayes in the hallways or presiding over a school assembly, and she looked every bit the serious administrator. Her bifocals were perched on her nose, her hair was honey-coloured, perfectly coiffed and swept up into a soft bun, and she was sporting the kind of sensible navy pantsuit that Hillary Clinton always wore. Ms. Davies was already in the office, as was the coach of the Westminster team, who was introduced as Ms. Griffin.

Anne and I were asked to retell the incident in the movie theatre bathroom, while Mrs. Chow recorded notes. They prodded us with more questions about the Instagram and Facebook postings and the decision not to involve our coach or any other staff members.

I reddened when Coach Davies asked me to recount what I had told her at the hospital, including our plan to have Danielle apologize by having her think that Matt was interested in her. We were also asked to give as much detail as possible about anything we had witnessed on the field that day between Mei and Helen prior to the big altercation.

I did almost all of the talking, since I wanted to take responsibility, and I could tell Anne was super intimidated, reverting to full "mouse" mode. They asked periodically if she had anything to add, and she kept shaking her head.

I was sure Ms. Davies had told them everything, and they were just looking for confirmation. They inquired if we'd had any further contact with Helen, and if we were concerned about our own personal safety. We said no to both. I thought the meeting was wrapping up when Principal Hayes took off her bifocals, placed them on her desk, and swivelled her chair to look directly at both of us.

She paused for a moment and made direct eye contact with each of us. Satisfied that we were paying attention, she continued. "In light of this incident, Helen has been banned from team sports at the high school level, so you won't see her on the field, but you do need to stay away from her. If you run into her, you need to exercise caution. Do not provoke her in any way. Is that clear?"

Anne and I both said, "Okay."

"Unfortunately, posting horrible pictures and hashtagging them and the like are not against school board policy. And while we're unimpressed with Danielle's behaviour on Instagram and other websites, we have no recourse in that regard."

Miss Davies piped in, "If I can interject for a minute here, I really think that we need to get in another guest speaker into the school. Someone who was the victim of cyberbullying, and devote an entire assembly. Get them really thinking about the implications of their posts and comments. You know, how quickly negative things get disseminated. Look at the long-term consequences of posting things that might seem 'funny' but do a real disservice to others."

Principal Hayes said, "Yes, that's a good idea. We need to keep tackling this problem again and again, but that's a sidebar right now. So, just finishing up here, the good news is that Mei is going to be all right. Frankly, we can't say for sure if the finger amputation was intentional. We have examined all the sticks from the game, but none of them seem to have been tampered with. So all we can assume is that she took a run at Mei but that it was a freak accident. Does that make sense?" Principal Hayes nodded to us, and we nodded back.

"I know you two spend a lot of time with her, so we want you to be an extra set of eyes and ears. Please use your mouths next time, though, if anything unusual happens, okay?" Both Anne and I nodded again, and we were dismissed from the meeting.

As we left the office and entered the hallway, still clutching our books from last period, we simultaneously slumped against the concrete wall. Anne said, "Okay, so Mei's Sasquatch comment was nasty, and Helen should never have messed her up that way, but Danielle is really ground zero here. Don't you think?"

"Yes, she was, for sure. And so she got kicked out of a game, that's barely any punishment. But really, what happened to Mei never should have happened and never would have if we had listened to you..."

"It was a mistake, you need to put it behind you."

"I honestly thought it was the right advice. I've been bullied before, and when I did, you know, 'tell on the bully,' it really went bad..." I trailed off for a moment.

"Is everything okay now?"

"Yeah," I lied.

"And remember, we all thought we had another week before we faced Helen's team. Let's just focus on Mei and just forget about the rest, okay?"

I took a deep breath and looked at my watch. I couldn't help but think that somewhere, in a parallel universe, I was sitting at Fireroasted Cafe, sipping a cappuccino with Cameron. Naturally, since I'd nailed Step Eleven, we were engaged in the perfect balance of clever and comedic conversation. Perhaps our fingertips accidentally touched as we reached for the packets of sugar...

"So are we still going to Mei's?" Anne said, bringing me back to reality.

"Yeah," I said. I really needed to fulfill Step Thirteen. I needed to make amends. Anne was right. I should focus on Mei and try to stop the self-blame. It wasn't helpful to anyone at this point. "Why don't we stop by

7-Eleven and grab a Toblerone and maybe some mags, like *Cosmo*, *Hello*, she loves that stuff." Guilty gifts, I thought.

"Perfect, I'll meet you at the front door in five."

*

We couldn't really get a good look at Mei's left hand, since it was all bandaged up and held in a sling, but she was in great spirits. You'd never know she was in any sort of discomfort. She loved being the centre of attention and was definitely still under the influence of painkillers. She told a lot of humorous hospital stories in a slightly loopy way.

Mei was especially entertaining when she talked about a young, hot plastic surgery intern. "So Dr. Max comes to see me. I'm waking up. And da first fing he says is, "Kweenex to wipe your dwool?" Surprisingly, she barely mentioned the game and Helen. She did make an inappropriate reference to 'Sasquatch,' but she mangled the pronunciation so badly, it sounded like 'Squash.'

"How much stuff are you on?" I asked incredulously. My stomach actually hurt from laughing so hard. I excused myself to use the washroom, partly to give my aching stomach a breather.

When I returned, Anne snapped to attention and gave me a guilty, surprised look, while Mei laughed like a hyena. I could hear a strange, metallic rattling noise, and then realized Mei was shaking a Ziploc bag up and down with her good hand, and the remnants of the cellphone were rattling around inside.

"It could be a new ringtone or somefing," Mei said as she continued to shake the bag. "We could call it clank. Get it, clank! Ha, ha, ha."

"Hand it over, Mei," I said. I swallowed hard and averted my gaze from Anne.

"Where is dat chocolate?" Mei slurred. "I smelled dit in your packpack but couldn't find dit, but I found dis phone."

I grabbed the phone from Mei, pulled the giant Toblerone from my backpack, and practically threw it at her. Then I put the phone back inside and zipped it all up.

"Ahhh, Nadine mad," Mei giggled as she fumbled around with the wrapper. She would have been hard pressed to open it with two good hands in her current state, and soon the bar fell on the floor, which she thought was an absolute riot.

"You said you dropped it in water?" Anne looked questioningly at me while unwrapping the bar for Mei. "What's going on?"

"Did big sis take a hammer and go smash?" said Mei, who was greedily inhaling the bar and already had a chocolate smear on her nose.

I was caught so off-guard, I didn't know what to say. I stood there trying to come up with some sort of explanation, but my brain blanked. I opened my mouth to speak but changed my mind. There was nothing to say.

"I was wight about Wachel. The nurse told me my fwend did a big fight at the hopital." Mei stopped talking long enough to stuff in more chocolate, and she then produced a huge yawn, but thankfully she covered her mouth. "Wow, I feel sweepy." And just like that, she curled up on her bed, shut her eyes, and was practically snoring before we left. Anne took the bar out of her good hand and placed it on her night table.

We tiptoed into the kitchen, and on our way out we warned Mrs. Chen about the chocolate mess. "Argh," said Mrs. Chen as she put down her magazine and got out of her chair to go deal with Mei.

As we walked down the porch steps, I knew I had to say something to Anne. "About the phone … I have my reasons. I just can't talk about it."

"Okay," Anne said quietly, and I suddenly felt about as low as I had during the meeting in the principal's office. She scrunched up her nose. "Are you all right? All that stuff you said about bullying?"

"I'm good," I said. "I am. Promise. But could you maybe keep it under wraps?"

"You mean from Cameron?" Anne asked as I nodded. "I guess, for now… It's just like with Mei, I don't want to keep things quiet that should be—"

I interrupted, "I get it. Appreciated." Less was definitely more here.

"Well, don't forget about practice tomorrow," Anne said.

"I won't," I replied as we went our separate ways.

CHAPTER 22

I had the luxury of coming home to an empty house and found the silence and stillness soothing after such a wild, unpredictable day. I dropped my stuff in the hallway and practically hurled my exhausted mind and body into one of the overstuffed white chairs in the living room. Immediately, my thoughts turned to Rachel and how she was going to keep dominating me if I kept letting her. For once, I needed to take the control, even though Rachel wanted me to believe that could never happen.

I was still deep in thought a few minutes later when, with the click of the lock, Rachel appeared. She kicked off her boots, practically bounced into the room, and happily dropped herself into the other white chair. "So I shouldn't have wrecked your phone. I kind of lost it, you were sooo awful at the hospital! I guess I was too. Anyway, *excusez-moi*."

"Do you mean sorry?"

"Do I have to?"

"Yes," I said, pushing her for a change.

"Okay," said Rachel, taking a deep breath. "I'm sorry. Satisfied?"

"Well, I can't just forget, but it's a start." And it was; Rachel had practically never apologized for anything before.

"You know me. I lose it, I lose control … sometimes," said Rachel.

I considered what she said. I had never heard her to admit to 'losing control.' I decided to take a chance. "I worry about you, you know. The anger and then the opposite, there's not a lot of … in between. Mom thinks it's because of the separation, but I don't know. Maybe it's something more, like, organic?"

"What?" said Rachel. "What are you saying? That I'm a mental case?" She was half-joking, but I could tell her back was up. I wanted to keep the conversation going, so I decided to back down.

"No," I said, unconvincingly. Of course I did.

"Good, because here I *am* apologizing, it's a bad time to be calling me crazy. As a matter of fact, I've been really pissed at you all day. Matt barely spoke to me at school. But he just sent a text from home. So you did help me out with the sibs. He wants me to go with him to find poetry books. There's this assignment. They have to go to a library." She seemed to be moving into one of her non-stop chatter "up" moods. "So he's making weekend plans with me already."

Hmm. Perhaps for Matt, the prospect of trying to navigate a real live library was quite daunting. Maybe he'd ask anyone for help. I kept that thought to myself, but I interrupted to curtail the verbal flow. "That's great. Reading poetry … sounds romantic." I knew I had had nothing to do with this, but I was happy to take the credit, especially with Rachel being so generous—first an apology and now a compliment?

Rachel paused for a second to scrutinize me and then decided to change course. "So what's your secret, Bean? You've had like zero friends forever, and suddenly you're Miss Popular." This time she waited for me to reply.

"Yeah, I wish. I have a couple of friends, from the team …" I purposefully trailed off. What was I going to say? Was I going to tell Rachel about all the steps? Part of me wanted to actually tell her how I *had* devised a plan *and* followed through. If I thought she would have actually listened to me, I would have tried.

"It's somehow all just *easier* for you," Rachel replied. She then suddenly got up from the chair. "What do you say? Shall I make a pot of tea for two?" she said in a fake English accent, smiling at her own joke. I thought how beautiful she looked when her face softened like that, and then she held out her hand to me as I got up.

"Sounds good. I'm in," I said. Rachel was in a good mood, and that worked for me. You never knew, maybe eventually I would try to talk to her. Really try. Perhaps one day we'd even be close again. But for now, this was about the best that could be expected.

We both walked into the kitchen, and it sort of felt like two former enemy soldiers, returning to the sight of a battle ("the battle of the cell phone") and finding that it had become in peacetime a cafe. We sat together as allies and enjoyed a venti soya green tea latte, hold the honey. I suspected that this was *not* the end of the war, but just a détente. I was pretty confident that something would push her over the edge, and probably soon.

Later that night I locked myself in the bathroom, and using a really small pair of tweezers I'd lifted from my mom's bathroom, and against all odds, I managed to extract the SIM card from the smashed phone. I was ecstatic. I could now text Cameron again. I carefully loaded the card into the fully charged and sanitized pee-pee phone, pressed the "on" button, and was fully connected. It had been a long twenty-four hours.

Despite the encouragement I had received from him over the last few days, I had this nervous feeling in the pit of my stomach as I looked up his name in my contacts. Even though I had just drunk a large green tea latte, my mouth felt stone-dry. I held the phone and hesitated. It was now or never, I decided. My hands were almost shaking as I started to type a message: *Did u have a coffee 4 me?? sorry that I missed it ☹ phone is wrking now ☺*. I almost added "and sanitized" but decided not to allude again to the toilet tale.

Xclent! doing chem, need coffee 2 keep me going, my brain is being slowly fried what r u doing?

Super tired, but have Fr test tomorrow I suck @ verb tenses, better study!

Try again tomorrow, coffee after school?

Love 2 but have fb practise. I added a couple of sad faces. Before Cameron could reply, I decided to be bold and texted again: *what about Fri?* I then immediately had second thoughts. Would he think I was moving too fast? Suggesting a Friday night coffee date to replace one originally set for Wednesday?

I have 2 work @ 5, but maybe a small cup of joe after skol?

Yes, where do u work?

Fruit and veg @ valu mart every Fri night!! Wed nite 2 if the papayas miss me!

LOL, *meet u at* FR *café @ 4? good luck with chem! sleep well.*

Toi aussi, au revoir ma cherie! replied Cameron, and my cheeks turned pink as I reread his salutation. It was difficult, but I did manage to turn my attention to the imperfect past.

*

Anne surprised me the next day. When we were eating lunch, she said that if I ever needed someone to talk to who wouldn't blab to anyone, she was there for me. "I'm good at listening. But I get not everyone wants to go there. It's complicated for us, isn't it? We have some overlapping family stuff. But I'm here for you, you know that, right?"

I smiled and said, "Thanks, it means a lot." And while it would have been awesome to unburden myself, in many ways that would have just further complicated things. It was nice, though, to know that I had a real friend.

And then just as we were leaving the caf and about to walk up the steps to the hall, Anne leaned in a bit closer and said, "I know he's my brother, but Cameron's a good guy, even if he can be a total slob sometimes. I think he really likes you, and as long as you like him back. Or, you know, tell him if you don't, well, then we're good." I practically tripped on the steps.

*

It felt like a month had passed since the field hockey team was last together, so much had happened over the past few days. Even though there was a lot to talk about, there was very little conversation. Danielle was clearly not her usual overconfident self and after a few minutes stopped even the pretence of trying. Ms. Davies abandoned the first drill at midpoint, called us off the field, and pointed to the bleachers.

"I was going to wait until the end of the practice to have this chat with you girls. I was hoping that getting some exercise might clear your heads a little, but I can tell that's not going to happen—you're all pretty distracted. Let me say that I'm so glad to see all of you. The last game was like a bad dream. I'm sure you're all aware that Mei's making remarkable progress. The doctors expect a full and complete recovery for the finger and hand."

Ms. Davies paused, retrieved a card from her coat pocket, passed it around, and continued. "It's a thank-you note from the Chen family. They appreciated the support we've given Mei. But don't let up yet. We need to continue to keep Mei and her family in our thoughts, and actions too.

"I know you're all disturbed by what happened at the last game. Perhaps you're worried about your own safety on Monday's game. I want to let you know that a lot of energy and resources have been directed at investigating the circumstances of the incident. The Warrior player has been dealt with in an appropriate manner. It was not a black-and-white situation, trust me, but she did utter a threat beforehand, and well, we all know what happened. She has been banned from playing team sports at the high-school level. That means you will never again face her on the field during the rest of your time at Elgin High."

Most of the team broke into spontaneous cheering, and Coach Davies paused until the noise quieted down. I didn't join in the cheering, and neither did Anne or Danielle. I was conflicted. Helen had really hurt Mei, for sure, but I didn't think the level of injury was intentional. And she had been fouled, too. Big-time. And while I didn't support violence, I didn't support cyberbullying either.

Directing her comments toward Danielle, Ms. Davies continued, "As we witnessed last game, the performance of just one player, both on and off the field, can undermine the good works of everyone. As a team, we need to be sportsmanlike toward everyone of the field. There can be no pride taken when we disrespect any players, or anyone for that matter. Got it?" She looked directly at Danielle, who nodded then looked at the ground.

I was surprised Danielle was being so, well, placid, but then I remembered her father expected her to get a field hockey scholarship at some elite US college. It's not like they needed the financial help with his big job and all, but I guess it was all about the prestige. I assumed she didn't have any other choice but to suck it up. But then again, maybe I was being too judgemental; maybe she was feeling guilty.

"Having said that, we need to look ahead. Today is a new day. And I have an update: the Warriors forfeited to us. And unexpectedly, just last night, the Bulldogs lost to the Lions, so they're out. The next game we play, then, will not be for the semifinals. It will be for the city finals. That game is this Monday, and we will be playing the Lions. So girls, we've made it to the end!" The cheering was loud and wild, and Coach Davies even started hollering herself.

In the midst of it all, Anne leaned over to me and mouthed a word I couldn't make out. I shrugged, so she leaned toward my ear, cupped her mouth and said, "Mei," and I nodded. The cheering was subsiding and the team was just starting to leave the bleachers, and I knew I needed to speak up. Ms. Davies was just grabbing the stack of pylons to set up another drill when I cleared my throat.

"This is Anne's idea, and I second it. I think we should dedicate this game to Mei. Let's win this championship, for her, or at the very least kill ourselves trying." Everyone was listening intently.

I paused for a moment to collect my thoughts, then continued. "The thing about Mei is that she's not our strongest player, and she's always joking around at practices. So she may not have *seemed* like a serious player, but she really was. When she was on the field, during a game, she gave a hundred and ten percent every second. And believe me, she trained hard off the field, too. The girl is gutsy. It's been awful for her, and she'd never let anyone know how much she's suffered. So in honour of Mei, I think we should all play with her spirit and give a hundred and ten percent. We know we're unbeatable if we do. Is everyone in?"

For a split-second everyone was quiet, and it was Anne who first piped up. "*In,*" and she put her hand in the middle of the circle. Soon we had everyone's hand, including mine, piled on top of each other in solidarity.

Wow, I thought. If we won the game, I'd be rocking Step Thirteen, and Mei would be so pumped. *Hmmm.* I quickly retracted that thought. *I should be repenting, not celebrating.* I wouldn't need to be making amends with Mei if

I hadn't been so stupid and blind. *Maybe I should aim for a tad more humility and less rocking of steps!*

Shortly afterward, as Anne and I walked through the back school entrance toward the change room, Danielle was waiting just inside. She grabbed Anne's arm and hissed at her, "Don't think I'm going to forget you lied to me, Lavery. About Matt."

"I know and I'm sorry…" said Anne.

"Damn straight," said Danielle.

I piped in, "She had to do it. Helen was so pissed for all your stupid posts. The hashtag Sasquatch wrist thing. You should have apologized to her anyway, trick or no trick. But it was Mei, she's the one who had to pay." Danielle pursed her lips, trying to formulate a response, but in the end all she did was huff before she headed off to the locker room.

*

In the spirit of pursuing Step Thirteen, I needed to visit Mei as often as I could. I left school right after field hockey practice without even mentioning it to Anne. It would have been too weird with the "elephant in the room" (the old broken cellphone, thanks, Mei!) hanging over us.

"She's feeling blue today, fair warning," said Mrs. Chen as we walked down the hallway to a solarium. "But we've had some good news. The doctor has given her the okay to go to school on Monday. It will be good for her to get back into a routine."

"Hey," said Mei rather glumly when she saw me. "*Quelle surprise,*" she continued and attempted a smile, but I could tell by her eyes she was putting it on for my benefit.

I told her about the upcoming game on Monday and how we were dedicating the game, win or lose, to the fighting spirit of our wounded comrade. I was waiting for her to fist-bump me, with her good hand, of course, or scream with delight. But instead Mei sat stunned for a moment and then burst into tears. And not just quiet, ladylike tears of joy, but huge, loud, emotional sobs. I scooted over and tried to give her a hug, but she pushed me away, not having any of that.

I felt awful, uncomfortable. But the tears ended as quickly as they began. Mei wiped at her eyes with her good hand as she regained her composure, ending with a little hiccup. "I'm touched about the dedication and stuff, but it's screwed up. I was part of the problem." Then she grimaced. "And my hand really hurts. I'm in rough shape." She massaged her left forearm with her good hand.

Moments later, Mrs. Chen checked in on Mei, and then she nicely but firmly suggested that her daughter needed to rest. "I'll text you tomorrow. Sorry your hand's hurting." I felt relieved as I left—I didn't know what to say to make her feel better, and her tears made me feel terrible. I spent most of the walk home beating myself up all over again.

My heart sank as I rounded the corner to our street and saw that the "Cat Mobile" (a combination of "Cam" and "Matt") was parked in our driveway. Naturally, my mom's car was nowhere to be seen. So were they having milk and cookies in the kitchen, or were they elsewhere in the house, doing something entirely different? I wasn't sure if I should even enter my own home.

I hesitated for a moment on the sidewalk and was relieved when Matt emerged through the front door. His black hair, which was normally perfectly coiffed, looked quite tousled, and one of the front parts of his red-and-white plaid flannel shirttail was untucked and hung out beneath his grey hoodie. While any other mortal would have put his head down and tried to skulk away at this point, Matt, of course, gave me a huge wave and a booming, "Hey, little sister!" I had to assume he called me that because he had blanked on my real name.

I responded with a weak half-wave and a barely audible "Hello," and that was all the encouragement he needed to walk past the Cat Mobile and head right on over to me. "You're home way later than Rach thought you'd be," he started, and then not so subtly added, "Not that I'm complaining or anything…"

"Yeah," I interrupted, not wanting to risk him delving further into why he wasn't *complaining*. "I had field hockey practice, and then I went to visit Mei." And to make everything perfectly clear, I added, "I'm just getting home, now."

"Hey, how's she doing?" asked Matt, clearly oblivious to my awkwardness. "I haven't seen her since, well, since that time in the hospital, remember?"

"Yeah, I do. She's okay," I lied. "Going back to school on Monday."

"Cool. Can I get her number? I'll text her a 'welcome back.'" He produced his cellphone a little too eagerly.

I stood speechless for a second, but what was I going to say? *No?* It was probably innocent enough, and I could just imagine how getting a message from Matt would practically make Mei's year. I was already sick of hearing her talk about it.

I reluctantly plucked my phone from a side compartment of my backpack and recited Mei's coordinates an octave lower than usual. Afterward, Matt put the phone back in his pocket and flashed his trademark *Yes, I am a beautiful person and I bet you're sorry to see me go* smile. Then he ran his fingers through his hair. What did Rachel and all the other girls see in all this phony posturing? He was practically a caricature of a school stud, and about the polar opposite of what I would want in a guy. Of what Cameron seemed to be.

I opened the front door to the sight of Rachel coming down the stairs in a bathrobe with a towel wrapped around her wet hair. While her appearance alone was not conclusive, her amazing mood combined with the state of her bed when I peeked in her room led me to deduce that the Rachel-Matt relationship had jumped to a new level. And I was pretty sure that this was a first for Rachel. *Wow*, I thought, *she must really like him*. She was pulling out all the stops here.

Rachel wasn't stupid. She knew I knew what had just gone down. She followed me into the kitchen, and I got to listen to her prattle on about trust and commitment. I had to practically choke down vomit when she tried to bring up the concept of 'soul mates.' I wanted to say, "You know, you couldn't ask for a more handsome or popular guy. If only he'd keep that gorgeous mouth shut, he'd be perfect."

Rachel started doing the mile-a-minute talking thing. All I needed to do was nod and smile every once in a while. Our kitchen conversation morphed into Rachel watching me make scrambled eggs for our dinner while she nattered on and threw back some grapes.

I clumsily chopped some peppers and olives, whisked, and cooked the eggs. And while part of me was totally repulsed, another part was dying of curiosity. As I sprinkled on grated cheese, I wanted to ask Rachel real questions like, "Was this your first time?" and "Was it nice? Did it hurt?" But I bit my tongue and kept nodding while she kept on talking.

I hadn't even kissed Cameron or had a date with him, but I couldn't help but wonder if that was his expectation in a relationship. If so, perhaps things would be getting way out of my league pretty quickly.

"Are you listening?" she said. "What's happening with Saint Cameron?" Maybe being with Matt was mellowing her. Rachel was trying to be nice, trying to engage me in a sisterly chat. But again, I didn't want to tell her anything. I knew that vague, evasive, or self-deprecating answers had worked best in the past with her, so I responded accordingly, "Yeah, well, I wish I had something to share, but sadly, no."

I was rewarded with a small smile, and then Rachel touched my arm and said, "Aww, and I was so looking forward to the double wedding." She offered to poke around a bit, mention it to Matt, and see if he could help. I graciously but adamantly refused all offers of help and said that he clearly wasn't into me and that I had moved on. I hoped she believed my lie.

Unexpectedly, Mom slipped into the kitchen. She seemed quite pleased that Rachel and I were having a sisterly heart-to-heart. She sliced up some fresh bread she had brought home and we sat at the table to a real family dinner, something that hadn't happened since Thanksgiving.

"Listen, girls, I have some news, and before I tell you, I don't want you freaking out, okay, Rachel? So your dad would like you two to visit him in New York. He's thinking December. For a weekend..." Mom paused and looked at Rachel, who barely reacted. Which surprised me—as I'm sure it did Mom.

"He knows this great boutique hotel right near Central Park. And he's made it crystal clear it'll just be the three of you. You could do some Christmas shopping, maybe see a play, whatever you want. And you don't have to set foot in his apartment. At all. So what do you think?"

"I'm in," I said without hesitation. I wanted to see Dad—it'd been almost a year. He'd pretty much stopped calling the house because it made Mom upset, although he had left a message on the machine to sarcastically thank us for the turkey dinner photo. Our recent relationship had been confined to email messages and the occasional call to my cell, since he hadn't yet mastered texting. Luckily, he wasn't on Facebook.

Rachel wore a neutral expression, but then she half-smiled and said, "I suppose … if Nadine's going, I'll go."

Mom exhaled deeply and said, "Okay, great. I do have a bit of, well, other news. I want you guys know that I'm signing the separation papers. It's really just a formality before the divorce ones. I'm not going to pretend to you of all people that this hasn't been brutally hard. And I've seen how tough it's been on you. Look, I've accepted that this is the next step, for all of us. We need to put this marriage behind us and move on with our lives."

My stomach sank at the news, and I felt this weird pressure on my forehead. I'm not sure why—I had gotten used to my dad being gone, just not the finality of it. But after that speech, I was going to have to figure out a way to accept that the leafy family tree of my imagination was really dead and gone. Instead of a rotting tree, I needed a different visual, something smaller and more alive, like a vine that had already taken root and was starting to grow up toward the sun.

It was better for Mom to get on with her new life and to keep moving forward. I guess for her to have accepted the pending divorce meant that she had also undergone some life-changing steps, just like me. But I assumed her inspiration was something other than an AA pamphlet.

I expected an outburst from Rachel, but she surprised me again by saying, "I guess at this point, you just do whatever you have to."

"I appreciate you saying that, I appreciate it very much." Mom paused to wipe at her eyes for a second.

"I love Dad, even when I didn't... Like him, you know?" Rachel started and Mom nodded. "But we're not kids any more. You don't have to keep protecting us. We know what happened. That Dad cheated—"

"Look, it's not that simple. It's easy to be the victim..." Mom interrupted.

"You don't have to explain..." I started.

"If you don't want to be protected, then don't protect me. It goes both ways. I would be a liar if I said that this is what I've wanted all along. I'd hoped it was just ... just an affair and that it would end, quickly. But it's not. People change and they are allowed to change. I want to move myself forward, too!"

Rachel nodded and then said, "I'd be crushed if I loved someone and then they're like, 'Sorry, not feeling it.' Like if Matt just up and ended it. If I was still feeling that way about him."

Wow, I thought, *the ice queen is really melting. This is good.* I didn't think I'd see the day that she admitted being vulnerable. And it was the first time she had offered emotional support to Mom in a long while. I guess being so into Matt finally allowed her to feel some empathy. Until now, the separation had been all about her. Who would have thought that Matt Lavery might be indirectly responsible for Rachel's possible emotional breakthrough?

Maybe this was the beginning of a turnaround somehow? Nah! Like a freshly perked cup of joe, she might have mellowed a bit, but I would bet good money she'd be back to her bitter self in a few days.

CHAPTER 23

I lay on my bed and stared at the ceiling, trying to process all that had happened that day. My brain was a jumble of thoughts, first and foremost being the official end of our family of four. It was like The Stewart family book, and all that had happened, the good and bad, was closing forever. No new pages were ever going to be added to that one. But I guess we'd already zipped past the first chapter of our second novel without realizing it.

With sleep escaping me, my thoughts kept churning, and I wondered about Rachel's surprising behaviour, and then how things would go after school with Cameron. Then I started thinking about the sheer number of major events that had occurred in such a short time span, starting with the field hockey game on Monday, which, unbelievably, had been just four days ago, and then all the stuff with Mei, and all the stuff with Rachel, and the stuff with Helen, and then the stuff with my parents, and the stuff with Cameron, and even stuff with Anne.

I wondered if it was because I was getting older that my life had suddenly started moving at a breakneck pace, or if perhaps I was going to be diagnosed with an inoperable brain tumour next week. Maybe God was trying to at least let me live a little before he pulled the carpet out from under me.

I finally did fall asleep but then woke up again in the middle of night and lay awake for what seemed like forever. *Oh well,* I thought, *I should at least think about what I'm going to wear tomorrow.* I mentally went through my clothes and settled on my slimmest jeans that made my legs look long and a newish off-white sweater that had a lightly scooped neckline and a cool, tone-on-tone pattern. It showed a bit of cleavage, and that was about all I could pull off.

I thought about wearing the silver Tiffany heart necklace my father had given me the last time I'd seen him. Clearly he'd known then he was leaving us for good and gave me a special gift with a message. I got up from my bed, opened my jewellery box, and pulled out the necklace. It felt cold as I secured it to my throat, and I touched the cool heart with my warm fingers.

I went back to bed and rolled around again. When sleep still didn't come, I grabbed my phone and looked at the stream of messages from earlier in the night. Mei and I had exchanged a few about the visit. She was depressed being stuck inside with her parents for so long and irritated by the pain but also worried about what might happen if she ran into Helen again.

We had texted back and forth, and in typical Mei fashion she had quickly shaken off her blues and was already joking about the TV movie that could be made. Her favourite title was *I Would Have Given You the Finger if You'd Only Asked.* I told her that Anne and I were going to come and hang out with her on Saturday night. Mei texted back seconds later: *so pumped … so bored … not lking hermit life* ☹.

The last set of messages from the day, only two this time, were from Cameron, confirming our coffee date. To my surprise, he had suggested we meet at my locker after school to walk over together. I'd just assumed he would want to be low-key about it and meet up at the café. It was cool that he didn't seem to care much about what others thought, and if we were going to go someplace together, that's just what was going to happen. No games, no subterfuge.

It was almost like Cameron didn't even realize he was in high school. I reread the message exchange as I lay awake in bed. And instead of feeling more excited and nervous, it calmed me. I put down the phone on my night side table and soon was fast asleep.

The next day at school was completely ordinary, and every little second seemed to stretch out to at least twelve minutes. I must have looked at my watch twenty times, and that was just before lunch. By the time I hit the cafeteria, I still hadn't seen Cameron at all. I ate my lunch with Anne, uneventfully, but was careful not to make a mess of my carefully selected clothes. I scanned the horizon for him a couple of times, but he was a no-show.

I tried to be nonchalant in front of Anne; I wasn't sure she knew what was happening after school. Just as we were headed back to class, she turned to me and said, "Have fun. A word of advice—don't mention music. He'll never shut up, and that would be very unfun!"

I ducked into the washroom at the final bell so I'd have a bit of time to prep. I had brought a toothbrush to make sure I didn't have any green bits in my teeth, and I spent a few extra minutes touching up the makeup I'd painstakingly applied that morning. *Maybe*, I thought, *it would be easier for me if I wore mascara more often and could get the hang of applying it properly*. Lastly, I put on some lip gloss and centred the Tiffany necklace. I surveyed myself one last time before relinquishing my spot to the girl behind me.

It seemed completely normal for Cameron to appear at my locker at the end of school. He made small talk with a few people who passed by as I gathered up my things for the weekend. I was a little on edge. I wasn't quite sure just how much to smile or just how much to talk. It was almost like I was floating nearby, watching myself perform as I did my usual "books from locker to backpack" ritual. And I felt that the performance should be going differently somehow.

It's fine, I silently reprimanded myself and forced myself to smile a little to coax my body into a slightly more relaxed mode. And of course just when I was trying to conjure up a bit of inner calm, who should come directly our way but Rachel and Matt, the Rat couple. She had her arm wrapped around his and was leaning in quite tightly. "Double date?" she asked, only half-jokingly.

"Uh, no," I said. "He's … we're just heading in the same direction … in search of caffeine…"

Both Cameron and Rachel looked at me a bit strangely, but Matt just nodded and said, "Cool, I think I hit my max today, enjoy the buzz. Forgot you were working tonight. I'm taking the wheels, okay? Thought we'd take a ... you know, *drive*." I wanted to gag. Was that some code word between them? God, I really hoped Cameron was as different from his brother as I was from Rachel.

"No probs. Remember it was Mom's car, right?"

"How can I forget—you always remind me, dude," said Matt.

"Have fun, kids," Rachel called out as they headed toward the parking lot.

Matt then turned back to us and said, "Don't go wild on us, stick to decaf!"

When they were out of earshot, Cameron said, "Should we live on the edge?" He gave me a sideways glance. I liked the way his mouth took on an ironic upward turn. He took my hand, and it just seemed natural, like we did this every day. It was surreal, a bit like a dream.

As we walked, our hands loosely swung back and forth together, and I touched my necklace with my other hand. For so long, it seemed that only bad things had happened since my Dad had given me the Tiffany chain. But now it felt that maybe I was moving away from the hurt of the past year. And at that moment, it stopped feeling like a dream, and it started feeling like my life somehow. Which was way better.

How long had it been since I'd started my twelve-step plan? And if I was really paying attention, I was currently at thirteen steps and still going strong. On the first day when I wrote down my goals, I said it would be amazing to even have the possibility of a boyfriend. And while having a cup of coffee with Cameron didn't make him my boyfriend, look how far I'd come. You never knew, reality always had to begin with possibility, right?

"Yeah, I think we can chance it, but let's not go too big. Maybe a tall?" I said, attempting to act natural. I definitely didn't want Cameron to know that he was the first guy to hold my hand since eighth grade.

"So is tall bigger than venti?"

"No, I think venti's bigger, but is that too big? It's seriously close to dusk," I said, referring to my parents, who never drank anything caffeinated after dark.

"Meaning? Are you like, of the Twilight persuasion?" Cameron tried his best to flash his incisors at me, but it looked so goofy, we both cracked up.

"I didn't realize you were a fan."

"Well, I wouldn't say that, the movies aren't bad—some action, some intrigue. At our family movie nights, Anne would always vote for *High School Musical*, and Matt and I'd want *Bourne Ultimatum* or something. So we'd end up with *The Hunger Games* or *Harry Potter*, or if Anne was real whiny, *Twilight*." We stopped and waited at the red light so we could cross the street over to *Fireroasted Cafe*. We were still holding hands, in case you were wondering ☺.

"I've read all the *Twilight* books. I especially liked the first one. But I loved *Harry Potter*. Dad and I used to read them before bed. He was good at voices, making each character sound different. Although I wouldn't say they sounded British." I paused and Cameron smiled a little, and I could tell he was really listening and that he wanted me to continue, so I did. "Sometimes if we were away at a hockey tournament and had a few hours to kill, we'd just sit in our hotel room and have this reading marathon. He'd try to trick me, you know do Dumbledore with the Snape voice. To see if I was paying attention."

"Nice."

"Yeah, it was. But eventually we stopped reading, and he watched the movies instead. I've read them all. I always liked the books better." The light turned green and we started walking again.

"Me too," he said, opening the door to the coffee shop and holding it open for me. "I didn't know you played hockey."

"I don't any more, but I did for years. What about you?"

"Yeah, I used to play too."

As we waited for the coffees, I decided to completely disregard Anne's comment about music. I recognized a song that was playing, so I asked Cameron if he knew it.

"That's Mumford and Sons. I really like it. What do you think?"

"Nice," I said. "So does your dad like the same stuff as Mr. Khan?"

"Absolutely not." Cameron laughed. "My dad's hardcore country, and he seems to just overdose on one artist, plays them over and over again. He's in a Garth Brooks phase right now, total OCD! I'm definitely feeling overexposed to that genre. Is yours a country music household?"

"Not really, we don't listen to much music, together anyway. We used to have these Sunday morning 'discos' at our house when Rachel and I were younger. Dad would be golfing, and Mom would put on some dance music, pop stuff. But then we got older, and it was just awkward, so that, I guess was the end of disco!" I said, and Cameron laughed.

And even though it was probably unusual to start a "date" talking about family stuff, somehow it just seemed regular. The whole coffee date, all fifty minutes or so, was … incredible. We talked and laughed as if we'd known each other forever. It was that easy, that comfortable, like we had this instant connection. I'd moved from having a full-on girly crush to a feeling that was deeper somehow. And although I could have been wrong because I didn't have much experience in the romance department, I thought he might be feeling the same way about me.

After we left the cafe, I walked toward the Valu-mart with him, still hand in hand. But then, without warning, he led me around the corner and kissed me behind an evergreen tree. And it was nice. And spontaneous. And well, really, really nice.

"I like you. You're easy to talk to, easy to look at."

"Thank you," I said graciously, uncharacteristically accepting the compliment like a big girl. And then added, "Same," looking Cameron directly in the eyes, and was rewarded with an adorable lopsided smile.

"Any chance you're free tomorrow night?" he asked softly.

"I wish I was, but I have plans to see Mei. She's going back to school on Monday, and you know, the whole thing has been pretty rough."

"Yeah, I get that. Hey, what about tomorrow afternoon? I have to find a bunch of poems. And we need to use, and I quote, 'real live books from a real live library.' Mrs. Valeriote, who I have for English—she's really good, by the way—thinks we need to like, hold the books, turn the pages, you know, to really get a feel for … the language." He paused to smile. "Maybe the better question is, do you want to come?"

I nodded and said, "Sure."

"Great. We can figure out this poem thing together. Is one-ish okay? Meet at the Central Library?"

"Sounds good," I said then hesitated a second and added, "It's funny, just the other day Rachel mentioned she was meeting Matt at the library this weekend to work on the same project." I then thought, *God, I hoped he isn't like Matt, in need of help with libraries or poetry or both.*

"Hmmm," said Cameron, "coincidence? I don't think that we carry some genetic poetry defect. I take it you don't want to run into them?"

"Yeah," I said.

"Okay, I'll find out what their plan is and let you know if we need to change ours?"

"Good. I'll text you before I leave, just in case," I said. "I don't know a ton about poetry, but I'm curious about this book thing you talk of…" We both smiled, and I added, "Say hi to the papayas for me."

"Will do. Bye," said Cameron as he touched my hand and held on for an extra few seconds before we parted ways.

CHAPTER 24

Later that Friday night, as I pushed the coffee date out of my mind and started to fall asleep, I suddenly jolted awake. And no, it wasn't the caffeine. It was the realization that with everything going on in my life, I had totally forgotten about school, the work part of it, anyway. *Oops*, I thought suddenly, *I've totally dropped the ball.*

Step Fourteen: Don't forget the school part of high school!!

I wished it was all about friends, boys, and sports, but unfortunately, there was work to be done. As I shut my eyes again and tried to still my mind, I was interrupted by Rachel coming in the front door. I couldn't figure out what was going on, but she was banging around like crazy downstairs.

I really didn't feel like talking to her, but then I heard a crash. I decided to wait till she was more settled to check on her. If she was wasted or something, she might either hug me or hurl abuse, both of which I preferred to avoid. Once I heard her leave the washroom, I gave her a few a minutes. When I thought she might be in bed, I knocked quietly on the door and entered.

"What's up?" she yawned. "Suck back too much caffeine with Cammie and can't sleep?"

I ignored her question. "It sounded like a herd of elephants down there. Thought I'd double-check." My eyes were adjusting to the dark, and I could see her lying on her side.

"Nice that you care, but I'm not drunk, just clumsy. I took out that old clock with my purse. I fell asleep in Matt's car and was only half awake when I came in. Of course, I feel wide-awake now, though. So … you didn't answer, you got coffee? With Cammie?"

"Yeah, but it was no big deal," I lied.

"As if. Matt thinks he's really into you. Any deets to share?

"No," I said emphatically but then quickly changed course. "How was your night?"

"Well," she yawned again, "too soon to start planning double wedding … yet. I think Matt's really hot and everything, and he was my first—oops, kind of slipped out. Good choice, though…" I kept a poker face while I swallowed my bile. "It was a bit weird, though … like he was pulling back. When I pressed him, he said he was just tired. He's not much of a conversationalist, maybe you've noticed. But I think he's really into me. I hope … maybe he's a little, I don't know, overwhelmed by his feelings. We don't have much in common, but we do have definite chemistry."

It was hard to know how to respond. My first thought was, *Well, you're both really into yourselves, so you have that in common*, but I knew that wouldn't go over well. I didn't want to say anything negative about Cameron's brother. And I also didn't want to say anything offensive to the easily offended Rachel on such a delicate subject.

Once again, I chose to be vague. "It's that the story of life? Girls … boys … miscommunicating … misunderstanding? Night," I said. I quickly and quietly fled the room.

*

The next morning, I lied to my mom and sis and told them I was going to Masonville Mall, but instead I went to the London Central Library to meet Cameron. The irony was not lost on me. He was already there, sitting at a long table strewn with poetry books of all sizes, and some looked pretty old. I paused and watched him from afar, and I could see his lips occasionally moving as he read a poem, and his brow furrowing as he struggled to interpret the meaning. It was cute how he pushed his bangs out of his eyes. When he finally looked up and noticed me, an amazing grin appeared on his face.

"Hey, perfect timing. I'm out of my depth here. Tell me what you think. It's Keats from 'Bright Star': 'The moving waters at their priestlike task, Of pure ablution round earth's human shores, Or gazing on the new soft-fallen mask, Of snow upon the mountains and the moors—'"

"Okay that's like, lovely," I said, pulling out a chair and sliding into the seat across the table. "Out there in space … looking down on the Earth. I'm not sure what ablution means, but it sounds like cleansing, maybe by the ocean?"

"Yeah, that sounds right," said Cameron.

"I want to see a real-live moor someday. I read this book one summer, *Return of the Native* by Thomas Hardy. We rented this cottage, and it didn't stop raining. I picked it off the bookshelf and just inhaled it. The moors, they were definitely part of the story."

Cameron nodded and said, "Yeah, Hardy's pretty famous. I think he writes poetry too." He then reread the poem while I paged through some of the volumes. He was concentrating, which was really cute, but then he looked up quickly.

"A breakthrough?" I asked.

"No … he says 'Eremite' earlier in the poem. Know what that means?"

I shook my head. "I guess you try to get the gist of it, even if you don't know every word."

"Yeah, especially with stuff from a different era. Try to figure it out from the context. I'm not even going to google it."

Cameron turned back to the poem again, but I decided I needed to make a bit of a confession before we continued, so I cleared my throat and then launched right in. "Here's the thing, while I'm pretty good at English, and I like to read and all, I've never been one for poetry, you know. A bit of a hater." I sucked in my breath and waited for his response.

"Really? It's even nicer that you came," he said with that little ironic upturned lip thing. "Don't get me wrong, it can feel like a slog, but the words and the sounds, can be, I don't know, hypnotic. And it's like a challenge, too, trying to figure out the meaning. Same with lyrics, you know, songs. They're pretty similar, lyrics and poetry."

"I get that. It's already growing on me, a bit. But no promises, okay." I took off my sweater and draped it on the back of the chair.

"Deal." Cameron smiled as he slid a musty anthology my way.

I looked through the list of poems at the front of the book and found several by Thomas Hardy. I turned to one of them, titled "I Have Lived with Shades." Despite what I had just said, I was quickly captivated by it, especially by a refrain about memory. It was repeated in a changed form several times: "O Memory, where is now my youth, Who used to say that life was truth?"

I wasn't exactly sure of the meaning, but the references to memory were intriguing. Was he referring to shades of remembering and about how memories change over time? Or was it more that he was too old to conjure up the memories that defined him? It really got me thinking, and I found myself enjoying the flow of the words.

Several hours later, and after lots of discussion and at least one heated debate, Cameron was pretty much done his assignment. I was feeling pretty good, since I had actually been fairly helpful, and I was also a little bit surprised at how much I had learned about poetry. More than I ever had. And it was really okay, after all. Maybe there was something to this book thing.

I was rubbing my eyes and starting to feel pretty hungry when I checked my phone. I had put it on silent when I first arrived at the library and had missed a few calls from Mom. I stood up quickly and told him that I had to run. And he apologized about keeping me out all afternoon. I would have paid money to spend the afternoon with him, even if it was in a sewer, but he didn't need to know that.

"Do you need a ride home? It's the least I could do after all your help."

"Sure, that would be great."

As I walked out the glass front door of London Central Library and onto the white limestone tiles, it took my pupils a second to adjust to the bright sunshine. I hugged my cardigan close. It was a gorgeous fall afternoon, a delicious mix of crisp and cool, just like a perfect apple.

"So Matt and Rachel, were they getting together to do the assignment?" I asked Cameron, riding shotgun in the Cat Mobile.

"He said they were going on Sunday. But then I heard there was some change of plans. He wanted to come with me, but I made an excuse. I'll help him later, he's not the most academic..."

Cameron dropped me off around the corner from my house. We kissed in the car before I got out (!). "I'll call you," he said as he squeezed my hand and smiled, and I knew he would. As I shut the car door, I practically had to stop myself from doing a happy dance right on the curb.

CHAPTER 25

It's amazing what a difference a trip to the salon can make. Mom looked ten years younger with a new haircut and some highlights. The style was both a bit shorter and a lot more up-to-date. She had these soft, lighter layers that framed her face really well.

We were sitting in the kitchen eating a takeout dinner of Pad Thai, mango salad, and shrimp curry. "I know I keep saying it, but your hair, it looks amazing!"

"Thanks … again." Mom smiled at me as she scooped more mango salad onto her plate. "I needed a bit of a change—a fresh start. Stephanie at the salon has been trying to get me to agree to it for months. But I just woke up this morning and felt ready. She was ecstatic. And lucky for me, they had a cancellation, so I got it done before I chickened out."

"So what made you go for it … today?" I forced myself to slow down. I was practically inhaling the food.

"You know, it's hard to explain, but I've just felt stuck for a long time. In the back of my mind, I guess I had this hope that we might reconcile. My friends all said it was a midlife crisis, that it might pass. So I waited and waited, and I couldn't really move on in some ways. I took the plunge with real estate, and that's worked out. But when the formal separation came, I realized I wasn't where I needed to be. I guess I was still in denial. It was ridiculous, despite the obvious, it hit me like a ton of bricks."

Mom paused to sip some white wine. "I was just keeping myself super busy so I wouldn't have to think or even be home. It was too hard. But at this point I'm glad we're getting on with it. It's given me a big kick in the you-know-what. It's an end but a new beginning too. It sounds corny but it's true. And a new beginning calls for a new haircut, right? Oh, and guess what? I joined a fitness club today!" She smiled and raised her glass.

"Cheers," I said. We clinked our glasses, and then we each took a drink in celebration, water and wine.

"Is Rach home tonight?" I asked.

It was proof positive that she was getting back into the parenting business when she replied, "Nope, out with Mr. Matt. So, what do you think of him?"

"Well," I said, deciding to both focus on the positive and be truthful, "he's from a really great family. Anne's a good friend and his brother Cameron's … nice. So I'm hoping some of those good genes rub off?" Mom frowned at me, so I continued. "So, what else—hmm, he's a super jock, most of the girls think he's totally hot. They practically fall over him. It can be a bit much."

"Really?" said Mom. "Sounds like he's the big man on campus. BMOC, we used to call them. It can be hard to be so … worshipped and not be full of yourself." She got up and started scraping the plates. "What about the fundamentals? Like, is he a nice person? What's really happening inside? And is he respectful and all the other stuff that a mother wants in her daughter's boyfriend?"

I thought for a bit and then I made a judgment call to confide in her, something I wouldn't have done even a few weeks ago. "Please don't repeat this to Rachel, but Matt's probably not great boyfriend material. He seems petty self-centred, like he knows exactly how hot he is. And I don't know, maybe he's had a concussion or two, but I don't think he's the sharpest crayon in the box. He does seem to really like Rachel, but he also goes through girls like water. I don't really see this thing lasting too, too long."

I got up and started to help tidy up. I was due to head out very soon. Then I thought of what probably had taken place a few days ago between Matt and Rachel and added, "He's a Romeo, so maybe you should have a talk with her."

"Okay, thanks for the heads-up. I appreciate your honesty. I'll have that talk, but I'll be casual about it, okay? I certainly don't know how it works in high school these days. But there have always been these good-looking playboy type guys like Matt, who, as you say, go through girlfriends like water. Rachel isn't stupid." Mom paused for a second before she continued. "Look, I know she's been way worse than usual ever since … well, you know. So thanks for being patient with her. And with me. It must seem like I'm completely oblivious, but I'm not. At least with Matt, she seems happier, definitely happier. "

Mom looked at me, and I nodded. It felt good to get some sort of recognition for not having killed Rachel—yet. While I would have welcomed the chance to talk more about Rachel and her moodiness, that wasn't going to be a short conversation, and I was already running late.

Mom paused for a minute, frowned, and then used the dishcloth to go at a mark on the granite island. She looked disturbed when it didn't go away, and I realized it was probably from the cellphone incident. She gave up on the mark and then looked directly at me. I picked up my phone and said, "I'm late," but she still wanted to talk.

"Let's keep an eye on her, okay? Her temper and her moods, it might well be something that eases off, you know. It could be triggered by hormones and is just part of, well, general teenage angst," said Mom.

"I don't think so," I couldn't help interjecting. "She might be acting better, but I don't think it's going away, just like that."

Mom sighed deeply and took a minute before she spoke again. "It seems like there's been a lot of improvement, like she's more in control of her emotions. I've thought about broaching the subject, but I don't want to upset her, not when things seem to be smoothing out on their own. I think I'll just give her some time."

"Maybe you should do the opposite? Talk to her now while she seems better, instead of waiting for another crash?"

"I think she's turned the corner. Let's not ruffle any feathers unnecessarily. Tea?" She reached for the kettle.

"No thanks, got to run." I said, annoyed and surprised. In some ways my mom seemed less oblivious about Rachel than I thought she was, but I also felt she was burying her head in the sand. She needed to talk to Rachel and then probably talk to a doctor. There was no way her behaviour was in the normal range. Was she schizophrenic? Depressed? Bipolar? I know I always joked around about her suffering from a mental illness, but I was slowly coming to the realization that maybe it wasn't just a joke.

"I'm off..." I said and started down the hallway, but Mom followed me.

"Hey, not so fast. What's the plan?"

"Going to Mei's house. With Anne," I said putting on my shoes and coat. "Her parents are making her stay home all weekend—they're worried about her going back to school on Monday and maybe getting her hand bumped or something. They want to max out the healing. So we're watching some black comedy from the eighties, I think it's called *Heathers*. Are you going out?"

"No, thank god. It's been a busy week, and I'm just going to drink tea, read trash, and relax. The gym will have to wait until tomorrow! Have fun, hon." She kissed my forehead and then walked to the living room, and I was finally out the door.

Mr. and Mrs. Chen were just leaving when I arrived. I could tell by the shoes at the front door that Anne was already there. Those two were an unlikely pair—yin and yang—but they'd grown closer, especially since Mei's finger amputation.

When I walked into the family room, they were both eating Twizzlers. Mei was lying on the couch and Anne was sitting on the floor. "It's twisted, sort of like *Mean Girls* but people actually die," said Anne, and then she paused to take another bite before continuing. "And they all wear shoulder pads and have big hair—very eighties. Oh, and they play croquet."

"So I've had this idea for a field hockey movie ... there's this player who gets her finger chopped off and goes ballistic, best part ... the title ... *Mein Girls*! Get it?" said Mei, laughing at her own joke. I went and got a bowl for the kettle-cooked popcorn I'd brought, and Mei hollered for me to bring some cokes and the bag of Doritos. We finally settled down to watch with lots of snacks. Maybe too many.

When we were halfway through the movie, Anne weakly spoke up and asked if we could pause. Mei jumped up and obliged. "My stomach, it felt queasy at dinner. I shouldn't have eaten all this crap," said Anne. "I should go. Finish the movie, okay? Text me what you think."

"You can't walk," said Mei, taking a swig from her coke.

"We're definitely calling you an Uber," I added, reaching for my phone.

"I'll call Matt," said Anne. "He'll come. He's got the car tonight, and he said he wasn't doing much."

As Anne went to get her phone, I puzzled over what she'd said. According to Mom, Rachel and Matt had a date, which made me wonder who was wrong. Better to keep my mouth shut, I thought. I didn't want the situation to get weird.

With Anne off in the front hall, making the call, Mei started talking about Matt. "Not bragging or anything, but Matt's been texting me. He even offered to drive on Monday so I don't have to take the bus. But my mom says she's driving me all week, no exceptions. Wouldn't it be awesome to see the look on everyone's face … me getting out of Matt Lavery's car! Oops, sorry!" said Mei insincerely to Anne as she returned to the room.

I was shocked by what she said and how she said it. I knew Mei liked Matt, but couldn't she be more low-key, considering Rachel was my sister and Matt was Anne's brother? But then again, when had Mei ever been low-key about anything? *Some friend she's turned out to be*, I thought, imagining how Rachel would react to Mei floating out of Matt's car.

Mei must have noticed my put-off expression, since she quickly said, "I know it's soon, but Matt and Rachel, it wasn't working out." Anne raised her eyebrows in surprise and excused herself again, this time under the pretence of using the washroom. I was pretty sure she was fleeing the conversation instead of heeding the call of nature.

I bet Mei's just exaggerating, her flair for the dramatic, I thought, trying to write off her version of events. But then I started to have this nagging feeling that it was somehow plausible. Wasn't I just telling my Mom he was a Romeo and that it wouldn't last?

Anger started percolating upward. Why didn't that bubble-brain Matt have the decency to break up with Rachel before he started moving in on Mei? And if he had broken up with Rachel earlier in the night, couldn't he have waited more than two minutes and then taken up with someone I didn't know? With the whole Cameron thing just starting, it was even more complicated. I could visualize Rachel in total freakout mood, wrecking havoc between Cameron and me.

Although—and this was probably a real long shot—maybe Rachel broke up with him? Hadn't she just said to me that they didn't have much in common? And like with science experiments as school … chemical reactions can only last so long, right? Just like chemical attractions?

The doorbell rang a minute later while Anne was still in the washroom. Mei almost tripped over herself to answer the door. Matt seemed to have forgotten all about his reason for coming as he stood in the foyer flirting with Mei in a very familiar, touchy way. Even though I could only partially hear what they were saying, I could see they were standing real close to one another.

"You need to get home," I said hastily the second Anne reappeared. But then I looked directly at her and was shocked. "You're really pale!"

She shook her head. "I suddenly feel a lot worse, and it's only partly because of my stomach. What Mei said—Matt and Rachel? Breaking up? How does she know, when we don't? Well, it looked like you didn't." I shook my head, suddenly a little nauseous myself. "I hoped this wouldn't happen. I didn't want my brother doing anything to upset your sister. It's bad timing for you with Cameron and everything." And then she gave a deep sigh.

"Don't worry, you need to just focus … on yourself," I started, trying to stave off the swirling feeling in my stomach. "Everything's going to be okay. You need to be okay. You can't miss the game on Monday… No way. And Rachel, trust me, she can take of herself." But despite my words, I wasn't feeling it.

I walked with Anne to the foyer and thrust her bag at Matt. He was a bit taken aback, both at seeing me, I assume, as well as by the aggressive gesture. He moved defensively away from Mei. I helped Anne with her coat and avoided eye contact with him as I gave her a gentle hug and told her to feel better soon. As they left Mei's house, I quickly grabbed my coat and bag and was out the door with barely a goodbye. Mei, who seemed stunned to have everyone leave so abruptly, yelled after me, "Hey, what's up? What about the movie?"

"I'm not feeling well myself."

"Oh come on," Mei started again in a teasing way. "It better not be an excuse because of me and Matt. You know I've wanted him, like, forever."

It was a good thing that I had all that breathing practice with Rachel, or I might have lost it with Mei. Instead, I stood for a few secs, silently composing myself before I spoke. "I can't do this, I'm leaving."

But then I looked at her hand, still bandaged, and was reminded of my sad part in all of it. I couldn't completely abandon Step Thirteen, even if she seemed intent on stealing my sister's boyfriend. I cleared my throat, and added. "The game, the championship—it's right after school. We're playing for you." I swallowed back the bitterness in my stomach that was lurching upward to my throat.

"I'm so there. Wait, it's Monday? Crap, I forgot, I have a plastic surgery appointment. I'll get it switched… Stay, let's finish the movie!"

I assured her I needed to go and started off again when Mei called after me, "I heard all about the fight at the hospital. Matt told me it's been all downhill since then. Nothing's happened … yet."

"For god's sake, stop shouting all this stuff out!" I said as I walked back up to her door. "I'm not sure what to say to you! Rachel and Matt seemed good. I don't want to trash him, but he seems like a player. I'd be careful if I were you."

As I walked away again, I thought what I couldn't say out loud to Mei. *Once your fifteen minutes of fame are over, I bet Matt will be long gone.*

A strong, gusty wind practically blew me home. I feared the weather might be foreshadowing the turbulence I faced when I arrived. I imagined opening the front door and Rachel twisting toward me, attacking me with the ferocity of a tornado. This was going to be huge. Not only had I failed to rehabilitate her romance but I also had a friendship going on with his new love interest. And just when my life was coming together nicely, it was about to come apart badly.

Mom would be home, though, so she might delay her revenge. But that could also work against me, as she'd have more time to plot. I also had to consider the remote possibility that Rachel might have bragging rights. That she dumped Matt.

I braced myself as I walked through the door and was unprepared to encounter a quiet home where eldest daughter and mother were contentedly sharing the couch with the TV on and a bowl of baked vegetable chips between them. The normalcy was startling. This was not one of the highly charged scenarios I had envisioned.

"Hey," Mom called cheerfully, "come join us. When's the last time we watched TV together, and on a Saturday night?"

Rachel rolled her eyes a bit but moved closer to Mom and touched the spot next to her on the couch, where I was to sit. The room was dark, save for the glow of the TV. I decided to play it safe, so I patted the surface of the couch with my hands first to make sure I wasn't going to sit in a vat of acid or on an open switchblade. All I felt was fabric, so I sat down carefully.

"You're home early. What gives?" asked Rachel. It was hard to read her expression, since she barely glanced my way and then started munching on a veggie chip.

"Nothing. I'm just really tired." An honest-to-goodness yawn came out of my mouth. "I want to get to bed early, you know, the big game on Monday and all."

"Well, we don't want to keep you up, Bean," said Mom. "But just stay for a minute, the show's ending. It's nice to have you both home. So, Rachel, you never said how your date went."

"Fine, better than I expected. Much better, in fact." Rachel adjusted the pillow behind her back. "He took me to a little place called Carlo's. It was really cute, we had pizza. It was totally empty, though. Then we tried to go for a walk along the Thames River..."

"Wasn't it freezing with that wind?" asked Mom.

"Yeah, it absolutely was, but Matt was a gentleman, he gave me his coat. He seemed a bit, on edge, like he wanted to say something … important. But the wind, and I was sooo shivering. We bailed." She smiled wistfully and then added, "I wonder what he wanted to say…"

"But then his phone rang, and Anne needed a lift, and blah, blah, blah, she ruined the moment." Rachel's mouth hardened a bit. "That family is freakishly attached to one another. He acted like it was some huge emergency, you know, drop everything. And he barely spoke in the car, came straight here. I guess you can't have Princess Anne riding in the back seat."

Huh, I thought, *that's really weird.* Who would you take someone out for dinner and a romantic stroll if they were going to break up with them? It was no secret that they had just become "intimate," so I couldn't even see Matt breaking up with her that fast. And that was when it hit me. It was Mei he was playing, not Rachel. Well, at least Mei had fair warning.

"So how was your night?" Mom asked me.

"It was good. No romantic strolls or anything like that, just hanging out, you know, watching a movie, eating junk food. I'm going to call it, I need some Z's!" I waved goodnight as I left the room and started up the stairs.

I checked my phone when I got upstairs and was disappointed that Cameron hadn't texted me. I knew if I kept the phone on the night table next to my bed as I usually did, I would be constantly checking it, so instead I decided to turn it off. I desperately needed some sleep before the game on Monday.

I had so many things swimming around in my head: the game, Cameron, and the library; Mei, Rachel, and Matt; my mom. It took me forever to turn off all those thoughts and fall into a deep sleep. I tossed and turned for what seemed like hours. When I woke up the next morning, the time on my old digital alarm clock read 10:09 a.m.

As I slowly sat up, my thoughts went directly to Cameron. I grabbed my phone, turned it on, and the red light started flashing. "Please be from Cameron, please be from Cameron," I said. As I scrolled through my messages, I was only looking for his name, and there it was: *hope u had a great sleep, thinking of u lots, can I c u tday? x C.*

I wanted to kiss the pee-phone, I was so happy to get the message. I had been thinking of Cameron almost constantly, but this whole relationship thing was new to me, and these things were complicated. I didn't want to appear too eager, so I purposely hadn't texted him the previous night, but then I had started second-guessing myself when I didn't hear from him. I started wondering if there was really *anything* between us. The antics of his brother last night hadn't exactly been a confidence boost.

There was so much to learn about dating. I didn't know how to play the game, and at the same time I didn't have any patience for that stuff. So it was nice to be reassured that I wasn't living in a dream world, and that the guy I had literally dreamed about liked me. He even said so after the coffee date. I reread the short message a couple of times, basking in a warm, fuzzy feeling, until I realized his message was almost an hour old. A response was definitely in order.

As I flipped through the other messages, a cold, hard reality began to replace the warm fuzzies. There were messages from two members of my geography class saying a meeting had been planned for noon that day to work on our group project. Due to the crazy events of the last week, I had pretty much neglected all my schoolwork. *Yikes*, I thought when I saw the deadline on the email—the project was due on Tuesday. And since we hadn't even started it, and it was pretty substantial, that meeting would take most of the afternoon today.

Hadn't I just made a Step Fourteen about not forgetting the school part of high school?

As I did a mental roll call of all my other subjects, I remembered the *Romeo and Juliet* test on Monday, and I hadn't even finished reading the play. The Leonardo DiCaprio video had helped somewhat, but it was a pretty modern interpretation, so I still needed to finish reading it and then study.

The other problem subject was Math. I was brutally behind on my homework, and we were working on the tricky subject of slopes. I really needed to get a handle on that one, too.

As much as I loved field hockey, maybe it was a good thing that the season would soon be over, one way or another, the next day. I needed to get refocused and caught up on school. I was doing pretty well in everything, except maybe science, but I needed to buckle down and get back on top of it all. The English test was on Monday, and then the game and the project was due on Tuesday. After that I could see Cameron again, anytime.

Better reply, I thought.

Slpt in, just woke up, been thinking about u 2. tons of hmwrk not free till Tues. I added a sad face to the message and pressed send.

A minute later Cameron sent back a message with twenty sad faces and a minute after that sent an apologetic text for monopolizing my time at the library the previous day. I responded that it had been my choice and that I would do it again, and that I worked best under pressure anyway. I decided not to make any references to last night and the Rat dilemma. Anyway, I didn't even know all the facts. I then texted my geography group and promised to meet them at noon as scheduled. When I checked the time, I realized that I needed to move it.

CHAPTER 26

The geography meeting went on forever, and I didn't get back until dinnertime. Even though Mom had made an impressive roast chicken dinner for the three of us, I knew I couldn't linger too long. I tried not to be too rude but ate rapidly then excused myself. I felt bad, especially since Rachel was rather silent, but I knew I couldn't afford to be distracted if I wanted to finish *Romeo and Juliet* and study for the test tomorrow.

I had barely thought about school for a while, but now that I was refocused, I didn't want to waste any more time. Besides, my life would settle down by Tuesday again, and I could make up for it then. Back in my room, the first thing I did was catch up on my texts. I quickly replied to Anne and then a member of my geography group who had a formatting question about the project. I took time to send a message to Cameron as well, secure enough in whatever we had to take the initiative for a change. Still, I was grateful when he quickly replied back that he hadn't wanted to distract me since he knew I was busy, but he was still thinking of me. He also mentioned that he would definitely be at the game tomorrow to cheer us on.

I had managed to push the game from my thoughts for most of the day. I found myself wishing we'd played this team before. It would have been much easier to predict their strategy and isolate their better players, I thought as I riffled through my backpack and found my rather too-pristine copy of *Romeo and Juliet.*

Even though I'd stopped studying by eleven that night and had flopped into bed by eleven thirty, I had still trouble falling asleep. *Argh, damn you, insomnia!* I rolled around and around, frustrated that when I needed sleep the most, it was elusive. I must have finally let my mind wander, since I woke with a start when my alarm sounded at seven fifteen. A couple of hours of shuteye would have to do. I wanted to put on my cleats and uniform and just play the game right then and there. Instead I brushed my teeth, showered, and dotted on more under eye concealer than usual.

When I finished with my hair, I made sure to wrap an elastic band around my wrist for the game. I found my cleanest jeans, layered on a few shirts, tossed my field hockey stuff in a bag, and jammed everything in my backpack—bags, books, and all. As I came down the stairs I noticed that Rachel's boots were gone from the shoe tray by the front door. I quickly dismissed any thoughts of her. I didn't have the time or energy to worry about her today, and besides, I rationalized, she had probably just left early to be with Matt.

I quickly made a lunch, stuffed an extra granola bar in my backpack for before the game, grabbed a banana to eat on the way, and left. I arrived at school around eight thirty—fifteen minutes before the morning bell. As I entered the main doors, I went straight to my locker to stash my field hockey stuff. I was still at my locker when I received a text from Cameron:

Just saw R & M. Maybe they had a fight? R seems upset, thought u'd want to know.

I quickly texted back: *Did u c M with a fetching formerly fingerless field hockey player?*

He replied: *Good use of alliteration, u r ready for the test! yes, how did u know?*

I texted back: *Women's intuition?*

I stood at my locker for a moment and thought through the confusing circumstances of the weekend. I had vowed not to think of Rachel today, but suddenly I had no choice. At first I struggled to try to make sense of it all, but it didn't take long to come up with a probable sequence of events in light of the new information from Cameron. Most likely, Matt had taken Rachel to the restaurant to break up with her, but it was too quiet and he must have known she wouldn't go quietly.

So instead of delivering bad news over pizza, he took her out to the Thames River for a walk. Because Matt was clearly a dolt, he hadn't factored in the wind or the water. It was probably too noisy for him to get his point across, and/or Rachel was too cold to stay and listen. When he got the text from Anne, he knew she was at Mei's house and he decided to bail. Rather than use the opportune moment in the car to end the relationship, he was using all his limited brainpower to plot his next conquest, so he lost focus. Or perhaps he knew that Rachel would freak, and he chickened out. Either way, he quickly dropped Rachel at home and raced over to see Mei.

I remembered hearing about twin transfusion syndrome on a news show once—it was when one of the twins took all the food from the other. I think the same thing must have happened with Matt and Cameron, but instead of food, Cameron took all the grey matter.

I needed to think about how I was going to deal with this. I checked my watch: 8:42 a.m. I had barely mentioned Rachel to Cameron; it had just seemed easier that way. He'd witnessed the fight at the hospital but otherwise he had no idea about our twisted relationship. I knew Cameron was giving me the heads-up, not as a defensive strategy, but so that I could take the offensive and comfort my big sis in her time of need.

A part of me wanted to find Rachel and see how she was doing; after all, she had been pretty good to me over the last little bit. But I needed to get through this day unscathed. If she would allow it, I would comfort her tomorrow.

In the meantime, I had to go back to my old defensive way of thinking. I quickly analyzed the situation. The only times I saw Rachel during the day were before school (that time being practically over), after school (when today I would have a game and a crowd would afford some protection), and occasionally lunchtime (here I was vulnerable). Anne would be a lousy bodyguard if push came to shove.

I knew what I had to do. I would return to my former sanctuary, the library, for the lunch hour, like the big coward I was. Rachel would quickly figure out the Mei angle, draw a straight line between Matt and Mei, find me in the middle, and I would ultimately be blamed for the breakup. It was ironic that the last time I ate lunch in the library turned out to be the end of Felix the mouse, and here I was to back to the scene of the crime, commemorating the end of the Rat.

My phone flashed again with a new message. This time it was from Mei, the cause of all my problems.

U were a bi#ch on sat nite but am so over it, fab 2 b back @ school, I may not c u 2day as I have a lunch d8, bet u can guess who! thx for dedicating the game to moi! but won't make it, super imp plastic dr. appt in aft! win it for me nad!!! xx oo me(i).

I was so angry at Mei. Because of her, I was in a panic. I knew she had it bad for Matt. I was pretty much the only girl at my school who didn't, after all, but why couldn't she consider my situation as the former girlfriend's sister? I guess it was somehow divine retribution that I'd sent Mei to get slaughtered by Helen, and now she might be the cause of my slaughter by Rachel.

And to think I'd been psyching up the team for a victory today in Mei's honour. Matt and Mei deserved each other—dim and dimmer. Didn't she realize she'd be tossed aside too, probably by next week? *No way I'm ever going to respond to this message*, I thought and hit the delete button.

Although it was hard to concentrate, I somehow survived Math first period and was grateful I'd tackled some of the weekend homework. It was a doubly cerebral morning since Science immediately followed. I hated the days I had Math and Science together; my brain always felt semi-fried afterward, and today my head was already spinning before classes even began.

As soon as science ended, I texted Anne and apologized that I couldn't meet her for lunch, that I was going to hole up in the library to study *Romeo and Juliet.* I had the foresight to bring my lunch with me to my morning classes, so I was able to take the back stairs to the library. I immediately tucked myself back into my old study carrel and managed to polish off my lunch before Mr. Khan even realized I'd arrived.

As I was poring over the play, Rachel appeared out of nowhere. Once again I had underestimated the enemy. "Here you are, just like Anne said. It's kind of like a reunion for you, no? Maybe you'll end up back here … friendless … again."

"What's up?" I asked neutrally, not reacting at all to her comment but thinking, *I wasn't sure how she'd be, and the answer is not good.*

"Since I've had like the worst day ever, I need something from you: your cleats. We have a soccer test in gym right after lunch, and you know how I suck at soccer. At least if you have cleats, you get the marks for full uniform. I need those marks."

"Why today of all days?" I spat the words out, the stress of everything getting to me. "You know I have the championship game. I need them. I can't play without them. So what are you going to do, cut off the spikes? So I'll slip on the field?"

"You and the stupid 'championship game'! As if. I'll lose marks if I don't have them. Just like you said to me at the hospital, 'It's not about you.' I promise I won't do anything to them. But I need them for third, and then ... I'll even hand-deliver them to you before fourth period. You've got English fourth, right?"

I was in a difficult predicament. If I said no, for sure she'd flip and do something. There was a chance she hadn't figured out the Mei connection yet and just wanted the cleats. And besides, with all the gym classes playing soccer, it would be easy to borrow cleats from someone if Rachel decided to destroy my pair. "Okay," I said as I checked my watch: 11:43 a.m. "Let's go."

She stood beside me as I opened my locker and grabbed the bag of field hockey stuff. It was hanging in the middle of my locker on a hook, and the cleats were sticking out at the top. I pulled out my cleats and passed them to her. "Room 202, like you said, before fourth."

"Whatever," Rachel said and walked down the hall. I locked my locker and looked at my watch; the lunch bell was going to ring in twenty minutes. *What the hell, I'm going back to the library*, I thought. If we lost the game, at least I'd ace my *Romeo and Juliet* test.

My third period class, which was drama, seemed to last about two years. I watched the clock mark the time, minute by minute. I was worried about everything: my cleats, Rachel, the test, and the game. But against all odds, Rachel was waiting outside my last period class, as promised, with the cleats in hand. Everything was intact.

I was so relieved, "Thank you!" I blurted out.

Rachel smirked but then added, "Good luck," and walked away. Okay, so that was a bit bizarre, I thought, but at least I had my cleats. So my punishment would be deferred—that was okay by me.

I walked into the English class, where Mr. Werstine was busy pushing the desks apart to prevent students from "helping themselves to the words of others." I spoke briefly to him about my need to leave thirty minutes early for the game, took my seat, put the cleats under my desk, and started writing away.

I felt good about the test and was so engrossed with the last essay question—"Is it better to love or survive?"—that I lost track of time and suddenly realized it was 3:07. I was running a few minutes behind schedule. I quickly handed in my test, grabbed my cleats, and headed off to my locker.

As soon as I opened my locker, I realized immediately something was amiss. The field hockey bag that was hanging in the middle was gone. I scanned the bottom in case it had somehow fallen, but it wasn't there or anywhere.

Damn, I thought, *damn*! I'd known she was up to something. Why had I given her my cleats? How had I fallen for this? What was I going to do now? Had she somehow memorized my locker combination when I'd opened it, or had she bribed the janitors? Either way, she wasn't going to just give me back my stuff, but I had to give it a shot. What did she have last period? Oh yeah, accounting, with the surprisingly dynamic Mr. Johnson. I knew where her class was, and that was where I decided to go. I quickly sent Anne a text telling her I got held up in English, that I would get to the field ASAP, and could she see if Ms. Davies had an extra uniform?

I made my way to Rachel's class and peeked in the window. She was sitting there, her accounting books wide open on her desk, but impatiently thumbing through a magazine perched on her legs underneath. It was so obvious, but probably Mr. Johnson didn't care as long as she wasn't causing trouble. One of the students must have seen me peer in, because seconds later, just as I was about to knock, Rachel opened the door.

She nonchalantly asked, "What's up?" But when I looked at directly at her, her face didn't register the expected cold, hard demeanour that Rachel normally assumed when being vindictive. Her appearance had changed since lunchtime. Her eyes now looked puffy, and her usually beautiful skin was blotchy. She was trying to put up a brave front, but I could tell she was extremely upset. Maybe the morning breakup with Matt was a shock, and it took her this long to process it.

I felt a twinge of sympathy for her, but I couldn't afford to waste my time or emotions. I had the championship game starting shortly, and missing uniform compliments of my distraught older sister.

"Uh, I think you know. My uniform, please."

"I don't have it," she said as she swallowed hard.

"Stop playing games. I mean it. I have no idea how you got it, but what matters is that I really, really need it. Now. You got me good, you won. So please, my uniform."

"Sure, okay. Well, I'll tell you where it is," Rachel said. She fingered her gorgeous hair in a carefree way, but I noticed her bottom lip quiver ever so slightly.

"That would be so awesome of you…."

"It's at home … your uniform," she said and abruptly turned around, shut the door, and walked back into the class.

I didn't hesitate. I opened the door, walked right in after her, and said in a low hiss, "So where? Where is it, in the house?" People were starting to look at us curiously, and Mr. Johnson was heading toward us, but Rachel could have cared less.

She considered my request for a minute, and then said, "Look around," just as the bell rang. As she grabbed her books and magazine, I could tell by the way she clenched her jaw that she wouldn't tell me anything else. Everyone in her class was on their feet; the game was to begin in fifteen minutes at 3:45. I had to get my uniform and then get to the field.

I checked my phone as I walked down the hall. There was a message from Anne: *Davies says 2 get out here asap & there r no extra uniforms, she's checking with Mei & we'll get back 2 u. c u soon.*

I had no time to waste and was in no mood to even feign politeness, so I barrelled down the crowded hallways, jostling anyone who got in my way. I headed out the back door and ran down the path. I could see that both our team and our opponents were already on the field warming up. Ms. Davies was talking on her cellphone on the sidelines as I approached. "Okay, yes, thanks, Mei, good luck with the appointment. Hopefully we'll see you out here afterward."

Ms. Davies hung up, turned to me, and said, "Can I assume from the way you're dressed that you haven't found your uniform yet?" I shook my head. "Mei's not going to be any help. Her mother couldn't get the blood off her jersey, so you know what she did? She just threw it in the garbage. Can you believe what a disposable society we live in? It seems a bit drastic, doesn't it? So what happened to yours?"

"It's at home," I said as Ms. Davies sighed.

"That's … disappointing. Look, I've already submitted the names and jersey numbers of all our players, so you can't wear anybody else's uniform. You could have worn Mei's since she's not playing, but otherwise you need to wear your own. And normally nobody would really care, but it's the championship game and we could forfeit if we start messing around. So go home, get it, and hurry back!"

I nodded and had to clear my throat, it was so dry, as the referee came over to consult with Ms. Davies. My heart started pounding really fast and I felt a wave of panic, but I steadied myself. I couldn't afford a meltdown. Deep breaths, cleansing breath in, stale air out and repeat.

I grabbed my phone and called Cameron.

"Hey, I'm coming. Everything okay?"

"No, it's not. I can't explain, but I need you to drive me home … to get my uniform and then back."

He paused for a second and then slowly said, "Really? You forgot it? Today? I'll be there in a sec."

I could see him walking quickly down the path toward the field. I mimed to Ms. Davies, who was still conferring with the referee, that Cameron was going to drive me home. She nodded and I ran up the path to him, and together we continued on to the Cat Mobile. As we pulled out of the school lot, he turned to me and said, "That really sucks, all this stress before the game. But it's kind of weird you forgot it..."

I wanted to scream, *Do you really think I'd forget my uniform, that I am that stupid?* Then I remembered he had no idea about Rachel. Still, it was annoying to me. Everything was annoying me. I was in a highly agitated state. I decided to keep my mouth shut. God knows what would start spewing out if I let the floodgates open up even a teensy bit.

I checked my watch and realized the game was starting in seven minutes. I looked straight ahead and blinked back the tears that were starting to form. We sat in silence for a minute or so as he drove, and I'm sure Cameron knew something was up, and he probably thought I was feeling unnerved about the game. If he only knew what was really going on.

"Worse case, you're a bit late, you miss the start. No big deal and just think, in an hour or so, you'll be in your uniform, holding that trophy ... you'll see, it's all good," he said as we pulled into the driveway.

"Just wait here, okay?" I practically barked, and I jumped out of the car before he even had a chance to put it into park. I fumbled with the lock for a second before it released, and then swung the door open. I didn't have a plan. I'd have to go room by room to find my uniform, and I'd have to look everywhere.

I opened the front hall closet and rooted around. I then went into the living room and looked on the chairs, the couches, under the cushions, in the fireplace, behind the curtains—everywhere. All I really needed was the jersey. I had extra socks upstairs, I could borrow pads from someone, and I could wear my gym shorts. Maybe I'd get lucky and find my jersey first.

If I were Rachel, where would I hide this stuff? I went upstairs and started ransacking her bedroom, looking in her drawers, under her covers, in her bed, in the closet, everywhere. Then I went to my bedroom and my mom's bedroom, looking under, behind, and in everything. Nothing, nothing, nothing. Wow, this was starting to remind me of that dream I had, where I was always searching ... *Okay, enough of that, keep your mind focused here.*

I went back downstairs again and into the kitchen. I opened the fridge and the freezer and the pantry and the dishwasher, until I came to the sink. I stopped cold. There was a large empty plastic ketchup bottle sitting in it. There was a knock on the door, and then I heard it open, and Cameron called out, "Hey, need some help?"

Between the empty ketchup bottle in front of me and Cameron coming toward me, I knew the gig was up. I had to let Cameron in on what was happening. I pointed to the ketchup bottle, and as calmly as I could muster, said, "I don't know where it is, but I think Rachel doused it in ketchup." Cameron looked at me really strangely while I peered in the stove and the microwave and then started opening the kitchen cupboards. "Maybe I can rinse it off and play in a wet jersey, that is, if I can find it," I said, trying to keep my voice even and some hope alive.

"So you don't know where it is? And you think Rachel did something to it? Like a prank? On the day of the championship?"

The poor guy, I thought. He was going to be so blown away by this. I started to feel a bit sorry for him, and that was good because I felt less sorry for myself.

"I can't explain. The only way you can help me is to keep looking. We gotta find the uniform or some kind of clue." I opened the cupboard and peered under the sink before using a fork to leaf through the garbage in the bag.

"What about the water on the floor?" said Cameron, pointing to a puddle in front of the fridge. "It could be from the fridge, or maybe it's from the ice maker."

"Yeah, it's probably the ice maker, but…" I came over to inspect the water and then stopped for a sec to think. Okay, so she doused the uniform in ketchup, but then what? I opened the pot cupboard, which seemed half empty. I quickly realized the large pasta pot was missing.

So she'd doused the uniform and put it in the pot. What next? She filled the pot with water, but spilled some on the floor. That would explain the water, but what did she do, boil my stuff? That didn't make any sense. And then—I'm not sure why, but probably because it was the most diabolical explanation—it hit me what Rachel had done.

The uniform was in the freezer, the big chest freezer downstairs. As I ran downstairs, Cameron wordlessly followed, close on my heels. I turned on the light in the utility room and then pulled open the freezer lid. And there it was, the pasta pot filled with frozen ketchup-coloured water. A red fabric mass lay encased in the ice. Rachel hadn't been lying. My uniform was at home.

I could barely lift the pot out of the deep freezer, it was so heavy. I carried it over to the laundry sink and started running hot water on the sides of the pot. Cameron stood speechless, watching. There was nothing else to do. After a few minutes I was able to dump out the contents into the sink, but the mass was still frozen solid. It was going to take a long while just to melt the ice, and then, if it was even going to be possible, I needed to get the ketchup rinsed off the jersey.

It took a moment to absorb what it meant. There was no way I could play. That was it; the season was already over for me. Instead of having to control my breathing so that I didn't fly into a rage, I had to struggle to breathe at all. I tried to take in the steam from the running hot water. I was so defeated.

"This—this is … wow … pretty … out there."

"Yeah," I said, and I rubbed my eyes, which were getting moist from the steam.

"So Rachel did this last night? Took your uniform while you slept? But forgot to let you in on it, you know, so you'd have time to fix it?"

I thought long and hard before I answered. Was I going to try to cover this up or come clean? Perhaps a few weeks ago I might have taken another approach. I would have tried to portray this as a tit-for-tat situation, retribution for a practical joke gone wrong, perhaps. But clearly what she had done was over-the-top. It was going to be hard to present this as some sort of normal sibling interaction. I had to stop covering up the problem, and that needed to be my first "step." And it had to start right then and there.

"Nope," I said loudly. The steaming water somehow helped my breathing, and I let the water continue to pour out of the tap. "She took it out of my locker during lunch today. I know that for a fact."

"Really?

"Yes." And then I added, "She borrowed my cleats, and she must have somehow figured out my combination, or maybe she bribed a janitor. I hear they have a list. So she took it, skipped class, and did this." I looked up to face Cameron and to see how he was taking it all.

"But how did it freeze so quickly? His expression was hard to read. "Oh … okay," he said.

"Yeah," I said. "It was the ice machine. A true stroke of brilliance. She filled the pot with ice, so she just added a bit of cold water, and presto. Then she plops it into the freezer, and it froze like that. She goes back to school, returns the cleats… Yadadada."

"Clever. Evil but clever."

"When I realized it was missing, I tracked her down. And guess what she said? It was at home, look around. She wasn't lying, was she?"

"Okay, soooo … why did she do this to you? Today of all days…"

"Well, let's see, you are my friend and Matt is your brother. And Mei is also my friend, and since Matt dumped Rachel for Mei, then that's my fault."

"Matt dumped Rachel for Mei?"

"Yup, so probably this ketchup is supposed to be the blood that came from Mei's finger. Rachel knew we were dedicating this game to Mei, and we were going to try to win it for her. I know, it's bizarre."

"Bizarre doesn't begin to cover this. I was thinking more like demented or insane." Cameron was shaking his head in amazement. He was actually taking it better than anyone should have or would have, but I was beyond humiliated. I sighed deeply to muzzle a sob. Here was the guy I was crazy over, and everything was going great, and we were just getting comfortable with each other, and well, God knew what he thought of me now.

"This is hard to explain, but I'll try." I began struggling to maintain my composure. "It doesn't make sense because that's not how Rachel works. I get blamed for her troubles, it's that simple. When she gets pissed, it's my fault. What can I say?" I looked at the red heap in the sink with the hot water pouring over it. It was starting to melt, but there was still a long way to go.

"You could say a lot. You don't have to take this stuff. I care about you, you know, what happens to you." Cameron shook his head and then looked at me directly in the eyes, and it was all I could do not to burst into tears.

As I fought to maintain composure, an image flashed into my head. I was closing the lid to Rachel's coffin, and just as it was shutting, I took one last look. Resting on the satin pillow was her head, frozen solid, encased in a mass of red ice.

Cameron was right, and I had already reached the same conclusion. I didn't have to take this stuff. Just as I should have done something before Mei played in the game with Helen, I shouldn't have let this happen either. I shouldn't have let all the millions of humiliations and tortures that led to this moment happen.

I wanted to drop on my knees and weep, but I swallowed deeply instead and realized the time for tears had passed. I shut off the water. "I already asked the coach, and they don't have any extra jerseys, so I have to watch," I said matter-of-factly. "I don't know what I'm going to say, but I'm going back. Win or lose, play or not play, I want to be with my team." Cameron nodded.

We drove back to the school in silence. I had nothing to add, and for sure Cameron was at a loss for words. I had gone from being his sister's friend to Rachel's sister to his potential girlfriend and finally to a member of some freaky, twisted family. As he parked the car, I was already holding on to the door handle, ready to make a quick exit. I assumed he would never want to have anything to do with me ever again.

Instead, as the car came to a full stop, he said, "Hey, not so fast." I let go of the door handle but stared out the passenger window. "Please. Look at me," he said. I sighed as I turned toward him. He pushed a strand of hair gently off my face and then touched his forehead to mine.

"Your sister clearly has problems. That doesn't reflect on you. I know Matt slept with your sister. I can't believe he just broke up with her, but I hope that doesn't make me look bad, right?"

"No, no, I don't blame you. I blame Matt. And Mei," I said.

"I know this won't make you or Rachel or anyone feel better. But Matt is—well, he's not what he seems. He acts a bit like a dolt, but he's really not. He can be lazy, so it's easier for him if people just expect less. I think he's got this, like, phobia of being dumped or something. So he never gives relationships much of a chance. Once he starts to get close to someone, well, he just rushes to end it. First. He wants to seem so cool, but he's just afraid, I think."

"I don't get that," I said. "You shouldn't be with someone if you don't really like them, and if you really like them, why do you want to dump them?" I shook my head. "I wish you'd told me that before. Maybe I could have warned Rachel, you know?"

"Oh, and then she wouldn't have frozen your uniform?" asked Cameron.

"No—well. Yes. But it might have spared her a little … from getting blindsided. You know."

"I guess I hoped it would be different. In my defence, I thought everyone knew his M.O. But still, I'm sorry."

"Okay," I said.

Suddenly I didn't want to leave the car. I knew the humiliation of not having my uniform was inevitable, and I was bent out of shape that I couldn't play. I just wanted to curl up in the fetal position and be transported to another place and time.

We sat in silence in the car for a minute, and then Cameron started talking again. "I knew there was a reason we hit it off, you know, aside from your interesting topics of conversation." He was teasing me, but I wasn't in the mood.

"Seriously," he continued. "We both, you know, struggle with our very different siblings. Of course, I'm talking about Matt here, not Anne. Matt thinks I'm uptight or something for not serial dating, and he thinks my interest in music is really … arty."

He paused and looked at me with those gorgeous hazel eyes. "He thinks I should pay more attention to appearances, you know, care more what people think. That's why he always wants to be the one who does the breaking up. But that's not a nice way to treat people. He should care more about that, and not so much about the other stuff."

I felt my heart jump, just for a second. Suddenly I wanted to really come clean about Rachel, talk it all through. But I looked at my team on the field and realized that this wasn't the right moment. *I will tell him, though.* It was time to leave, and we both silently got out of the car. Cameron went to the bleachers and sat with Matt.

I went over to talk to Coach Davies on the bench. She did a double take when she saw me still without my uniform. She opened her mouth to scold me, saw how upset I was, then shut her mouth again and patted me on the leg.

"It's a tie game, 1–1, and we're just about to break for the half. The Lions are a good team, very offensive, but we're holding our own. Anne and Estella are doing real well, but they'd be doing better if you were out there. Danielle, she's solid today. It's a real tribute to her that they've only scored once, because they've taken many, many shots. We've got to keep our fingers crossed. Look at the bench, without you and Mei, it's empty. All hands on deck."

The referee blew the whistle to signal halftime, and the Elgin Eagles jogged slowly off the field and headed toward us. The team seemed to be in pretty good spirits as they grabbed Gatorades and water bottles to hydrate. Coach Davies called everyone together for a huddle.

"Good work, girls, good work. Those Lions are a strong team, lots of shots on goal. Danielle, outstanding job, keep up the good work." Danielle nodded but didn't smile. "Claire and Nakeisha, keep doing what you're doing, but be a bit more strategic. They seem to come in wide, and we need to stay on that, okay? Watch those shots from the side. Anne and Estella, good work, keep pressing them on the net. Take a few more chances, sometimes you get lucky, right? By the way, good goal, Anne, you put us on the board."

Ms. Davies paused as the referee approached the huddle, stopped a few feet away, and pointed at Danielle and Ms. Davies to come and speak to her.

Ms. Davies raised her eyes at Danielle, and then they both walked over to confer with the ref.

The ref's attempt at privacy was only for show, since we all could hear loudly and clearly exactly what she was saying. "Goalie, I have received several complaints about foul language. I could eject you from the game right now, but since this is a championship game and I have only heard it second-hand, I'm giving you a warning. But if you swear or even take the name of the Lord in vain just once, you are out of here, got it?"

Danielle, who was looking at the ground during this short speech, looked up when she finished and gave a quick but defiant nod in the ref's direction. Ms. Davies seemed stunned, and then turned away and walked back to the huddle as Danielle trailed behind.

We all reconvened, and Coach looked directly at Danielle as she finished. "Girls, be relentless but make sure you play clean. As you can see, we have no one on the bench, so if someone's ejected, we'll be down a player. You know what's at stake here, let's do this."

The whistle sounded and the players returned to the field. The second half started uneventfully, but then Anne, Nakeisha, and Estella, with the help of the midfielders, got into a groove, and our offense began to dominate. Unfortunately, the Lion goalie also seemed to find her mojo and was successful at saving a few good-looking shots. While most of my focus was on the opposing goalie and our offensive players, I noticed a scuffle downfield.

I tapped Ms. Davies on the shoulder and pointed toward Danielle, who was visibly freaking out. Even from our vantage point it was obvious the opposing team's defensive players were mouthing off and harassing her. "They're trying to get Danielle kicked out. I'm going to the ref, right now!"

And just as Ms. Davies got up to protest the harassment, Danielle's unmistakable voice could be heard shouting, "*You're* the bitch!"

The referee blew her whistle, pointed at Danielle, and announced, "Elgin goalie, you're out of here." Coach Davies immediately approached the referee to challenge the ruling. The other coach leapt off her bench to challenge our challenge. Things deteriorated, and pretty soon the ref and the coaches were all arguing with each other.

The referee then blew her whistle long enough and loud enough for the ruckus to subside. When she had regained control of the situation, she firmly reiterated her original ejection. "She was warned, and she swore so loud my ears practically popped. She is out, period. The game will restart in five minutes."

Coach Davies looked furious, but she kept it under control. The players on both teams returned noisily to their benches. The Lions were high-fiving each other, believing their victory was imminent. The Elgin Eagles, losing their goalie and being down a player, were despondent.

Danielle walked up to the bench and enraged, threw down her mask and pads and even ripped off her gold lamé top, revealing a *Yale* t-shirt underneath. *So much for the field hockey scholarship at some elite US college.* Anne went over to Danielle and said, "Those players were awful, I'm sorry."

"And what about you, Saint Anne! You lied to me at the last game. And now he's with *your friend*, Mei!"

Danielle came right up to Anne and shoved her face right at hers. I could see the spit flying out of her mouth as she spoke, while Anne stood there paralyzed. "You owe me, and I'm collecting! They'll last two seconds, so you better tell Matt about me … how awesome *I* am, the gloves are off."

As Anne reeled back in surprise, something inside my brain snapped. Danielle was talking to Anne just like Rachel talked to me, and there was zero chance I was going to stand on the sidelines and let her push Anne around. I somehow sputtered out, "You want it? You got it! I'm going to tell Matt exactly what you said!"

Danielle hissed, "You wouldn't dare," and Anne stood speechless. Coach Davies was still arguing with the ref, but the rest of team watched me saunter up to the bleachers. I leaned over to Matt and said, "Sooo, Matt … when you've had enough of Mei, you see our goalie, Danielle? Well, she's ready. You might want to be careful with that one, though, she's threatening your sister. That's all, so back to the game!"

Matt initially looked confused but then glared at Danielle, who in turn glared at me. She punted her goalie mask and stormed off. As I turned to head back, Cameron touched my arm and said, "Good one."

I nodded and walked to the bench. Ms. Davies had already gathered the players around. "That was totally unfair," Ms. Davies said, "and I will protest this to the league. Danielle may have lost it, but those girls were intentionally going after her. I wish she'd told me earlier. You girls are tight-lipped about when you need to speak up."

She glanced intentionally at me and then sighed deeply. "Well, this game isn't over yet, and I, for one, am fighting mad. I know we're going to be down a player, and it will be tough, but we can do this. Claire, you're the backup. You need to get suited up. At least the ref agreed that if anyone harasses the goalie, even just once, they'll be thrown out too..."

And then I saw Cameron running toward us from the bleachers. He'd picked up Danielle's top. He turned it around as he approached the huddle and said, "There's no number ... on the shirt. You don't have to be down a player. Nadine can play goalie." When he saw my stunned look, he pulled me aside and quietly said, "This is the only way you can help. I've seen you play. You have got good reflexes. You'll do just as well as anyone else, and at least you'll have a fighting chance this way. I'm sorry, I didn't think ... I should have asked you first ..."

I took the shirt from him and nodded. Everyone cheered. Coach Davies ran over to the ref, who pulled out his roster sheet, rechecked the paperwork, and gave us the thumbs-up. For a few tense moments I stood holding the goalie equipment, before I awkwardly donned the pads. I almost laughed when I realized I'd be playing goal wearing jeans. At least I still had the elastic for my hair.

As I assumed my position in goal, I prayed, begged, and pleaded to whatever higher power might exist in the world to keep the play down the field, as far away from me as possible. Even though we'd dominated, the score was still tied 1–1. I couldn't let in a single goal. The pressure was so much greater than at that very first game, when I'd practically developed lockjaw from all that stress-relief smiling.

I had to get a grip here! Playing a super-important but unfamiliar position in a championship game sucked, but those were the cards I'd been dealt. *Wait a second*, I thought. Had I really been dealt these cards or had I picked them myself? Damn it! If I'd done stuff differently with Rachel, maybe I'd have my shirt and be playing forward. While it had been therapeutic to visualize Rachel's funeral, it hadn't solved anything.

And if I'd handled the situation with Helen differently, maybe Mei would've been here to play, too. Now we were down two players, indirectly due to my own failings. But I had just stood up for a good friend, and that made me feel powerful, which was really good because I was tired of feeling powerless. I couldn't keep letting all this rotten behaviour slide. Maybe I was finally ready to make my move with Rachel.

It took about a second after that thought to quickly refocus when the play came down field toward the goal. I hated to admit it, but I completely panicked. I had to calm myself down when the opponent entered the scoring circle. Breathe, breathe, and keep breathing. I watched that ball every second. I didn't even blink, and when she shot the ball, I knew exactly where it was going, and I reached out and deflected it. It was an easy save, but it was a save nonetheless.

Looking back, I can honestly say that I didn't play too badly. I saved a couple of okay shots but was lucky enough not to have anything too hard come my way. My team played well, but it was frustrating that even though we dominated offensively, their goalie, unlike me, was really good and we just couldn't get a shot in. The Warrior offense heeded the ref's warning and didn't harass me, so I wasn't too distracted. At the end of the second half we were still tied 1–1. For the first time in my life I would have been happy with a tie. Or maybe a rematch with Danielle in goal and me in my jersey…

"Sudden death," said Coach Davies. "That's how we decide a tie-breaker—sudden death. The first team to score wins. It's simple, girls. Let's get there first. Nadine, you're doing great. Hang in there." I nodded but felt a bit of bile start to make its way up my throat. I swallowed hard and thought, *Win or lose, it will soon be over. Just keep it together.* I needed to get back on that field and, like everyone else, give it all I had and let the chips fall where they might.

No, no, no. What a sucky attitude, I thought. Where was that killer instinct I used to have on the ice? I needed to get those chips to fall where I wanted them to fall. Coach Davies practically took the words out of my mouth. "Okay, Eagles, it's taken guts to get where we are, and it will take guts to get where we need to be. We deserve this victory, so let's take it from them!" Everyone cheered. It was just the adrenaline burst we needed.

As overtime began, the same pattern emerged. We kept a press on their goalie but were once again shut out on the scoreboard. Luckily, I didn't face any real tricky shots, or we would have died suddenly.

At about the eleven-minute mark my resolve paid off. I somehow managed to save a ball that was passed from one player to the other and then fired wickedly hard at close range. I deflected it just as it was about to go into the bottom right hand corner of the net, and no one was more surprised than me. The rest was like a Cinderella story, with Anne scoring a few minutes later after an unexpected breakaway. We'd won. My teammates lifted Anne up in the air. Everyone embraced and cried and shouted and high-fived each other.

Suddenly, the stress of the hour, the day, the week, or maybe my entire life just overcame me. I staggered over to the bench, and in the midst of the celebration, I put my head in my hands and started to break down. It took about two seconds before Cameron was at my side, and in front of everybody, he embraced me. Then Anne joined in, and Claire and Estella, and Ms. Davies and the entire team, until Cameron and I were at the centre of a huge group team hug. It was over! And I had a shiny medal hanging around my neck to prove it.

CHAPTER 27

As Cameron pulled into our driveway, he turned to me and said, "Are you sure you'll be okay? I could be backup, just in case?" I shook my head.

"Seriously, I'm freaked out about you being all alone with Rachel. Who knows what she might pull."

"I've got this. I finally—and absolutely —feel that I've got to do something. It's not going away. I guess I practiced telling Matt about Danielle."

"You need to be careful. You know, make sure she's not concealing any ketchup bottles or anything. What about your mom, can't she help?"

"She's kind of in denial. And I've been too terrified of Rach going public, embarrassing me. I'm ashamed to admit this, but someone got hurt because I was afraid to stand up to a bully. It's time, it has to end, and now you know. And like you said before the game, you can't get too … fixated on what others think."

"Seriously, maybe you should start slow," Cameron added, and I nodded.

"Keep me posted, okay?"

I said, "For sure," and squeezed his hand.

When Cameron drove away and I opened the front door, the house was still in shambles. Amongst the mess I could see Rachel's boots and backpack in the front hall. I felt tired but confident and unafraid. I walked into the kitchen, drank about a gallon of water, and actually laughed out loud when I realized the ice machine wasn't working, probably from overuse. As I went upstairs, the disaster scene continued, but when I reached the top, Rachel's door was shut tight.

Remember, I thought to myself, *this is a step, an important step. You can't just snap your finger and expect it to go away. Cameron said to go slow, and that was probably good advice.* I wondered if I should give the step an official name. *Nah*, I thought. If I survived this, I'd either be dead or be done with steps.

"Rachel," I called out loudly as I knocked on her door once, twice, three times. There was no answer, so I slowly turned the handle and pushed open the door. Rachel was lying on her bed, curled up. I hadn't expected this. I thought she would be gloating because she had ketchuped my uniform and perhaps was plotting to relish Mei. Instead she looked pale and withdrawn, practically defeated.

"Hey, what's wrong? Are you sick?" I asked.

"What do you care?" she mumbled.

"Because I do," I said.

She sighed and said, "Well, I don't, so just go away." Then she rolled over.

"I know you're upset. Matt was a complete jerk."

"And Mei's a bitch."

"Why don't you get up, Rach, we can talk?"

"Well, my life kind of sucks right now, so why should I get up?" This was starting to sound very familiar, like me a few months ago. *My name is Nadine, I'm fifteen, and my life completely sucks.*

"Look, I'm really sorry about what happened. Matt wasn't nice, and neither was Mei—I don't get why so many girls would practically kill each other for a chance to be with him …" Rachel snorted but I continued, "and you know, Matt will dump her in the end, and she'll be miserable soon enough …"

"So, that's it? You just say they're both assholes, she'll get what's coming to her, end of story?" Then Rachel paused for a second and added quietly, "Well, what about me? I thought we had something, but he threw me under the bus."

I took a deep breath and thought, *This is good.* Well, it wasn't good that Rachel was so hurt, but she was acknowledging her feelings. It had to be a two-way street, I needed to open up to her as well. "I know you feel awful. I hate that garbage about time healing everything. It's not going to be good, not for a long while, anyway. And I'd be crushed if the same thing happened to me, with Cameron."

Rachel nodded and said, "You didn't fool me, not for one second. I knew you guys were into each other." I shrugged, admitting the subterfuge, and then wondered if I shouldn't wait until she was in a better emotional state to really confront her. It was definite progress that despite her black mood, she wasn't lashing out in anger. But I knew it was best to seize the moment while we were both being honest. Before I lost my nerve. Even though she was clearly upset about the breakup, there was no time like the present. I couldn't let this crazy situation go on any longer.

So I began, "We both had rough days today. You've treated me like crap before, but this was by far the worst. You knew how much that game meant to me and how *stressed* I'd be. With everyone wondering what happened. It was brutal, and then I couldn't play."

"Why do you take it so seriously? It's just a stupid game."

I decided to ignore the comment. "But then I had like, this epiphany. Someone started threatening Anne. Hey, stop smiling! Anyway, I decided then and there that I was done. No more rolling over. A switch just flipped, and I fought for her..."

"Just get to the point, please. And then leave me." Rachel rolled her eyes in disdain.

"Hear me out, it's the least you can do." I did my best stare her down. She sighed but kept quiet. "You know, you completely screwed me today, but I, well, I survived. Anyway, I'm not going to tiptoe around you anymore, pretend this crazy stuff isn't happening. I'm done. So be warned, the days of Nadine the doormat are over, okay?"

Rachel moved into a full sitting position, looked directly at me, and said, "You know, you only got exactly what you deserved."

"What? I got exactly what I deserved?" I repeated incredulously. I was tempted to throw up my hands and leave, but then my anger flared. "So why? Why did I deserve it today? I had nothing to do with the breakup. Why did I need to be punished? Humiliated."

"Well, today it was mainly because you're friends with the bitch that stole my boyfriend. But also because of the usual shit."

"What usual shit?"

"Please! You think you're sooo great. You'd never played field hockey before, and now you're some big superstar. And you go on forever about the stupid championship. And then Cameron? It's just too much! You've had it too easy. You needed to be taken down a notch."

"I've had it too easy? Are you kidding me?" I gasped. "You're the beautiful one, looking like a million bucks in sweatpants. You always have guys after you." Rachel blew some air out of her mouth impatiently, but I could tell she was listening. "You know, when you're on, you're unstoppable. You're the life of the party. So you're not amazing at sports, but you're smart, and you know it. It might help if you cracked a book now and then. And what you did today was twisted, completely twisted, but pretty ingenious."

"Yeah, I am pretty good at the tortures. But, okay, well, let's see..." She counted on her fingers as she talked. "You were Daddy's little 'Disney princess of hockey,' for like years … Mom's little rock and sporty, smart, with your little field hockey friends, la, la, la. Like I said, you don't even try."

"I've worked my butt off! I practically had to crawl out from under a rock. I forced myself to get a life. It was like a job. I worked at field hockey and I worked at making friends. So no, nothing fell into my lap."

"Well, for the record, I liked you better when you were a loser. But what you're saying is bullshit. It's easy for you."

"You have no idea. I really tried and I had to learn." I thought of Helen. "Nothing was handed to me on a silver platter. You could turn things around, you know that. You could."

"Yeah, right." Rachel paused for a second, but then she said something that really surprised me. She looked right at me and said, "So … how do I recover, especially after this?"

Then I looked directly at her and said, "Are you ready to hear the truth? And not retaliate?"

She snorted and glared, but I held my gaze.

"Okay, fine, I'm ready," Rachel finally said.

"So I've watched you, and unless you're working something, like with Matt, you barely break a sweat. But for the last month or so, you've made an effort, with me and Mom and Matt. I know it's easier to be nice when you're happy, but if don't try when you're feeling bad, then you get stuck, you know." I waited for a reply, but Rachel didn't say anything.

"You say your life's crap right now, but are you willing to do something about it? It's work. You don't have to be Miss Congeniality or anything, but you could absolutely make your life better. There're some nasty kids at school, but most are not. You can make a real friend or two, if you try."

"Well," started Rachel, scrunching up her face, "the truth is, I keep everyone at arm's length. I don't have a real friend."

"So maybe you need to stop that and pull people closer. Make the first move, show some interest, talk and listen, really listen. Suggest something they might like to do."

"You know, that's about the opposite of what I usually do."

"So what do you usually do?" I asked.

"Try to get them interested in me."

"Hmmm. Well, you are an interesting person, I'll give you that, but it's got to be more of a give-and-take. Being interested and interesting."

Rachel nodded. I think she got what I was trying to say. She sighed deeply and said, "My brain hurts, everything hurts. Can we continue our 'how to make friends' lesson later?"

I knew I had pushed things unbelievably far, but there was one more thing I really needed to say before I lost my nerve forever. And it was huge.

"Look, Rach, there isn't really a good time to mention this but ... well, it seems you're a bit, I don't know, maybe depressed a little—"

"OMG, so I'm crazy too!" she practically howled, but I decided to keep talking, just quickly.

"Well, you've got trouble sleeping, and you get in these pretty black moods that seem to really last. I googled it. We all get moody and stuff, but you seem to be up and down well, more than most," I managed to spit out without getting spit in the face.

"Okay! So to recap, I need to get friends and get signed up for shock therapy. So … my people, are they in the psych ward?"

"That's not what I mean, and you know it. You've been on a better path lately … recently. It's hard to say this stuff, and I know it's got to be hard to hear it. I'm not saying go to the psych ward. But I do think that everyone could use someone to listen to them at times, you know, so that you can vent or just figure stuff out…" I held up my hand and continued talking really quickly to keep Rachel from interrupting again. "I know I could have used someone to talk to, especially, like, all of grade nine. It's hard being a teenage girl—we have so much pressure to be pretty and thin and to party and put out and then not be a slut. And don't even get me started on the mean girls. And to top it all off, every month, our bodies are on this crazy hormonal rollercoaster. It's too much!"

"God gave the easy stuff to the guys."

"Yeah, and my point is there's lots of help out there. Look, I'm not an expert, I don't really know anything. But it seems that you're suffering, and that's why you want me to suffer too. There are lots of people out there who may be able to help, you know. You could make an appointment with our doctor? She's really nice, just see what she says. Think about it, okay?"

Rachel looked at me silently. So I repeated myself, "Please, for me, just think about it."

"Okay, fine. I'll think about it," she said. And I felt a huge weight lift off my chest. Rachel and I sat there quietly for a minute, and then she added, "It's nice that you care."

"I do care." We sat silently again for a minute, and even though my timing wasn't right, I couldn't help myself. I had to tell her what happened at the game. "And, so…. just to let you know, we won the championship. I ended up playing goalie. I crushed it."

"You little bitch!" she cried, but I could tell her insult was only half-hearted. "I skipped gym today, now I've got two detentions, we're all out of ketchup, and you still won that stupid game."

"Yup."

"After Matt dumped me, my brain was just spinning. The frozen ketchup idea just came to me. It was so perfect. But as soon as I was done, I just crashed."

"You looked upset in Accounting," I said. "It was almost perfect. It was Cameron's idea that I could play goalie without a uniform. I could've killed him at the time, though."

By this point Rachel looked tired, and I knew I had to wrap it up. "So, sorry to foil that malicious plan of yours."

I can just leave now, I thought, *and be fairly confident I'll get through the night unscathed. Maybe we can talk further tomorrow.* But then I thought, *No. I have to stop being a coward. It's now or never. I couldn't keep walking away.*

"I remember when we were good friends, so you don't have to look too far … because I'm here. We could get there again if you wanted. Not all huggy and stuff, but just, respect. Have each other's back, that sort of thing?"

"I've listened to you, go on and on … every bloody thing you said. It's time to shut up and leave me alone."

"As soon as you say, 'I'll have your back.'"

"And then you'll absolutely leave?"

"Only if you mean it," I said and held my breath while I waited for Rachel to respond, either verbally or physically. I was really unsure which way she would go at this point.

She sat silently for a minute then finally sighed and said at a much lower decibel level, "Okay, okay. I'll try … to have your back." She then plopped back down on her bed and flung her pillow over her face. It wasn't exactly a ringing endorsement, but it was a beginning.

"And I'll have yours," I said but there was no reply.

As I left her room and went to mine, I thought, *I'm not dead, so I guess I'm done with the steps.* This was a huge victory. I'd finally confronted Rachel, and somehow it had gone okay, better than expected.

While I knew that our original family tree was dead, I suddenly had an image of a vine growing around the trunk and encircling the branches. Who knew, maybe someday that vine might even have a few flowers? It was a nice thought, and I smiled briefly, savouring the moment. But then I noticed my cellphone. The light was flickering. I had new messages. How could I sit and savour?

I picked it up and scrolled through the texts. The first one was from Cameron: *Hope it went ok with r? Come by the store tmrw if you need ketchup xxoo.*

I replied, *Went great, ok, I will.*

A date? texted Cameron.

Sure, I texted back.

Yes ☺.

Even though it was only nine thirty, I was spent. I shut off my phone and my light and crawled into bed. As I closed my eyes, for some reason my mind wandered to the funeral scene I'd imagined so many times. My brain immediately placed me where it always did, leaning right over Rachel's dead body. But this time, instead of doing something evil to Rachel while she was dead and powerless, I just started to cry. And the teardrops fell down my cheeks and landed softly on Rachel's still face.

Then the tears started streaming down my face for real. It had been a day of wild extremes for me, both good and bad. But the breakthrough with Rachel had been the best thing by far. For most other people it was just another gloomy Monday night in November. But somehow for me it seemed like a new beginning. And as I fell asleep that night, I was hopeful.

ABOUT SUSAN MARSHALL

After four kids and a career at the *Globe and Mail* newspaper and Seneca College, Susan Marshall decided to stay at home, becoming a specialist in offspring dispute resolution. Writing had always been a much-loved activity, and she is now happy to have a pursuit that allows her to work at home in sweat pants, drink loads of coffee, and engage in random fits of exercise when she needs a break. An avid reader, Susan loves e-books and falls asleep nightly to the soft glow, oblivious to what happened on the last page. Currently residing in Toronto, Ontario, Susan lives with her husband, Mark, three sons, a daughter, a dog, and a cat.

BOOK CLUB GUIDE

1. There is an old saying that it "takes two to tango." Do you think this saying is relevant to the Nadine-Rachel relationship?
2. "I knew there were lots of reasons why grade nine sucked so badly, but one big reason was fear. I was shy and afraid of putting myself out there. Somehow I had to overcome all this fear if I was make a go at this personal improvement thingy."
   Discuss fear as a motivator for the big decisions in Nadine's life. What role does fear have in your life?
3. "From experience, I knew that fighting back only made things worse. Much worse."
   In this excerpt, Nadine is speaking of "fighting" Rachel in the figurative sense. Do you think her assessment in accurate? Why or why not?
4. "I know I always joked around about [Rachel] suffering from a mental illness, but I was slowly coming to the realization that maybe it wasn't just a joke."
   Do you think Rachel is afflicted by a mental illness, and if so, which one? What would you do if you thought a sibling or friend might be suffering from something similar?
5. Do you think that sibling rivalry always exists, and if so, does it last a lifetime? Why are sibling relationships so complicated?
6. Would you say the ending of *NemeSIS* is happy, sad, or ambiguous? Speculate on what might happen if one more chapter was added to the book.

7. Are there any bullies in your family? If so, how do (or did) you cope with them?
8. What is the worst thing a sibling has done to you and what is the worst thing you have done to a sibling? Conversely, what are the best things you've done for your sibling or vice versa?
9. Do you think Nadine was successful in fulfilling her steps? Putting yourself in her shoes, would you have taken a different approach?
10. What might the long-term future hold for the two sisters?

WRITE FOR US

We love discovering new voices and welcome submissions. Please read the following carefully before preparing your work for submission to us. Our publishing house does accept unsolicited manuscripts but we want to receive a proposal first, and if interested we will solicit the manuscript.

We are looking for solid writing—present an idea with originality and we will be very interested in reading your work.

As you can appreciate, we give each proposal careful consideration so it can take up to six weeks for us to respond, depending on the amount of proposals we have received. If it takes longer to hear back, your proposal could still be under consideration and may simply have been given to a second editor for their opinion. We can't publish all books sent to us but each book is given consideration based on its individual merits along with a set of criteria we use when considering proposals for publication.

THANK YOU FOR READING
NEME*SIS*

BlueMoon
PUBLISHERS